PERILOUS DESIRE

This was worse than she had thought—that he should imagine himself in love with her!

"Oh . . . honey . . . " he whispered, and drew her to him gently. The hard lean body pressed to hers and he tilted her chin when she would have hidden her face against his chest. "Darling . . . oh, sweet—" His lips found hers, parted them, pressed a warm masterful kiss on them, urged her to respond. Betsy could not, she felt limp and weak and helpless.

He nuzzled his face against her soft throat, kissed the vulnerable place under her ear, brushed against her cheeks, returned to her mouth. His kiss was harder, more demanding. Betsy could not answer. She was afraid—afraid of the drumming of blood through her body, the traitorous weakness that made her long to lean on the strength of a man, any man, even this tough, hard man so quick with his fists and his knife—

What could she do? She had better string along with him, until she could get away. But where could she go, how to escape?

Also by Louisa Bronte:

GREYSTONE TAVERN
GATHERING AT GREYSTONE
FREEDOM TRAIL TO GREYSTONE
CASINO GREYSTONE

Published by Ballantine Books

MOONLIGHT AT GREYSTONE

by Louisa Bronte

BALLANTINE BOOKS • NEW YORK

Library of Congress Catalog Card Number: 76-11802

ISBN 0-345-25060-5-150

Manufactured in the United States of America

First Edition: September 1976

Moonlight at Greystone

1

"Taxi, miss?" the gray-uniformed station manager asked.

"Thank you, no," Betsy Olsen replied wistfully. If only she had the money to afford the luxury of a cab! "Perhaps, you would be kind enough to give me directions to Greystone Tavern, sir."

The station manager obliged, pointing, and Betsy picked up her shabby suitcase, tucked her thin black clutch under her arm, and set off toward the hill that separated Saymore from Long Island Sound. What a lovely place, Betsy thought as she looked back, noticing the two old white-steepled churches and the old-fashioned frame buildings which comprised the sleepy town. How nice it would be to belong to such a clean, simple community, to make one's home here, to settle down . . .

Wearily, Betsy climbed the hill, her distination the small island where Greystone Tavern stood—and had stood for nearly two centuries! Betsy hoped to find refuge at the tavern; she had come by chance, and hoped that Chance would be kind to her.

At the top of the hill, Betsy paused breathlessly. She sat on a tree stump and looked out upon the old Boston Post Road and beyond it the waters of Long Island Sound lapping at the shore. Removing the blue felt cloche from her head, Betsy ran a hand through her thick wheat-colored hair, trying to alleviate a headache that she knew was caused by hunger. She had left New York early that morning, going without breakfast—and now it was past noon! Yesterday? A cup of coffee and a dry cheese sandwich. No wonder she felt so weak! The doctor had told her she *must* regain her strength, or she would not see another winter.

1

Pulling the shabby white fox coat more tightly about her slim frame with one hand, Betsy coughed convulsively, then massaged her vulnerable throat with the other. She could *not* get pneumonia again; the two bouts with it last winter had nearly finished her. That was why she was in the country now—the doctor had recommended rest, country air, fresh milk, and vegetables. He told her she had to get away from the city if she wanted to survive.

And what difference would it make to anyone if she didn't? All her hopes and dreams were shattered during the Great War. In this October of 1924, it seemed an eternity since she and Lowell had made plans for the future, *their* future. Now she had to make her own plans since Lowell lay in an unmarked grave in France, Betsy's future buried with him. That war had taken the only person she cared for, and now there was no one in the world who cared. Certainly her theatrical circle didn't care; she had not even been able to find a walk-on part in the past six months.

Betsy removed a stone from her worn black suede pump, then rose and began walking down the hill toward Greystone Tavern, her collar turned up against the wind blowing chilly off the Sound. Betsy looked around at the glorious autumn trees—the leaves in beautiful shades of red, brown, and yellow, falling softly and lying like a warm blanket on the ground. Watching as the oaks, maples, and fruit trees that abounded on the hill bared their branches to the cloudy sky, Betsy thought of the drastically different world she had left: New York City, its hard sidewalks, the hot steaming cafés, the endless impersonal auditions, and the wind whistling down the streets, caught between the tall, unfriendly skycrapers. Maybe Uncle Hubert wouldn't take her in, but Betsy knew she could not return to her hard-luck life in New York. Not ever.

Betsy puckered her pretty mouth and began softly whistling "It ain't gonna rain no more, no more," defiantly at the trees, at the wind. A sharp bark almost at her ankles startled her so that she jerked around, her pulse pounding. Blue eyes wide with alarm, Betsy stared at a dog that had suddenly appeared, head cocked to one side, surveying her. It barked again.

Betsy eyed it cautiously. It was a medium-sized dog, nothing too frightening. It would have a black glossy coat, if it hadn't been so dusty. Wistful brown eyes stared up at her, the stump of a tail tried a tentative wag. A cocker spaniel, Betsy thought, noting the large floppy ears that framed the intelligent, imploring face.

"I suppose you're hungry," she sympathized. The tail wagged more eagerly, he came and pushed his nose against her white hand. Betsy bent down; her fingers slowly cupped the little head, the chin, tickled the amazingly soft hair, getting as much comfort as she was giving. "I'm sorry, but I'm hungry also, doggie. But I haven't got a thing to eat. I hope Uncle Hubert is feeling charitable."

He licked her fingers, as though in sympathy. Lifting her suitcase again, the dog trotted along beside her, importantly, eagerly.

"Go home," Betsy said patiently. He paused, perked his head aside to listen to her voice. "Go *home,* doggie!" The word "home" stabbed at her like a shrap knife. "Oh, I suppose you don't have a home, either, doggie," she muttered, her hand to her aching chest.

"I wonder what your name is?" she murmured to the dog, who marched beside her now, evidently firmly attached to her. "If you were my dog, what would I call you? Let me see. Pooch. Spot. No, your coat is all black, such a lovely glossy black. No spots. You look Welsh, all dark and sweet, like the Celts. I would call you—let me see—Bryn," she said, thinking of some ancient poetry. "Yes, Bryn."

The newly christened Bryn barked approvingly and danced ahead of her, scuffling through the autumn leaves, then racing back eagerly to his new mistress.

As they neared the bottom of the hill, Betsy sank down on the grassy slope, once more needing to catch her breath and ease the pain in her chest. Bryn sat up beside her, close enough for her fingers to weave through his silky coat. "There it is, Bryn, home for a couple months, the winter if I'm lucky. Am I lucky?

Haven't ever been. Maybe I could be now. Has my luck changed? I'm twenty-seven, Bryn. It's about time. Goodness knows, I've tried all I can, and I'm so weary of trying."

Bryn gazed at her keenly, as though trying to understand all she said. He made sympathetic noises in his throat, as though trying to answer. What a sweet dog he was, Betsy thought. She could never take him back to New York, her previous landlady had had a fit when someone smuggled in a little Pekinese. All landladies were like that nowadays, they didn't want to bother with animals and children. Children. Not much worry about that. Her hopes for marriage and children were buried in France with Lowell Reece.

But that was in the past now, Betsy scolded herself halfheartedly. She looked down the hill, and toward her future. Greystone Tavern did look old; the greystone was severely weathered and there was a pile of charred timber leaning against the old walls. Betsy wondered idly if there had been a fire recently. The curtains were drawn, and the place looked so still, but of course it was just past noon. Suppose Uncle Hubert was gone? What would she do then? A panicky feeling rose in her, choking her, causing her breath to come fast and uncomfortably.

Betsy rose, picked up her heavy suitcase, and trudged on. The spaniel rambled ahead of her, raced back with a stick in his mouth. Betsy laughed at Bryn's antics, grabbed the stick from his mouth, and flung it down the hill. The dog raced for it, enchanted with play. She reached the road, set down her suitcase, rubbed her aching cold fingers. The wind was stronger now, as though a storm might blow up.

Wearily, Betsy crossed the road, feeling as though she had crossed a barrier between one life and another. Actually, when she had given up her apartment, put her two boxes of possessions in storage, and taken the train that morning, she had put her previous life behind her. The dreams of taking Broadway by storm were dead. An actress needed more than a little talent and big hopes to make it. Betsy knew she needed a manager, a more dynamic personality, drive, ambition, health—now she knew she had none of those.

Her heels resounded on the planks of the worn bridge that connected the mainland with the little island on which Greystone sat squarely, its sturdy front facing north, and beyond it the blue Sound. Behind it, some stables had fallen to ruin, and lay in a heap of old weathered timbers. She saw a well, with a bucket. Was that how they got their water? How primitive was it here? If she had not been so weary, Betsy might have felt apprehensive. As it was, she was too tired to be particular. Anyplace where she might lay her head for a time would be shelter enough. She could endure poor conditions.

Betsy walked up to the huge carved front door. She knocked once, then more loudly. Finally she could hear footsteps as someone stalked along the hallway. She drew back, waiting.

The door opened. The slim graying man who stood there had a familiar face, changed though he was.

"Uncle Hubert," she said, choking a little. "It's Elizabeth—Betsy Olsen."

"God in heaven," he said, staring. "Whatever in the world are you doing here?" He made no move to draw back and welcome her.

"I—I lost my job—in New York. I—I wondered if I might—might stay here a little while. I can cook," she added bravely. "I knew you had a restaurant here."

"I have a cook," Hubert Olsen said shortly. Then something in Betsy's frail countenance drew his keener attention. "You come a long way. Come on in, Betsy."

He drew back, and opened the door enough to let her in. Uninvited, Bryn bounded in, to survey the new surroundings curiously, and give a brief bark. Uncle Hubert gave him an unfriendly look.

"Brought your dog, have you? Dogs ain't usually welcomed in a restaurant. Folks don't like it."

About to disclaim him, Betsy changed her mind. Maybe Bryn had run away and someone was searching for him, but until she found out for certain, he was her dog. He had adopted her on sight, and she was proud of that.

"I'll keep him out of the way," she promised, stepping in with her chin up to hide her uncertainty. The hallway was wide and dark, the open beams seeming to give more height to it. Two hall tables held unlit oil lamps, Betsy noted, with a pang. Didn't Uncle Hubert have electricity?

To her left was a dimly lit room, shuttered and dusty. She could make out shabby white curtains, dark torn draperies of once-red velvet.

"I don't use it," Hubert said rather apologetically. "Too much trouble to fix it up. They had a ways back, but the lines were torn down in a storm and were never replaced." He gave her a nervous side glance. "You for wet or dry?"

Betsy was too weary to be cautious. "I have a little nip now and then, I don't care one way or the other."

She thought he seemed relieved. "I serve meals in the taproom—well, it used to be the taproom." He indicated the room to the right. "Nice old place, wooden panels, don't take much care to keep it up."

She thought the room looked nice with the panelling. There was a huge stone fireplace to the side, and a long pine table down the center of the room. Old captain's chairs were set about for comfort, and some ladder-back chairs were around the table. Betsy thought it looked rather primitive and masculine, but handsome, and clean.

"You'll be hungry, unless you had lunch?" It was half question, half answer.

Betsy was much too hungry to be proud. "Yes, I am hungry. If you have some tea or coffee—or a sandwich—and maybe something for Bryn," she asked shyly.

"Sure. Come back this way. We can eat and talk. I was just getting lunch." Olsen led the way to the back of the hall, then to the right, into an enormous old-fashioned kitchen. The big black stove was the only concession to modernity. The huge sinks were white porcelain with rusty faucets. "We use sea water for washing," he said briefly. "I bring bottles of water for drinking over from Saymore. Got a Model A, myself," he added proudly.

"I noticed the well in the back."

"It works sometimes, when the water is smooth. When the water is brackish, look out, got too much salt in it." He indicated a place. Betsy sat down, wriggling out of the warm white fox coat, revealing her short gray skirts halfway up to her knees. Uncle Hubert gave her a disapproving look, but said nothing. Short skirts were all the rage in New York, but, Betsy surmised, Saymore was probably behind the times.

She wondered what Uncle Hubert would think of her one evening dress, the flimsy blue chiffon with the irregular hem which she had made herself. It had thin spaghetti straps, and a low square neck which revealed much of Betsy. There was no need to shock him, she mused, she had three cotton frocks she could wear, and probably wouldn't have occasion to wear the evening dress, anyway.

Hubert Olsen set a plates of whole wheat bread and slices of cold roast beef before her. To Betsy, it looked like sheer heaven. She made a sandwich of the beef and bread with real soft butter, mustard, and lettuce that looked garden-fresh. Uncle Hubert sliced some tomatoes carefully, then set them before her.

"Like some milk?" Betsy nodded, her mouth full. "You look a mite peaked. Down on your luck?"

"Yes," she said baldly. "I had two attacks of pneumonia last winter. I couldn't get work in any theater, so I took a waitress job for a while. Two weeks ago, I fainted three times on the evening shift. They sent me home and said to rest up, and come back when I felt better. I stayed home in bed two days, and went back. They had filled the job."

"Too bad," he said, moving to the icebox near the kitchen door, and peering inside. He drew out a large bottle of milk, and set it before her with a glass. She poured it out unsteadily. Bryn gave a muffled whine, sitting up alertly beside her. "Go ahead, feed him," he said, brusquely, but not unkindly. "He looks hungry, too."

Betsy put some meat and milk in a dish, and set it before Bryn. The dog went to it, daintily, she noticed proudly, but definitely hungrily.

"Have you eaten?" Betsy asked her uncle presently. Hubert shook his head, and sat down opposite her.

He ate a sandwich and drank some coffee, pouring out some for her. Betsy sat contentedly over the coffee, warming her cold fingers on the coarse white mug. Never had a meal tasted so good! Under the table, her slim feet wriggled out of the old pumps, and the blisters eased. Bryn had curled up near her feet after his feast and was sleeping peacefully.

Finally Hubert leaned back, his face gray and troubled. He looked different, Betsy thought, harder, more tense. He was her father's older brother, and years ago they had been close, but Betsy had not seen him for about eight years. Hubert had changed from a gay, middle-aged bachelor often out on the town, to an old man, graying and weary—his eyes shifty and unhappy. What had happened to him? Was his business poor?

"Well, we'll talk," he said finally. "Mind my pipe?"

She shook her head.

He filled it slowly, tamped down the tobacco with stained fingers. "Well, I expect you want to stay here, Betsy, for a time. But frankly, I can't have you stay."

"I—I would work hard, Uncle," she said tautly. "I don't mean to sponge."

"Wasn't thinking about that. You can't stay here, a young girl, alone, pretty."

"I'm twenty-seven, past being young and pretty, thank you, anyway." Her tone was bitter. "Please, Uncle, I don't have anywhere else to go. I hate to beg—but I just can't go anywhere. There's nowhere else to run to."

"Trouble is," Hubert said, drawing on his pipe, "it's dangerous here."

The words hung in the air between them. Betsy caught her breath. It was so quiet in the tavern she could hear the old grandfather clock in the "taproom" ticking and the pendulum swinging.

"Dangerous?" she whispered.

"You're no fool. I shouldn't have to spell it out. The restaurant here never did make money. I leased it for five years, come three years this winter, from Ned Palmer, a farmer nearby—brother of Jonathan, the last owner of the place. But Betsy—I couldn't make a go of it just by the restaurant, though I got a fair cook."

Hands twisting together, Betsy was thinking quickly. The Sound gave access to the Atlantic. Greystone was isolated and close to New York City and all of New England by railroad and automobiles. That explained his question when she arrived.

"Rumrunning," Betsy murmured.

He gave an alarmed start. "Don't say it—don't! You see, Betsy, I had to do it. They bring in the loads from the coast and store it here. Someone picks it up. I get a fair amount of money for it, enough to keep me going. Otherwise I'd go under, Betsy, you got to see that!"

"Yes, yes, I see."

"So you can't stay here. Them rumrunners, they're a hard, cruel lot. You can't be around here. I can't have you. My own brother's daughter: he would never forgive me."

Betsy brushed a weary hand across her eyes. All she could think of was this huge tavern, beds aplenty upstairs, and her feet hurting her so, and her stomach satisfied for the first time in weeks. "I want to stay anyway, Uncle. They won't bother me, I'll stay away from them."

"They come and go when they please. There's no staying away from them. You got to find another place to go."

"There *is* nowhere else, Uncle. I have nowhere to go. I could help with the cooking, the cleaning," Betsy said stubbornly. "Please, Uncle—the doctor said some time in the country would do me a world of good. Please—I won't be a bother—"

"You'd have to promise to keep your mouth shut, no matter what," Hubert said weakly. "I could get killed if you talked, you see that. There's federals all around, come a-snooping. Thought you was a fed when I went to the door." He attempted a smile, failed, fell back against the straight chair. "Elizabeth, please, girl, go on your way. Don't get mixed up in this."

"I have nowhere to go," Betsy said wearily, and put her head down on her arms. She was so tired, she could have fallen asleep right there. Hubert Olsen drew a hard breath, reached out awkwardly, and patted the shining flaxen hair.

"All right, Betsy. You can stay, for a little while. But if you get into trouble, don't blame me! And don't talk—not to anybody. You never know who is in the feds' pay."

Betsy breathed a deep, relieved sigh, feeling a weight fall from her shoulders. "Thank you, Uncle Hubert. I will keep my mouth shut, I promise. Nobody will learn anything from me. It isn't my business, anyway."

"That's a good girl. Well, we'll manage. I'll show you your room upstairs. Suppose you want the mutt with you."

Betsy stood up, feeling for her pumps with her aching feet. "Thank you again, Uncle, you're so kind. I won't be a nuisance—"

The hard knock at the kitchen door jolted them both. They stared at each other, paralyzed with fear. Betsy's hand went to her throat. Before they could speak, the door opened, and someone big and red-haired walked in.

"Hello there, may I come in? How are you, Hubert?" The man's voice was beautiful, the words clipped and precise, not like the slur of country folk. Betsy turned around slowly to see a tall, handsome man wearing a neat gray pin-striped suit and highly polished gray shoes. He in turn was staring at her with startled pale green eyes—the tired girl with stockinged feet, a dog at her heels. "Well—well—who is this? Hubert, you continue to amaze me! I never dreamed you brought girls here." The light jovial voice jangled Betsy's tired nerves.

Hubert stood up, introduced them shortly: "My niece, Elizabeth Olsen, late from New York City. She has acted on the stage, but right now she's come to help me with the restaurant. Betsy, this here is Bradford Schuyler, from Saymore, formerly from Newport." His tone warned her.

The man came forward, holding out a big carefully manicured hand. Betsy put hers into it, and felt the warmth folding over her cold fingers while she took in the gray-and-red silk tie and the diamond ring on his pinky finger. "Well—well," Bradford Schuyler said softly, staring down steadily at her. "A rose in the desert. A beauty—and you were hiding her. I never knew you had any relatives, Hubert."

"One brother. This is his daughter, all the kin I have in the world." Hubert was short with him, frowning. "You go on upstairs and make yourself comfortable, Betsy. The front right bedroom, where the rose spread is, that's yours. And take the dog with you." Bryn was interestedly sniffing the stranger's shoes.

She started to leave, but Bradford put his hand on her arm. "Just a moment. You don't mean she is going to stay here, Hubert?"

"For a short time she will be helping me with the cooking and cleaning. I'm going to build up the restaurant this winter, and she has waited tables before. Besides, Betsy is a good cook, and sews darn well."

"Hubert, as much as I relish her presence, she can't stay here! Betsy," he said, turning to her, still holding her arm with easy possession. "You don't realize, my dear, that this part of the coast is very dangerous these days. There are rumrunners about—aren't there, Hubert?"

"Yes," Hubert said shortly.

Bradford laughed softly. "And I should like to have a drink of your exquisite brandy, my friend!" he drawled. "Come, join us in a drink, Betsy. If you are set on staying!"

"No thank you, I just ate," she said, looking from her uncle to the man, trying to understand the threads that ran erratically from one to the other, the undertones of their conversation. The man warned her about rumrunners, then asked for a forbidden drink!

Hubert got out a bottle of fine brandy, with a Jamaican seal on it, and two glasses. Bradford released Betsy and sat down.

"Sit for a moment, girl," he said easily. "Let me tell you about the problems of living here. You're too pretty to run around Greystone. There are some hard characters—thanks, Hubert." He raised his glass to Betsy, his green eyes studying her as he drank several swallows.

Hubert motioned Betsy to sit down. She poured herself another cup of coffee, and sat sipping it while they drank and talked. Apparently Bradford Schuyler wanted to take over the lease of Greystone, and argued with Hubert over it.

"No, Schuyler, I promised Ned Palmer I would keep it for the whole five years," said Hubert, with weary patience. "I promised to run it myself. I couldn't go against my word."

"I would pay you well. You could stay on here, Olsen, keep the lease, but let me run it. *I'd* soon have it in the black."

Schuyler remained long enough to have two glasses of brandy and flatter Betsy with his compliments, then left.

After the sound of his car had rattled away, Hubert said shortly, "He is one of the reasons you should not stay here, Betsy. Don't forget that."

"Why, Uncle?"

"Why! He is a bachelor, Betsy, and has many girls. He treats them all alike, with flattery and compliments, and then forgets them as soon as they are out of sight. Watch out for him. You go on up, now, get some rest. If you decide to leave, Betsy, I'll drive you back to the station in time for the evening train."

2

Betsy awoke with a start in the dark room and, in a moment of panic, could not remember where she was. She heard a movement at the foot of her bed and sat up, frightened. Then she remembered.

"Bryn?"

The dog whined his response as Betsy yawned and slipped out from beneath the warm down comforter. She groped in the darkness for her suitcase and found some matches in a pouch. She struck a match and lit the oil lamp on the bedside table. Soon a warm glow spread throughout the room, chasing the shadows away. Bryn wagged his tail happily at his mistress.

Betsy walked over to the lovely rosewood dresser to peer into the darkened mirror. It looked like it needed re-silvering, but aside from that minor point, Betsy had been surprised by the sparkling condition of her room. In the lamplight, the furniture glowed with its recent oiling, and she noted with approval that the rose spread matched the rose and gray braided rugs and rose curtains—a far cry from the shabbiness she had expected. Apparently, her uncle kept a room prepared for guests.

Finding the bathroom next to her uncle's room across the hall from hers—the one in her room was completely out of order, though it had been an elegant one when the room was furnished in fin-de-siècle elegance—Betsy was pleased to have an abundance of hot water as she rinsed her face from her nap. She had certainly been exhausted! But sleep had refreshed her, and once again she was ravenously hungry.

Back in her room, she unpacked her few possessions. Then she opened her makeup case, but closed it again.

There was no need for rouge and powder here, and she would save money that way, too.

She found an old blue cotton shirtwaist that came almost to her ankles. As she tied the belt low on her hips, she thought that its modest length would please her uncle. She liked the dress, the blue matched her eyes, and it was cut to fit better than the shapeless flapper dresses that were so fashionable now in New York.

When she was ready to go downstairs, Bryn was waiting by the door, wagging his tail in anticipation of his dinner. Betsy patted him and a cloud of dust rose from his coat.

"The first thing we do, Bryn, is brush that dirty coat of yours and have you looking like a proper dog!" Bryn whined happily at the affection in her tone.

Everything was dark but for a lamp in the hallway. Betsy hesitated, but fresh hunger drove her on. She went into the dark kitchen, found matches, and lit the kitchen lamp. The cavernous fireplace yawned before her, empty of wood. She assumed her uncle just used the stove.

She filled the kettle with fresh water from a bottle standing near the stove, and searched for the coffee can. Then she heard steps thumping on the cellar stairs, and hastened out into the hall to open the cellar door for him.

Hubert came up, wearing a heavy black coat and thick boots. She gave him a surprised stare. Why would he need a coat to go to the cellar?

But it wasn't her business, she had promised to keep her mouth shut. And that went for questions, she had decided.

"Evening, Betsy. Feeling better?"

"Much better, thank you, Uncle. I was wondering whether to fix supper."

"I haven't eaten. You a good cook?"

"Pretty fair," she said happily. "What would you like?" He told her, and she found meat in the icebox, and some onions, celery, and tomatoes, and began putting the meal together. While she cooked, he was removing his boots and hanging his coat on a hook behind the back door. He looked tired and dispirited.

He sat down at the table with his pipe. When the coffee had boiled, Betsy set a cup before him. "You look like your mother," he said suddenly. "She was fair like you, with blue eyes. Remember her much?"

"Oh, yes. I was fifteen when she—went. Father died when I was eleven."

"I remember. You were a thin young thing. Wondered how you and your mother would manage."

Betsy felt an old feeling of resentment swell up against her casual uncle who had come to Robert Olsen's funeral, said a few proper remarks, and gone away again. Her mother had had to struggle hard those next few years, running the little boardinghouse she had set up in her old home in Princeton, New Jersey. The effort had worn her out. Besides, after her husband had died, Jane Olsen had not wanted to live. "A one-man woman, that's me," she said to her daughter in an effort at lightness, when she refused the offer of an elderly lawyer in town.

After her mother's death, Betsy had stayed with a girlfriend until she was sixteen. Then, unable to bear receiving charity any longer (and her girlfriend's mother had let her know often that it was charity), Betsy left Princeton and went to New York. She had cooked, washed dishes, gone to night school, auditioned in the theater, until she met Lowell Reece in an acting class. They had had an all too brief affair. Lowell had wanted to marry her, but the draft came, and he went away to Europe, leaving Betsy with more hope than she'd ever known in her short life.

"Not meet any young men in New York City?" Uncle Hubert asked curiously.

"You always meet young men in the city, Uncle, but they aren't usually serious," Betsy replied, turning the meat in the skillet.

Lowell had been serious, and sweet. Betsy remembered his kisses, his caresses, his caring for her. For a short time, she had felt warm, wanted, eager for life. The nights in his arms had been like a glimpse into heaven, the heaven her mother had known with her father. When he was gone, she had written to him, begging him to be careful. There had been a long gap between his letters. Then a little bundle of them arrived, along with a letter from his commanding officer. "I sincerely regret to inform you, Miss Olsen—"

Lowell had wanted to fight as a pilot with the French Air Force instead of on the ground with the American Expeditionary Force. She could see how it would be more glamorous, more exciting for him. His letters had contained a boyish excitement. Yet she had wondered over and over if he might have lived had he gone into the American army. Still, many had died—many . . .

Why did men have to lead such exciting lives? Couldn't they be content with the drama of everyday living? They had wanted to marry, have a family. It had been decided that Lowell would be an actor and Betsy would remain home and have children, and keep his life comfortable. How ironic, she thought, bending over the plate of sliced vegetables, that Lowell had died and she had gone on the boards, and on tours, with sleepless nights on trains, shuddering in the cold mornings as they waited for transport to the next theater. Betsy wondered how exciting Lowell would have found that life.

She sat down to eat with her uncle, and he praised her cooking, and expanded enough to tell her a little more about his business. His cook came Mondays through Fridays, and stayed longer if he had guests overnight. She did the cleaning, though she grumbled about it.

"I could help there, Uncle," Betsy offered quickly.

"You going to stay?" he asked dubiously.

"Yes, I want to," she said firmly. That comfortable bed! Warm water for washing up. A place to stay and hang her clothes, and not worry about the rent due. Not having to run out on a cold morning at five to wait tables for sleepy breakfasters. She drew a deep breath of relief when he nodded.

"All right, we'll try it."

"Thank you," she said, profoundly grateful. "I'll try to help all the time and earn my keep, I promise you."

"I ain't worried about that. It's your safety," he told her wearily. "Remember what you promised. You don't tell anyone about anything."

"I promise."

He wandered away to the taproom, and helped himself to some brandy there. He was sitting, reading the newspaper, when she peeped in later. He seemed buried in it, as though he didn't want to talk. She and Bryn went to the room across from the taproom (as Uncle Hubert called it)—the room at the left as one entered Greystone. Betsy had heard that it was once an elegant casino room, with an extension that doubled its size. The extension had been removed, and it now appeared to her to have been a smaller restaurant room—for private parties?—than was the "taproom" across from it. Most of its tables had been removed, and the room was desolate-looking. She and Bryn soon left and retreated to the comfortable kitchen.

Betsy wondered if she should offer to fix up the private dining room, so it could be used as lodging for the overnight guests. She could mend the curtains if they were still in good enough condition. And she would keep her promise to do the cleaning, so his cook wouldn't have to do it. She wondered about the woman, decided she could wait until Monday to meet her. It was Saturday night.

New York would be gay and bright with lamplights and signs sparkling. In the theaters, it would be curtain-raising time. Before facing the audiences who would make or break the plays, actors would tremble with nerves, putting on their costumes with shaking hands, peering at themselves in the makeup mirrors to see if the foundation looked good, the rouge natural, the mascara-framed eyes bright enough. Her elbows on the kitchen table, Betsy propped her chin in her hands. Once that had been her dream, but she was disillusioned. It was all make-believe. The outside world did not often see or recognize the tawdry world of the actor. The audience did not question what lay behind the stage presence. They did not know that the actor had waited years for the part, that he had starved, begged, stood in lines, ridden cold buses from one section of America to another, waiting for his big chance.

And for most of them, that big chance never arrived.

"Oh, Bryn, it was all such foolishness," Betsy sighed. Bryn started up from his comfortable place before the stove, and padded over to lie over her slippers. She felt his gentle fur rubbing her ankles, and she reached down to pet him under the chin. "Life is so much simpler when you don't want anything but food, shelter, and clothing, isn't it? Well, from now on, that's all I want. Just that, no more."

Just to remain alive. Not to wish for the gentle touch of a man's arm about one's shoulders, the kiss of love and possession, the yearning for hopeless goals. Not the love, the marriage, the children. Not the acting, the big part, the great chance. Not the pounding of Broadway's pavements, not the scrubbing of dishes in dirty kitchens, the snarl of the harassed boss. Just peace and quiet, the touch of an affectionate dog on one's slippers, a warm kitchen in which to sit. It was enough, thought the tired girl.

Abruptly Bryn rose and went over to the cellar door. Then she, too, heard the slight sounds, like the muffled bang of a wooden object against something harder. Then footsteps resounded on the stairs.

"Uncle?" asked Betsy. She hadn't seen him go downstairs. Perhaps there was another entrance to the cellar, she had forgotten to ask him about it—no, she had resolved not to ask him. Betsy picked up the small oil lamp on the table beside her, went to the door and opened it.

She held the lamp high, so her uncle could see to come up. Bryn was growling softly beside her. She peered down into the darkness.

"Uncle?"

A dark shape was ascending the stairs—someone dressed in black, thumping in black boots. The head lifted, startled eyes took in the lamplit girl in the blue dress and the small black dog at her feet.

"What—who are you?" the man asked as he reached her. Betsy looked at the sparkling brown eyes, the tight strawberry-blond curls that clung to the well-shaped head, the broad shoulders in the shabby black pullover.

She backed up nervously. He came into the kitchen, and behind him came two other men. "Uncle!" Betsy called, and Bryn barked imperatively at the nervousness of her tone. "Uncle!"

"Who's she? Who's that girl?" The second man, middle-aged, small, with black straight hair and black eyes, was speaking in a strongly accented voice. Italian? Betsy thought so. He was glaring at her with disapproval.

"I don't know. An angel, I think; haven't seen one lately, so I'm not sure." The first man was grinning, looking over Betsy with frank admiration, from her head to her heels and back up again. The grin made creases in his darkly tanned face.

Another man came up silently behind the other two. He was slight, with gray eyes. In fact, Betsy thought, he was all gray—gray overalls, gray shirt, gray hair, smoky gray eyes that looked her over expressionlessly. He had one hand in his bulging pocket; it seemed overlarge, to Betsy, perhaps he had a gun.

Uncle Hubert came out to the kitchen and looked grimly at the trio. "Didn't expect you tonight. It's coming up to storm."

"All the better," said the Italian man, turning to him. "Won't be out looking for us in this. Who is she?" His thumb jerked toward Betsy.

"My niece. My brother's girl. She come up today. Don't worry, Gino, she'll keep her mouth shut."

"Introduce us," said the first man, blue-gray eyes laughing down at Betsy. She felt very slight and fragile beside his tall lean body as he moved closer. "Who are you, sweetheart?"

"Her name's Betsy Olsen," said Hubert. "She's my niece, I told you. She won't matter. Got the stuff?"

"We're ready to unload. Got a cruiser offshore. We got thirty cases of the best," Gino said, dismissing Betsy with a glance. "Vic, you go down, and help unload."

"I'm Victor Halstatt," the man said solemnly to Betsy, paying no attention to the order. "You're beautiful. Are you going to stay here?"

Betsy nodded, unable to speak, her throat choked up with fear. So these were the rumrunners! They looked tough and hard, like men playing a part on stage. Only this was real. She glanced timidly at the dark Italian, who was scowling at Vic.

"Vic, I told you—"

"Keep your pants on, Gino," said Vic easily, not taking his gaze from Betsy. "Honey, do you realize this isn't the safest place in the world? Your uncle has some company sometimes."

She did not attempt to answer. Hubert and irritably, "She knows. She'll keep her mouth shut. She promised. She is going to help with the cooking and cleaning. Down on her luck. Won't be here long."

"Oscar, you stay here in the kitchen with the girl. Hubert and Vic will unload while I take a look around. I bet the feds have been nosing around—"

Vic turned and glared at the small gray man. "Oscar isn't staying with the girl," he said flatly.

There was a pause, as though he had flung down a gauntlet. Gino cleared his throat. "Okay. Oscar, you nose around. Vic, you and me will unload. Hubert, you stay here."

They accepted this. Hubert sat down heavily in the kitchen chair, motioned Betsy to a seat. She put her hand on Bryn, who was growling uneasily at all the strangers. They waited. Vic went down the stairs with a clatter, followed by Gino. Oscar disappeared silently out the back door.

Betsy and her uncle heard the thud of cases being set down. It seemed to take years, but it was actually less than an hour before the two men came up again. Oscar had reappeared, and leaned against the wall beside the door to the hallway, his hand in his pocket, his gray eyes watching Hubert and Betsy.

"All set. We'll see you again soon." Gino handed a packet to Hubert, and received another in exchange. Gino opened his, riffled through it, counting, with a line of concentration on his dark forehead. "Okay. Good. Same arrangement. Come on, you two."

Vic hesitated, then came over to Betsy. "I haven't heard you say a word, honey," he murmured.

Betsy swallowed. She didn't think she could speak. They waited, the other two men looking her over with cold curiosity.

She rubbed her throat. "I—I don't have—much to say," she finally whispered.

He grinned down at her. He bent and whispered in

her ear, "Look, honey, I'll see you next time. Ask Hubert about me, he'll tell you I'm okay. If you get into trouble, let me know, huh? I'll be back."

He waited. She managed to stammer, "Thank you—"

Oscar came up behind him. Vic whirled about, and suddenly, like a magician on a stage, he produced a knife in his lean brown hand. "I told you not to go creeping about me," he snarled, and Oscar backed up two steps. The laughter was gone from the blue eyes.

"Come on, you two, no fighting," Gino said smoothly. "Come on. You can do your courting some other time, Vic. I don't think the gal likes you, anyway," he laughed.

Gino went down the stairs, Oscar following him. Vic hesitated. Hubert said, "You best go. You know Gino."

"I know him. You take care of this little girl, huh?" Vic touched the shinning wheat-blond hair lightly with his fingers, grinned at her, and disappeared down the stairs into the darkness.

Betsy went limp. She had never been so frightened in her life. Those quiet deadly men—that knife! She wondered whether the man named Oscar had kept his hand on a knife in his pocket, or on a gun.

Hubert waited, as though expecting her to question him. When she did not, he shrugged, went to the kitchen door, and went out. Rain splashed against the windows, and still he stayed out. When he came back, his head and coat were wet. "They left, I saw the boats going. Reckon they got the cruiser a ways out. You won't talk," he warned.

Betsy shook her head, still numb from those awful men.

Hubert descended into the cellar to count the cases. She wondered what he would do with them but would not ask. No questions, no trouble, she thought. She shivered as she remembered the warm touch of Vic's hand on her head. He was a dangerous man, she thought. *Hard, dangerous, like them all.*

When Hubert came back upstairs, he returned to his paper, grumbling about the weather. Betsy got out a large brush and a newspaper, and set the paper on the floor. She soothed herself and Bryn by brushing him until his black coat shone. His loving, intelligent eyes watched her as she brushed him, and he cocked up his ears when she began to hum "Somebody stole my gal" to him, so she sang it to him softly. She had a little soprano voice, not enough for the stage, the stage managers had told her.

But it was a sweet voice, and Bryn approved, howling along with her when she sang "Toot, toot, tootsie, goodbye!" Going through her song repertoire with "Way down yonder in New Orleans," "Linger awhile," "When lights are low," Betsy stopped when she began to sing, "Rememb'ring—". The song was too sad for her, there were too many memories of Lowell tied into the song, so Betsy returned to the pretty songs, the gay songs that did not remind her of all she'd lost.

Betsy was so tired she slept late into the morning. She lingered in bed, enjoying the warmth of the blankets on this rainy day, and the rythmic snoring of her dog—what luxury!

When she finally got up, Betsy found a note at her door. "Going into Saymore for supplies. You can take a bath, the water's hot for once. See you about noon. Hubert."

Betsy thought that was nice of him, and prepared to do just as he suggested. She soaked in the hot tub, singing out loud, for there was no one to hear but Bryn.

It was past eleven when Betsy had dressed in her blue shirtwaist and gone downstairs. She looked into the icebox for something to fix for dinner. From a distance, as she opened the windows, Betsy heard bells. Bells?

Then it struck her that it was Sunday morning, and they were church bells from Saymore. With the best night sleep she'd had in years behind her and with dinner to prepare—she was happy.

"Oh, Bryn, this is so nice, isn't it?" He wagged his stump of a tail. Betsy put on a roast to cook in the big iron stove. She had figured out how to work it by now, and just when to add pieces of wood that Hubert had stacked in the corner of the cold fireplace.

As she was settling down to her coffee, she remembered the men last night, but deliberately shook off the thought. Uncle Hubert would protect her from them, and besides, they would never be there for long, just long enough to make their "drop." Betsy wondered where they tied the rowboats when they came up through the cellar. But she wouldn't go downstairs, not unless her uncle told her to get something from the pantry down there. She had no curiosity at all, she told herself firmly, and was perfectly content not to know. Buttering a piece of whole-wheat bread, Betsy put the events of last evening firmly away as she marveled at this newfound abundance of food.

Uncle Hubert returned about one o'clock, looking satisfied. His Ford rattled into the yard from the bridge, and halted with a jerk beside the back door. He came through the wet grass. The rain had stopped, and a watery sunlight shone through the dark clouds.

He carried no supplies. She was about to ask him where the supplies were, but she closed her mouth on the question. No questions.

She fed them a big Sunday dinner of roast beef, baked potatoes and cream, the last of the tomatoes, a dish of spiced apricots. She drank a big glass of milk, and sighed with pleasure.

Bryn kept her company all afternoon. She found some good books in the middle bedroom upstairs; the Palmers—Megan and Jonathan—had lined its walls with bookshelves, and it must have been a library before Uncle Hubert had made it into a bedroom for guests. The books were *The Four Horsemen of the Apocalypse* by Ibanēz, *Main Street* by Sinclair Lewis, and, surprisingly, a brand-new copy of *So Big* by Edna Ferber. She planned to read them all. Hubert had retreated to his newspapers. He sure didn't talk much, but Betsy had no quarrel with that. She could talk to Bryn.

It was after supper, while she was doing dishes, that a thin middle-aged man appeared at the back door. Hubert came through the hallway promptly. "Hello, Alva," he said, as the man stepped in. "My niece, Betsy Olsen. Betsy, this here is Alva Stern, from the grocery store."

"Howdy," the man said, revealing rotten yellow teeth as he smiled. Betsy thought he was greedy-looking, with a sharp curious nose. He was about five feet four, not much taller than Betsy.

Alva carried in a box and dumped it casually on the kitchen table. Betsy saw tomatoes, some greens, a couple cuts of meat. Curious, that he should deliver the groceries on Sunday.

"She know?" Alva asked, indicating Betsy with a jerk of his head.

"She knows, but she's not interested. The cases are in the cellar. I'll help you bring them up."

Betsy realized then, with a start, why the man had come—he was the contact! Hubert had gone into Saymore to tell him that the cases of rum had arrived.

They loaded Alva's car and he drove off. Betsy had gone up to her room with Bryn while they worked. She didn't want to see or hear them. She sat on the bed after she had made it and picked up *So Big*. Bryn whined and licked her fingers.

"I'll just stay out of it all," she told him firmly, but with an increasing feeling of dread, Betsy wondered just how out of it she could remain . . . and for how long.

3

Betsy wakened early Monday morning to a dark, stormy sky. But her room glowed pink and cheery in the lamplight, and Bryn rubbed against her ankles as she brushed her hair and swirled it into a wavy silvery bob just below her ears. With a pang Betsy recalled the long flaxen pigtails of her girlhood. Her mother had brushed out her hair with one hundred strokes every evening and told her stories when she was not too weary from work. Sometimes Betsy sat on her mother's knee and they sang together. Betsy had loved that intimate time of soothing strokes and fairytales, security, and peace.

She had cut her hair soon after her arrival in New York. All the girls were cutting their hair, and Betsy had few regrets. The long hair had tangled and snarled, the braid was hard to manage alone—everything was harder to manage alone, she thought sadly. Bryn looked up at Betsy and whined as if to remind her she was no longer alone.

When she went downstairs, Betsy was surprised to hear the rattle of pots and pans. Bryn bounded ahead of her into the kitchen, and gave a bark of surprise. Betsy, curious, walked in to find a pleasant-looking middle-aged woman with gray hair tied into a neat bun at the nape of her neck. The woman wore a shapeless gray dress and black shoes with laces.

"Well, you must be Betsy," the woman said with a smile. "I'm Florence Cunkle, *Mrs.* Cunkle. I come to cook and clean. So you're Hubert's niece from the city?" A sharp glance accompanied the remark.

"That's right. How do you do, Mrs. Cunkle? I do hope I can help you out," Betsy said.

"Sure can. This place is too big for the few what come here," Mrs. Cunkle said, turning back to the stove. Her plain face was flushed with heat as she flipped the bacon slices with a spatula. "Hubert said that you might give a hand with the cleaning. I get mighty tired of doing every room every week."

"I'd be glad to. You—you keep everything looking beautiful."

The woman looked pleased. "Thanks. It was different ten years ago. I worked for Jonathan Palmer when he ran the Greystone. We had so many diners, times we didn't know where to put the bodies." She laughed softly. But the Palmers gave up lodging guests—except under special circumstances, and then the downstairs bedroom, the one across from the kitchen, would be used. They made Greystone their *home,* and they and their children had the whole upstairs to themselves. But speaking of overnight guests, now we have maybe two or three in a week, if that. The railroad, with its sleeping cars, hasn't helped us any, either."

"Well, with the automobiles, it might change back," Betsy said optimistically as she sat down at the table. "People might be getting out to the country more, and will want a nice restaurant to come to. In New York City, lots of people are buying automobiles."

"Nasty noisy things they are," said Mrs. Cunkle, breaking an egg deftly into the simmering skillet. "Mark my words, folks will go back to carriages. Nobody in his right mind wants them gasoline fumes up his nose. No, it's fashionable right now, but it'll change, you just see."

Betsy felt dubious, but decided it would be more tactful to keep her mouth shut. It seemed that all the situations in her life eventually required that—keeping quiet.

Mrs. Cunkle was a good cook. She set bacon and eggs, hot breads and marmalade before Betsy. Betsy dug in, then fed Bryn, who was sniffing hungrily at the fragrant odors.

"Where is Uncle Hubert?" Betsy asked over her coffee.

Mrs. Cunkle gave her an odd look. "Went into town," she said shortly. "You know anything about his business?"

"I don't pay any attention," Betsy said hastily.

Mrs. Cunkle nodded briskly, her gray bun bobbing. "Don't, either. Don't pay to mess in other folks' business. I don't know nothing, don't want to know. Live longer. My man wasn't so careful. Died fifteen years ago."

Betsy thought there was bitterness and cynicism in her tone. Her back was to Betsy as she bent to the floured board and pounded the dough for a pie crust. The rolling pin moved smoothly until the pie crust was thin and even. Then she flipped it into the pie tin and began slicing around the edges with swoops of her sharp knife.

"I'll do the rooms," Betsy offered and went to fetch the mop, broom, and dustpan. Mrs. Cunkle nodded, her conversation drying up as abruptly as it had begun.

Bryn trotted along with Betsy for company. She started with her uncle's room, tidied the sparse articles on his dressing table, picked up a shirt to be laundered, and mopped vigorously. She changed the sheets, decided to do a laundry before the storm came up. It was rumbling away to the west, and might take much of the day to come.

She went downstairs with the sheets and shirt.

"Tub's in the cellar," Mrs. Cunkle said, noting Betsy's industriousness approvingly. "It's all right to go down. Ain't nothing down there."

So she knew about the rumrunning, thought Betsy, her mouth set. Well, it was none of their business. She went into the hall and down the stairs reluctantly and found the sinks in an ill-lit part of the cellar. She found the water hot, and filled the tub for washing. Betsy let the sheets soak while she went up to do her own room. Bryn trotted along with great interest, poking his nose at the mop, sneezing at the dust, rolling over a rug she picked up to shake. He was a sweet nuisance, and Betsy rubbed his stomach before pushing him off the rug.

Hubert came back from town and settled himself in the office—a small room across from the kitchen and next to the back hall door—at a desk, with papers spread about him. The accounts, said Mrs. Cunkle.

Betsy put the sheets on the outdoor line to dry. She

wondered what they did in the winter. Maybe they strung lines across the cellar, which seemed reasonably dry. She shivered at the brisk wind, and hastened indoors again.

She was down washing out dresses and Hubert's shirt when she heard heavy footsteps upstairs. It didn't sound like Mrs. Cunkle, who had a light quick step for all her bulk, or her uncle's slow, dragging gait. These steps were quick and sure and solid. Had the rumrunners returned? Surely not in daylight!

Betsy wrung out her dress, put it in the next tub to rinse, and turned to the shirt.

"Who's in the cellar?" demanded an authoritative voice. Betsy stiffened again, Bryn gave a short sharp bark.

"My niece," said Hubert's voice, with weary patience. "She come to stay for a spell. She's doing the wash."

"I want to see the cellar, anyway. We'll go down and make ourselves acquainted." Boots clattered on the stairs.

Betsy looked up from the tubs to meet the eyes of two men who came down. Hubert was behind the strangers. The first one was an uncharacteristically tall Oriental-American, six feet, probably. He was maybe in his mid-thirties, with jet-black hair. Something in the way he carried himself reminded her of the sheriff of her home town.

The young man behind him was tall, lean, with brown hair, hazel eyes, maybe mid-twenties. A little unsure, but covering it with a brisk manner.

Betsy waited, her soapy hands resting on the edge of the tub. Hubert caught up with them. "My niece, Betsy Olsen, from New York City," he murmured.

"Howdy, ma'am," said the first man, gazing right through her. He was slender, but all muscle under his gray shirt and dark-gray coat. More rumrunners? No, somehow she did not think so.

"Betsy, this here is Mr. Ming, with the Treasury Department of our government," said Hubert. "And this here is his assistant, Mr. Burton."

"Robert Ming," smiled the older man, holding out

his hand. Betsy held up her soapy hand to show how wet it was, but he reached out and gripped it firmly, anyway. His palm was calloused, his fingertips rough. "How are you, Miss Olsen? Decided you'd like the country better?"

"Down on my luck," she said frankly. "I have tried acting, but my voice isn't strong enough, and my health isn't good. Uncle said I could stay awhile and help out here with the cooking and cleaning." Might as well get it straight from the start, she thought.

"Jim Burton," murmured the other officer, when Mr. Ming reluctantly released her hand. He was blushing a little as she held out her hand, and he shook it solemnly also. His eyes were admiring as they studied her heart-shaped face, the high cheekbones, the large blue eyes. "Gee, I think you would make a swell actress. I'd come to see you anytime."

"Thank you. I'm afraid it takes more than looks," she said, with a bright artificial smile. "You have to have lots of talent, training, and then the breaks."

Mr. Ming was listening to them alertly. He waited politely until Betsy finished speaking, then he turned to Hubert. "Like to look around down here," he said pleasantly, but it was an order nonetheless.

"Sure, sure, if you want to—*again*. This here is the part we use most. I keep the vegetables here in winter, saves running into town. The wash tubs is here. We set up lines in winter. Have to soon. The floor opens so we can tie up the rowboats beneath."

"Show me that again," Ming demanded.

Betsy, unable to repress her curiosity, followed behind as the three men went over beyond the shelves of supplies to the center of the cellars. It was an immense, shadow-filled place mostly bare of contents. Hubert carried an oil lamp, raising it high to show them the way the stone slabs slid back at the touch of a lever.

"Opens right to the Sound, huh," Burton commented, bending to study the open waters of Long Island Sound. A rowboat bobbed on the slight waves below. "Built on stone foundations, I see. Pillars to hold up the foundations sunk into the water. You can come right in from outside."

So that was how Hubert had come in, Betsy thought as she watched her uncle's cautious face. How old he looked, holding the lamp high for them, the gray of his face matching the gray of his hair. The lines were carved deep beside his mouth and nose, and around his eyes. For an older man, he was playing a dangerous game. She wondered if he was strong enough to keep on. Sometimes he rubbed his chest, as though his heart hurt him.

The men kept on talking. Robert Ming poked around the cellars, studying the cement floors as though he expected to find evidence. Betsy wondered if the smell of the liquor would linger. Surely not, since the cases were probably not opened. But the men drank, her uncle had bottles of brandy about. Would they not question that?

Betsy went back to her tubs, rinsed the dresses and shirt, and took them up to the outdoors to peg them to the line. Mrs. Cunkle, preparing the luncheon for them all, paying little attention to the men tramping into her kitchen and out again, was composed. They poked around, opening cupboards, talking to Hubert for a time.

Sometimes the tones were sharp, sometimes soft and muffled. They were questioning, questioning. Betsy took the last load of clothes out to the line, and brought in the dry sheets. Mrs. Cunkle was working with a hard, worried line to her mouth, a stoop to her ageing shoulders. She had luncheon about ready.

"He won't ask *them* to lunch, I'll be bound," she muttered in an un undertone to Betsy. Betsy nodded.

She was folding sheets when the men came out again to the kitchen. Mr. Ming was looking grim, Hubert exhausted.

"Nice to meet you, Miss Olsen," Mr. Ming said, pausing beside her. "You plan to stay long?"

"It depends."

"Well, if you see or hear anything, you'll let me know?"

Betsy looked blank and indifferent, watching the sheets as she made neat folds and patted them on the table. "I'm not sure what you mean, Mr. Ming," she told him finally. "I'm just staying here for a time. Nothing is my business."

"Knowing about a crime and concealing information—that happens to be considered a crime, Miss Olsen," the Chinese Treasury agent said, his voice sharpened with a touch of anger.

Betsy kept on with her work, her soft mouth stubborn. She had promised her uncle she would not get involved, and she wouldn't. And she knew from the newspaper accounts that the federal agents had to catch someone in the act of transporting liquor, or concealing it in his house, before that person could be charged.

The officers finally were ready to leave. Betsy went to the front parlor, pretending even to herself that she was going to look over the curtains there. Instead she peeped at the two men from behind the closed draperies. They walked slowly as they crossed the bridge, their heads together, talking earnestly. Once across, Mr. Ming finally shook his head, Mr. Burton stood and faced him, his hands outflung. Then both men climbed into a black sedan they had left parked near the Boston Post Road and departed.

Betsy took a look at the curtains, fingering them. If they were washed once, they might fall to pieces. They were delicate and old. Still—she might risk it, washing them gently, soaking them. And she could mend the lace edges.

She went back to the kitchen. Hubert had taken out his pipe, and moodily, silently, stuffed it with tobacco.

"Luncheon's about ready," ventured Mrs. Cunkle.

"Ain't hungry. You go ahead and eat," and he walked out.

Mrs. Cunkle shrugged. "You want to eat, Miss Olsen?"

"I guess so. Do you?"

"Might as well." She filled their plates from the stove. "I'll just set his back to warm. He'll be hungry later, once he gets over this." She put the covered pans back into the oven, and to the back of the stove.

They sat down and ate, slowly, both thinking of the officers, the secret operations of the rumrunners. Gloom had settled over Mrs. Cunkle's pleasant features.

When the meal was over, Betsy went outside to collect the dresses and shirt. A couple of shirts she'd found hanging on pegs in Hubert's room were shabby at the cuff, and had dangling buttons, so Betsy cleared the table and began searching the cupboards for a sewing kit of some kind.

"Want thread and needles?" Mrs. Cunkle asked.

"Yes, please, do you know where he keeps them?"

"Don't know about him. I was cleaning upstairs when I come across a real pretty sewing basket. Reckon it belonged to one of the Palmers years ago. I keep it here, to do a bit of sewing." She opened a cupboard near the kitchen door, and took out a lovely rosewood sewing basket, with little drawers and a cloth top fastened with a draw ribbon of pale blue. It was old, but lovingly cared for, the rosewood was shining.

"Oh, how nice!" Betsy took it, stroking it with her sensitive fingers. "I wonder if the thread—"

"Got fresh, threw out the old that had rotted. There's some embroidery silks that I left, and the needles are still good. Go ahead, use it. It makes me upset to have a thing not used. Like people. God put them in the world to work, and be used, and fulfill His purposes," said Mrs. Cunkle, unexpectedly. "Makes me upset, when they ain't used right."

Betsy thought about her words as she explored the lovely work basket. She drew out the little cunning drawers, looked at the rows of threads, the neat lines of needles on black cloth, the sharp sewing pins, the hooks and eyes, the snaps and buttons. There was everything to delight the needlewoman's heart, including twists of brightly colored embroidery threads, large-eyed needles, a silver thimble, and an open gold thimble. She tried the gold one, and it it fit her. She sat down to sew Hubert's shirts, humming happily.

Bryn padded over to her, and flopped on her shoes. She reached down and scratched his ears, then returned to her work.

"Your dog?"

"Well—yes, I guess so. That is, he followed me here, and he seems to like me. I—I wondered if someone had lost him," Betsy confessed.

"People throw out strays, no more feeling than stones," said Mrs. Cunkle. "No one claims him, I'd keep him. Nice animal." She reached down, lifted his ears, examined his head critically, and stroked down his legs. Bryn whined happily at the attention, and licked her work-worn fingers. "Nice dog," she said brusquely. "Keep him. Anyone inquires, you'd know, have to give him up. Otherwise, he's yours."

It was as though she had set a seal of approval on Betsy's ownership, and the girl glowed. She had never owned a dog, never owned anything, she thought. She finished Hubert's shirts, and looked about for the next task.

Mrs. Cunkle had decided to wax the hallway furniture and floor. She hummed tunelessly as she worked. Betsy went back to her bedroom, and took out the dresses she had hung on the wooden pegs in the closet. She brought down a couple that needed mending. They were the short, cheap, but pretty flapper dresses, with gauzy fabrics, butterfly sleeves. One was of a silky blue-green, another of yellow. She found threads that went rather well with them, and set to work.

Mrs. Cunkle returned, panting from her task, and sat herself down across the table. "Pretty clothes," she said. Betsy held them up for her inspection. "My land. Do city folks wear them that short?"

Betsy gazed at the irregular hems of the recklessly short dresses, the irrepressibly gay freedom of the waistless tubes which ended in flounces. About the low necks were more flounces, and the sleeves were short, just to her elbows. "I guess so. It was the style there," she said. "All the girls in the show wore them."

"My, my," said Mrs. Cunkle, and into her plain good face crept an expression of wistfulness. "When I was a girl, it was to the ankles and below, or Pa'd have the whip to me. Just think. Now you wear them halfway up to your hips."

"Styles are funny things," Betsy said cautiously. Mrs. Cunkle had obviously not discarded the styles of her youth, and her dress fell to the tops of her laced shoes. It was shapeless and drab, doing nothing for the pink-cheeked woman. Betsy sighed, thinking that all too soon, she herself would be old and gray, resigned to the status of spinster, wearing gray and black and dark brown, and a bonnet.

Her blond head bent above the blue-green gauze, she sewed the butterfly sleeve which had somehow caught itself on the buttons of a man's coat, at a dance. When she had pulled away, it had ripped. Last winter, she thought, she had been to a dance with a man, who had it been? Ted, or Billy? She couldn't even remember. He had wanted her to go back to his apartment, she did remember that. He had promised her some really good booze—only she would have had to stay the night. She had taken the subway home alone. Somehow affairs had had no appeal anymore. Maybe she was old already.

"I remember my mother in a dress with a train a foot long," Mrs. Cunkle was saying. "She was wearing it to church, and when she got home she found a dead mouse in the train. If she didn't let out a screech and a holler!"

Betsy shivered. "I can imagine! I guess shorter dresses have their advantages. I wonder how they ever kept their dresses clean. Why, the fabrics alone would have been impossible to wash."

"Oh, land, yes. I remember Ma wearing a silk taffety that spotted if you looked at it. She never cleaned it. She finally had to throw it away, so filthy dirty you'd have been ashamed to use it for rags. I like cottons myself, you can stick them in a hot tub and swish them around and get them clean."

Mrs. Cunkle fixed herself a cup of tea and some coffee for Betsy, and they talked spasmodically for a time. Then Mrs. Cunkle roused herself to start the dinner.

"Himself will be hungry," she prophesied. "It's always like this. He worries himself into a state so he can't eat. When he calms down, he eats like a horse. You'll see."

Betsy opened her lips to ask if it happened often. Then she shut her mouth firmly. No talk, no questions. The less she knew, the better off she was.

4

A traveling salesman, a rather old man, arrived on Tuesday evening and remained until Thursday morning. He was a Mr. Rowe, in his sixties, small and stooped. When he carried his heavy case of supplies, he walked all bent to one side, it was so heavy.

"Things used to be different," he confided to Betsy as she served him breakfast in the taproom. "I can remember I had to make reservations ahead of time to come. Now I walk in and there's a room. Ain't natural. I remember Casino Greystone full from top to bottom, with noise and music half the night. A lively place then, sure was."

Uncle Hubert was out. She sat down opposite Mr. Rowe to serve his coffee and help herself at his urging. He seemed lonely and sad. "But you still come to Greystone."

"Yep. Have a couple customers yet in Saymore, and this is pretty handy. Have to walk from the railroad station, though, and my case gets heavy. Don't know why I keep on. I should get me a job back home and settle down."

She tried not to smile at the elderly man's sober appraisal, talking of settling down at sixty-two, his admitted age.

"Wife died a few years back. She used to nag me to get a job at home. But I couldn't do it, I hungered for the road, the traveling, seeing new faces. Would you believe, I have customers and friends in two hundred cities and towns? I counted up once."

"I believe you, you have a way of talking and being easy with folks," Betsy said sincerely.

His face brightened up, his eyes glowed. "Thank you,

35

miss. Why, in my day, I used to go to a town, and not be able to leave for two days beyond my schedule. They would just beg me to stay over and show my line of brushes and supplies to a couple more friends, and have dinner with them." Rowe drew a deep sigh. "Wife couldn't understand it. She never left her home town to go more than twenty miles by carriage. Said as how her home was good enough as any she had ever seen. We never had no children. It was a great disappointment to us both. Maybe I would have settled down then."

"Children make a difference," she said slowly, tracing a pattern on the worn surface of one of the oak side tables. She had decided not to disturb the long pine table in the center with its worn silver epergne neatly placed with some last autumn flowers in it. The bright crimson and yellow of the marigolds and dahlias made a bright spot of color in the dim firelit room.

"You're not married?"

"No. My—fiancé—died in France."

"Ah—you seem too young for that." He patted her arm quickly with his thin dry hand and withdrew it quickly, as though embarrassed. "Too bad. Marriage can be a fine thing, when two folks work together for a goal, have a nice lot of children to raise . . ." He sank into musing.

Betsy finished her coffee, and made to stand. It brought him back from his contemplation. "Ah, my dear. If you would heed an old man's advice?"

She smiled. Lately no one had even tried to give her advice, except to tell her she had to pay the rent more promptly, or she ought to take care of her health if she wanted to keep her job. "What is it, Mr. Rowe?"

"Youth goes so swiftly," he said wistfully. "Be happy while you can. You're a lovely young lady. Find yourself a fine beau and marry him. Have children. You'll live again in them. The old ways are best. Marriage, a home, children. Peace. I'm an old man. I lived a wild life at times, but I'm tired. Wish I had a real home to go back to."

"So do I," she said, under her breath. "But wishing won't make it come true. And Uncle Hubert is—kind to me."

She was sorry to see Mr. Rowe depart, lugging his heavy cases, stooped and weary before he was out the door and across the bridge. Going on and on, never to stop until death caught up with him in some shabby small-town hotel—to still the restless spirit which drove him on relentlessly.

Betsy thought about his words at intervals in cleaning and laundry, in cooking and taking care of Bryn. Find yourself a beau, indeed, she thought bitterly. Men, in her experience, wanted a brief affair, and then they departed, their animal instincts satisfied. Who wanted a home nowadays?

Mrs. Cunkle went home early on Friday afternoon. She had cleaned up Mr. Rowe's room, and it looked as though it had never been occupied. Betsy noted in the first-floor bedroom the two large old-fashioned beds, the four immense posters on each. She thought they had probably held canopies at one time, long ago.

The great tavern seemed quiet that night. Betsy sat at the kitchen table after she had washed the supper dishes, and with a lamp beside her she went on mending her worn underclothing. She hummed to herself and Bryn, some of the old songs, and he grumbled a happy reply to her. Uncle Hubert was sitting in the office, going over accounts. She wondered how he could make a living with one salesman in a week, and then with a queer chill she remembered his moonlighting. That was how Uncle Hubert made ends meet. The rum, and his payment for sheltering it.

Greystone Rum. It sounded like an old brand name. She half smiled, then felt the chill feathering down her spine again. He would be in deep trouble one day when the federal officials finally caught him in the act. They must strongly suspect him now, to come so often and nose about, as he said. Mr. Ming would not quit until he had discovered the link between the rumrunners and the sales in the rest of the state.

It grew dark earlier these nights. Betsy glanced out the window, and saw night descending on the waters of the Sound. Presently it was black outside, with little light from the moon or stars, hidden by clouds.

Sitting in silence, Betsy heard the soft rowboat oaring

before she heard footsteps in the cellar. She went stiff, so did Bryn. He began whining and went over to the cellar door.

She went swiftly to the office. "Uncle—they are coming."

"Get upstairs," he said quickly, but it was too late. The men were coming into the hallway, barring her way.

Vic was in the lead, his quick happy grin when he saw her making her feel dread. He was so big, so strong—and he liked her. She knew what happened to stage girls when a big man began to like them. She eyed him warily, tried to slip around him. His big arm caught her by the waist.

"Hello, honey, I thought of you all week," he said cheerily.

"That why you did such a lousy job of work?" asked Gino Pescara from behind him. "Dames, they cause nothing but trouble!"

"Can I help it if that lousy damn boat of yours made me sick?" said a feminine voice, in something of a whine. Betsy looked into the kitchen, then went in swiftly.

A woman sat on the hard kitchen chair, recently Betsy's refuge. She was a big blond woman, in her thirties probably, with pink frills about her throat, and huddled into a shapeless black coat. Her face seemed green in the lamplight, a plump round, heavily rouged face with much mascara about the eyes.

"Dora, you wanted to come along, you wanted excitement," Gino said with tired patience. "You got only yourself to blame. You got your excitement, so shut your mouth."

The woman moaned, clutching her throat. Betsy grabbed a pan quickly, and the woman vomited. The smell of liquor was strong in the kitchen.

Vic watched, his mouth set in a tight, hard line. "She's drunk," he told Betsy. "Don't worry about her. She can take care of herself." He leaned against the wall, watching her with bright blue-gray eyes.

"She's sick," Betsy said. "Uncle, should I put her in a bedroom? If she could lie down—"

Hubert shrugged. "Whatever Gino wants."

"Do what you want. I got the cases. We'll bring them into the cellars," Gino said, turning from Dora disdainfully. "Oscar is standing over them. Everything all right here? Anybody come last week?"

"The feds came the morning after the cases got picked up. So their news is behind as usual," Hubert told him, as though casual about it, but his eyes belied his concern.

"They're coming closer. We might have to change our dump for a while," Gino said softly. Vic paid no attention to them, his gaze on Betsy as she held the woman's head. The woman was warm, feverish.

"Come on into the bedroom. I'll make you comfortable," Betsy urged gently.

"Only if Gino says so," she said with a groan. "Gino, it's all right I lie down for a while?"

"Do what you damn well please. I know you ain't coming again on a trip of mine! Come on, Vic, stop mooning! We got work to do."

"You don't have to take care of her," Vic said again.

Betsy gave him a look of dislike. "I'll do what I please," she said sharply, and helped the woman to rise. She was like a ton of blubber, hard to move, hard to direct, but Betsy got her moving toward the first-floor bedroom, and through the door. When Dora saw the beds, she moved faster, and finally flopped onto the nearest one before Betsy could even strip down the bedspread.

"Ahhh, a bed that ain't moving. God, I can't go on one of them damn boats again," groaned the woman. Betsy moved her gently to one side, got the bedspread down and the blankets apart. She helped her to slide into the bed.

"I'll bring a hot-water bottle for your feet," she suggested.

Dora opened her eyes blearily. "You're good, a good girl," she muttered. "I need a drink. You got some brandy?"

Betsy hesitated. Then she shrugged. It would make the woman more sick, but if that was what she wanted . . .

She went out to the kitchen, found the hot-water bottle, put a kettle on. "She wants some brandy," she told Hubert, with careful lack of expression.

Hubert looked grim. "She's had enough," he said. He went down the cellar stairs, leaving Betsy alone in the kitchen. She heard the men working, grunting as they moved the heavy cases up from the rowboats into the cellar, piled them carefully on the floor of the cellar.

Thunder rumbled, lightning flashed. Betsy glanced out the windows worriedly. From the black rolling clouds moving more rapidly overhead, she guessed the storm was coming closer.

Vic came up first, rolling down the black sleeves of his thick pullover. "I've been thinking about you all week, honey," he said, as she returned to the kitchen after settling Dora. "Couldn't get you out of my mind."

It seemed to Betsy that all men thought about was sex—and making more money. "It isn't necessary," she said sharply. "I am sure there are plenty of girls about—more willing and easy to handle."

"Hey—don't prickle!" Vic gave her a quick grin. "I mean, I was worried about you. You didn't know what you were getting into when you came here, did you?" His eyes were sharp.

She kept her face expressionless. "I just knew I was coming to my uncle's. I don't care what he does for a living. It's no business of mine."

He sat down on a kitchen chair, hooking it to him easily, flipping it around, straddling it so his arms could lie along the back. He studied her intently, flaxen hair to flat-heeled shoes. "It could be trouble for you, sweetheart," he told her. "Did the feds see you when they came?"

She tightened her soft mouth. "Yes," she snapped.

"What did they say?"

She gave him an exasperated look. "If you want to talk business, talk to my uncle! I'm not involved."

"Yes, you are, honey, whether you want it or not. Just being here, you are involved. You're prettier even than I remembered," he added, looking slowly down her again.

He probably fancied himself as a fast worker with

women. She could see how the ladies would be attracted. He was sturdy, tall, good-looking. A girl might be tempted to run her fingers through the tight strawberry-blond curls, caress the tanned cheeks and the lean cheekbones, trace the laughing, sensuous mouth—Lord, what was she thinking? Men were trouble, and this man looked like double-trouble!

Gino came out to the kitchen. "Dora's sleeping," he said shortly, with a frown. "Vic, you fixed the motor yet?"

"Not yet. I've been unloading cases."

"Far as I can see," said Gino, "you're unloading a line on a pretty girl. Get busy! This ain't what I pay you for. You can relax when we get back to Havana."

Vic turned his head slowly, gazed at Gino. His cheekbones seemed more taut, the smile was gone. Gino moved uneasily. "You in a great tearing hurry?" Vic asked very softly.

"As much as you are," Gino said. "Come on, Vic. You know about engines and Hubert's got some tools. Go on, get a move on. It might take hours to fix that damn engine."

Vic finally shrugged and stood up. "See you, sweetheart," he said to Betsy, and clattered downstairs. After a few minutes, Oscar Kawecki came silently up the stairs and into the kitchen. He looked over Betsy as though she were a bug he wanted to examine.

"What kept him?" murmured Oscar.

"What you think?" Gino said irritably. "A dame. He got a million dames in every port. Never saw such a guy with dames on his mind. Trouble is, they come too easy for him. He ought to look for someone like Dora. Talk about trouble—" He snorted and left the kitchen.

Betsy felt horrible about being near Oscar Kawecki. "Excuse me," she said hastily, and slid past him and into the hallway. She hesitated. If she went upstairs, he might follow. She fled to the taproom. It was empty.

A man followed her. Betsy looked around, eyes wide and frightened. But it was Gino.

"Dora's awake. She wants some brandy," he said briefly, and went to the cupboard near the bar. He touched some spring, a panel slid aside. He reached in, took out a fresh bottle, made a mark on the pad on the counter. "Got glasses?"

Silently she handed him a glass, but still he reached out. She handed him another one. "Thanks," he said. "Listen, doll, don't pay no mind to Vic. He's not a bad kid, but he craves excitement. Stay out of his path. He eats little girls like you for breakfast."

"I'm not little, and I'm not young. I've met his kind before," she said bravely. "And I mean to stay out of his path."

"Smart girl," he said, still standing there, bottle in one hand, two glasses in the other. Deliberately he looked her over, his glance lingering on the rounded young breasts, the delicate white throat. "Say, why don't you come on down to Havana with us? Got room on the cruiser with us. We'll give you a good time in Havana. Nice and warm, and lying out on the beaches. Bet you like to dance, a girl who moves as nice as you do."

"No, thank you." She managed to keep the quaver from her voice, and kept her hands rigidly at her sides.

"You'd like it. Bet it's dull for you up here. Nothing going on in this here tavern. No fun."

"Gino!" Vic's voice rang through the room. Gino swung around, to find Vic behind him, a heavy wrench in one hand, his hands grimy with engine grease. The blue eyes blazed with fury, the face was hard and grim. "Get away from her. Get away, I tell you! You want trouble from me?"

Gino managed a shrug. "No trouble. Just thought the pretty gal might like a good time in Havana. Why don't you persuade her, Vic? She might listen to you!"

He went out, a smug little grin on his round face. His black eyes flickered as he looked back over his shoulder at Betsy, standing beside the bar.

Vic waited until the door closed after him. Then he demanded, as though he had a right to know, "Was Gino bothering you?"

"No one bothers me," she said, with quiet composure. "I mind my own business. Let me pass."

He looked as though he would stand in her way, but he finally moved aside and let her through the door.

Then he followed her to the kitchen, still clutching the wrench.

The kitchen was empty. From the windows, Betsy saw the thin shadow of Oscar Kawecki move past. He was stalking around the gardens, around the house.

Betsy shuddered, put her hands on her shoulders. She could not relax until these men had left. Bryn gave a whine. She started, looked down at him, bent to pat him, "All right, boy," she murmured, and he came to rub against her legs.

"You come downstairs with me, watch while I fix the engine," said Vic finally. "I won't be easy unless you're right under my eyes. I don't trust Kawecki."

She didn't trust any of them. "I'm all right here," she said, with reserve.

He scowled. "Your uncle is down there," he offered. "We're both working on the engine, it's drawn up into the cellar. Come on down. Bring a lamp."

Lightning cracked outside, sounding close. She was so edgy she gave a great start.

"Come on," Vic said more gently, and gave a jerk of his head toward the cellar door. "Come on, Betsy. You look like a lost child like that. Bring the pup if that makes you feel happier."

She would feel safer near her uncle, frail though he was. She finally nodded, took the lamp, snapped her fingers for Bryn, and they followed Vic down the stairs. His jacket off and his sleeves rolled up, Hubert was trying to find the trouble by the light of a couple of candles.

"Don't you have electricity here?" Vic asked. "Think you'd want it, a cold place like this."

"Too hard to get it from the mainland," said Hubert. "Cost a fortune to bring the wires over, have to be over the bridge, or underwater. Didn't think it was worth it. We got plenty of lamps."

Vic found a dusty chair for Betsy and wiped it with a rag. She thanked him primly, and sat down to watch curiously. Bryn curled up in her lap, hanging over the edges, but feeling warm and comfortable to her, his little heart pounding against her legs.

The two men muttered over the engine. Vic finally

took off more parts, and spread them over the cellar floor. He crouched down on his heels to spread them with his hand, searched for the pieces he wanted, and began meticulously to put them together again. He was completely absorbed, like a child, Betsy thought. A very dangerous child, who played with guns and knives as well.

She could see the gun handle as it stuck out carelessly from his belt. She knew he carried a knife, he had produced it like lightning when Oscar came up behind him. She was curious about him. She wondered where he came from, he spoke good English. He moved with ease, he had manners.

What made a man like him turn to rumrunning? And to associate with men like Gino Pescara, and Oscar Kawecki, whom he obviously hated? The money, the excitement? Or something more?

"Ah, that's doing it," he muttered at last. He turned on a switch, listened intently to the purring of the motor. "Like I thought, it got some grease down in the rods. Now I can put it back together."

Hubert nodded, and began helping him lift the heavy engine so they could assemble the rest of the parts. Hands moved deftly, big tanned hands that could work with precision on small engine parts—or hold a woman's waist until she knew she could not get free until he chose to let her go. She remembered the hardness of the fingers curling about her waist.

They were finally satisfied. Vic stood up. "All it takes is setting it in the boat," he said. "I'm going to see if Gino is ready to leave."

Hubert stood up, slowly, swaying a little, as fatigue gripped him. His face was gray and weary. "Uh—got me in the back," he muttered. "Ain't used to bending down like that."

Vic looked at him with concern. "Want some help?"

"No, I'll manage." He waited, then walked like an old man to the stairs, held the railing carefully with both hands, and hauled himself up the narrow passageway.

Betsy got up, and Bryn bounced up the stairs before

her. Vic followed slowly, just behind her. She could feel his warm presence at her back.

In the kitchen, he gave her a grin, and held out his filthy hands. "Mind if I wash up here?" he asked.

"I'll get you a fresh towel."

"Thanks, sweetheart."

She thought of telling him not to call her affectionate names, but it would probably just make him worse. She brought the towel and laid it on the drainboard next to the basin where he was sloshing cheerfully in soap and water. His arms were covered with curly, sun-bleached hairs to his elbows, his fingers were long and strong with hair on the backs of them

Lightning cracked, much closer to the tavern. Vic looked out the window in front of him, his eyes narrowed keenly. "The waves are higher," he said. "Where's Gino? We better get going, if we go before it breaks."

"I'll get him," said Oscar Kawecki, appearing from the dark hallway like a gray ghost. He rapped sharply at the door of the bedroom. Gino came out, scowling.

"Dora's still sick."

"I sure am," said the voice from the bed. "I'm sick as a dog. I ain't going on that cruiser again. God, I'd sink!"

Gino looked at the other men helplessly, his hands outflung, palms up. "What am I gonna do with her?"

"Leave her," said Oscar expressionlessly. The smell of liquor came strongly from the bedroom.

Gino scratched his head. "Can't do that. She'd talk to the feds if she got scared enough."

"Want me to take care of her?" asked Oscar, with a shade of mockery, his hand to his belt where a knife lay in its sheath.

"God, you bastard, don't make jokes like that!" said Gino sharply. "She's my woman, I take care of her!"

"If you don't, I will. She's a risk. You shouldn't have brought her along." Oscar was leaning lazily against the wall. Though still rinsing his hands, Vic had turned from the sink to gaze at Oscar.

Betsy thought how lean and powerful he looked, like

a panther ready to spring. His body was like a coiled spring—no, like an animal, that was the best way to describe him, she decided. He was like some jungle animal, taut and merciless.

"We got to take her back," he said slowly. "We can't leave her here. Tell him, Gino. You can make her go with us. We won't sink. She's just scared and sick."

"I can't go!" came the wail from the bedroom. "God, I'll be sick and die—and you won't care!" She began to weep noisily.

Gino winced, and glanced at Hubert.

The older man frowned, then said slowly, "You could leave her here, pick her up next trip. If she stops drinking, so the feds don't smell the stuff, it'll be all right. We always have visitors."

"I'll talk to her," said Gino, his eyes brighter. "Once she's better, she can go back all right. Or I'll get her a train ticket." He went to the bedroom and shut the door. They heard his voice, decisive, overbearing, overriding the weak protests of the sick woman. Finally he returned, dug some money from his pockets, laboriously counted out some bills, and pressed them in Hubert's hand.

"You don't need—we can take care—" Hubert began.

"I pay for what I get," said Gino. "You take care of my woman, you and your little gal here. Okay? Then I pick her up next trip. Only don't let her drink, and don't let her talk."

"I'll put the liquor away where she can't find it," said Hubert in a low tone, his back to the bedroom. "Betsy is a good girl. She'll take care of her—won't you, Betsy?"

"I'll take care of her," Betsy promised, with relief. The sooner it was taken care of, the matter settled, the sooner these men would be on their way.

5

It was after seven o'clock. Thunder rumbled closer, lightning flashed and sparked dangerously near the windows. Betsy decided to make some hot tea for the restless Dora; maybe she would settle down.

The men went downstairs to the cellar; she could hear their voices grumbling, arguing. Finally they came back up.

"Waves are high," Gino said to Hubert, looking troubled. "Goddamned unsafe out there in a small boat. How long do these storms last?"

Hubert looked to the windows meditatively. "Apt to last all night," he said finally. "Just getting worse."

Gino swore gloomily. He paced back and forth in the kitchen. Oscar leaned against the wall and watched him. Hubert was filling his pipe. Vic was staring at Betsy, standing at the huge black stove, waiting for the water to boil.

"We best stay the night," said Gino abruptly. "We can leave as soon as the storm lets up. Leave the engine where it is. The boat may swamp with that heavy engine in it. Got the boat tied up tight, Vic?"

"Yeah. I double-checked it, got two lines on it," said Vic. "Are we invited to stay the night?" His tone was slightly sarcastic as he turned to Hubert.

"Sure, sure, we got plenty of beds. I'll show you one of the rooms upstairs," he said to Vic. "There's three beds in it," and a nod of his head indicated the bedroom where Dora lay. "We can fix you up easy."

"Okay." That was settled as far as Gino was concerned. Oscar went out, padding softly in his rubbery shoes. He was so quiet, so quick and gray, like a ghost stealing about, that he made Betsy shudder.

47

"If you want some supper, Betsy will cook, she's a good cook," said Hubert, with an effort at cheerfulness. "You fellows hungry?"

"She don't need to wait on us," said Vic shortly. "We can do our own cooking."

Betsy gave him a shy glance, noticed how his eyes kept gazing at her steadily. "I'd rather do the cooking than have men messing up my kitchen," she said with a slight smile.

Gino gave a short laugh. "That's honest! Just fix me a couple of sandwiches, that's a good girl. Dora, she won't eat, I reckon."

He went to see to Dora, and tell her they were staying. Hubert said, "I'll set the table in the taproom, Betsy. What will you fix?"

She went over to the icebox, bent over to see. "There's some chicken, I can fry that quick. And we have fresh corn and tomatoes. Mr. Stern said it was the last corn of the season," she said, then caught herself. He was the man who would come to get the rum. She should not even have said his name.

She took out the chicken, began cutting it up into pieces, and got out the flour. She set the skillet to frying, and put the chicken pieces in after flouring, salting, and peppering them. Soon a savory odor began to fill the kitchen.

Gino and Oscar came back. Gino had a pack of cards in his hand, and flipped them restlessly. "Have a game, Vic," he said.

"Not me," said Vic, tipping the chair back dangerously on its legs, watching Betsy.

Oscar gave him a disgusted look. "Hanging around the dame," he said, in his soft voice. "I'll take you on, Gino. How about Hubert?"

"We'll get him in. More fun with three. Better with four," said Gino, in Vic's direction. When Vic did not reply, Gino shrugged and left the room.

When they were alone but for Bryn, Vic said, "What made you come here, Betsy?"

"I was broke, I had been sick," she said briefly. She set a lid on the skillet, and turned her attention to the corn. She put on a big pan of water, and began to shuck the corn stalks.

"Tell me about it," he said.

"What do you care? It's the same old story," she said.

"I haven't heard it," he told her. "Come on, honey. We might as well talk. It'll be a long night."

She did not plan to share it all with him! Bryn went over to him as he sat at the table, and curled up on his shoes. Traitor, thought Betsy. She thought Bryn was *her* dog, and there he went curling up at that man's big feet.

"Tell me about you. Hubert is your uncle?" Vic was coaxing her, his voice smooth and charming. She bet he charmed girls right into his arms, birds off the trees, and so on. That look on his face, as though she were his sole interest in life, that intent interested look.

"Yes. My mother was married to his brother. Father died when I was eleven."

"Go on. What happened then? How did your mother manage?"

He seemed really keen on it. She shrugged to herself.

"Well, Mother took in boarders . . ." She went on, told him about her life until her mother had died. "Then my girlfriend said I could come to live with her." She paused, thinking of the cringing year, avoiding her girlfriend's mother because the woman always made her feel like a charity case.

"How long?"

"A year. Then—then I quit school and went to New York—"

"Backtrack," said Vic, reaching down to rub Bryn's ears. The small black spaniel whined with pleasure. "Did you finish school at sixteen? I bet not. What happened?"

"Well—I wasn't really welcome there," she finally admitted. "My girlfriend's mother made me feel—well, I wasn't earning my way. I worked after school in a grocery store, then after Christmas I got a job as a waitress. I gave her all the money I made, but she still— well, made me feel—"

"Not wanted," he said crisply.

She flinched. "Yes," she agreed dully.

"Some women are like that. Cold as stones to someone

not their own," he said, as though thinking aloud. She wondered if he met many women like that. Betsy had, since her mother had died.

"So I went to New York, got a job. Went to acting school—someone said I could act, and I had always sung. But my voice wasn't strong."

She hesitated, then decided to skip Lowell Reece. She told him about the acting school, the amusing crazy things she had done with her friends. The repertory group, the nights on the buses on the road. He listened, then interrupted.

"How about boyfriends? I bet you had plenty."

She turned the chicken with a knife and fork, her back to him. "Some," she said.

"A special fellow?"

He sounded sympathetic and warm, and she had not confided in anyone for so long. "Well—yes, a fellow. We—got engaged."

"What happened to him?"

"He . . . was drafted. Lowell decided that he would rather fly. He had been stunting some with a friend, he was a pretty good pilot. His mother was French, so he went over to France, joined the French Air Force."

Betsy came to a complete halt. Her throat seemed dry. She poured herself a glass of cold water, and took a couple swallows. There was a long silence in the kitchen. Bryn whined, and Vic reached down to rub his head with his long clever fingers.

"Didn't come back?" he asked finally.

She shook her head. "I . . . got his letters . . . a letter from his commanding officer," she said dully. "He crashed. Got a medal for . . . shooting down two Germans. That's all. The end."

"I might have known him. What was his name? Lowell what?"

"Lowell Reece." When his question struck her, she turned about to look fully at him. "Did you—know him? Were you over there?"

Vic's face was strange in the lamplight, hard-planed and brooding. "Didn't know him. Knew a hundred like him. I was a mechanic in the Lafayette Escadrille. You hear about that?"

She nodded, her floured hands clasped tightly together. "I know. You went over . . . enlisted?"

He said, "Yep. Crazy fool. Still am. I thought it would be exciting. I crave excitement. Have to be driving on, and in the middle of action. I got bullets in my hip, a knife in my shoulder. And I learned plenty about the insides of planes. But excitement? Not so much as learning about what fear is in your guts."

"Excitement!" she burst out bitterly. "That's all men want—excitement. Don't care about a woman at home, just so they can have action and something blowing up in their faces. I know all about that!"

She turned back to the cold water and flour, beat it vigorously, then set it aside to wait for gravy-making.

"You hate him because he didn't come back alive," Vic said slowly.

"Hate him!" she gasped, then whirled around to stare at him with wide blue eyes. His own were understanding, his face relaxed and smoothed from the hard lines. He nodded, and his blond curls gleamed in the lamplight.

"Yep. I know how it is. Something happens, and you hate inside. Love is hate turned inside out, and hate is love turned inside out. Both sides of a garment, you might say. The way I hated my folks for dying when I was a kid, being thrown out on the street to make my way when I was thirteen. I hated them all. My parents who had loved me, and died. The relatives who could have taken me in, and didn't, because I was a wild kid, and they had children of their own. I remember them talking about me in the front parlor. I snuck down the stairs in my bare feet, shivering in the cold, but I had to know which one would take me in. I heard my dear old Aunt Marie who always gave me candy at Christmas— she said she couldn't endure to take me. And the others as bad. They decided I should go to an orphanage. So I ran away, with a sack on a stick like Huck Finn." He gave her a grin, without amusement, his teeth showing as his lips curled back in a snarl. "Sometimes I have to laugh, thinking about them waking up the next morning, all prim and proper, ready to inform me that they would pay for me to go to an orphanage, and me gone!"

He flung back his handsome head, and laughed aloud. But she knew instinctively there was no joy in him, only bitterness.

"I know," she whispered. "I know how you feel. Alone in the world, and scared. Oh, God, how scared I was." She put her floury hands to her cheeks for a minute, remembering the sick helpless feeling when she knew she was completely on her own.

"You got flour on your face, honey," he said, then got up, and in a single fluid movement, was over to her. She had no time to shrink back. He wiped her cheeks with his fingers, looking down at her, holding her face in his big hands. Strong enough to crush her head between his hands. Fingers like steel clamps, only they were gently stroking her flushed cheeks.

His sensuous mouth was too close to hers. She thought he was going to kiss her. She moved wildly, put her hands on his wrists and pushed him away. "I—I think the chicken is burning," she gasped.

She could feel him behind her when she turned, and lifted the lid of the skillet, to poke at the chicken.

Lightning cracked at the windows, and rain suddenly drummed against the panes. She jumped as though she had been shot.

"Oh—it's coming down," she whispered.

"Sure is. I'm glad I'm inside where it's cosy and warm, and not out in a dinky boat on the Sound," he said easily, and went back to his chair.

"I wish—wish you'd tell me more—about France," she said, searching frantically for a way to cover her own confusion. To keep him talking—he seemed to like to talk—to keep him from coming close—she must. She took out the tomatoes and celery and cucumber, and began to slice them into a large dish.

"If you want to hear," he said, indifferently. The closeness between them seemed broken, and she felt relief. As she went on fixing the dinner, he talked.

He told her about France, the muddy fields, the wide airstrips, the tin huts where the men had eaten and slept. He told her how they felt when one of their planes did not return. When she shivered, he went on hurriedly to talk of Paris, a couple of leaves, the French girls and how they laughed and sang. Dance, how they could dance, he said, and snapped his fingers, and sang a French song in a husky, rather good voice. Bryn enjoyed that, too, and sat up and barked, made them laugh.

"I bet you can sing, honey, you have a pretty voice," he told her.

"I sing a little," she admitted. "But, as I said, my voice wasn't strong enough for the stage."

Hubert came back to the kitchen, eyed Vic sharply, with displeasure. "Think you'd rather come and play cards," he said. "I wonder that Betsy can fix dinner, with you here bothering her."

Vic did not stir from his chair, but looked up lazily from under thick eyebrows. "I'm not bothering her," he said, very gently. "We're talking, aren't we, sweetheart?"

"I don't want her bothered," Hubert said, with unusual firmness. A nerve twitched in his thin cheek, his eyes shifted from Vic's hard gaze.

"Dinner is ready, Uncle," Betsy said hurriedly. "Will you take in this tray?" She handed him the tray of cold vegetables, and added, "I'll bring the chicken and corn. Are they ready to eat?"

"More than ready. Come on, Vic," said Hubert.

"I'll eat out here," Vic said, not rising. "I like it out here." He was deliberatcly insolent, baiting. Betsy's breath caught in her throat.

"All right, Vic," she responded swiftly, when her uncle would have protested. "You can tell me more about France. I'd like to hear about that." She flushed at her uncle's look, but she didn't want him in trouble, not with Vic, who was so swift with his hands, with his knife, with his temper. His moods seemed to change faster than a west wind.

She took in the chicken and corn. Gino eyed the plates hungrily. She set them down before him. Oscar laid down the cards, moved to a seat at the long pine table next to Gino.

"I'll bring coffee," she said, and departed.

While she was brewing the coffee, she laid a place before Vic. "Another one, for you, honey," he reminded softly.

"I ate earlier," she said.

"You can have something with me. It may be a long night."

"I usually go to bed early," she told him, then flushed.

"Not with that storm howling, Betsy," he said. "I reckon we'll all be up late. I got a restless feeling in my bones."

"Have you?" She felt troubled herself, uneasy, with a strange fear gnawing at her. "Oh, I wish it was over. I hate storms. They make me feel—oh, anything could happen."

"Anything can," he said absently. "Want me to feed Bryn?"

"I will."

He disregarded her, and went to the icebox, poked around, found Bryn's food, and put it in a dish, with some fresh water. Bryn whined with pleasure, and settled down on his special mat to eat and drink. Resignedly, she set a place for herself opposite Vic. The man was used to having his own way.

She took a big coffeepot in to the men. They were eating hungrily, in silence, even her uncle across from them. "Good food, honey," said Gino, that was all.

When she returned to the big warm kitchen, Vic had piled both plates full and set hers down. "Oh, that's too much," she said sharply.

"You don't eat enough. You're thin as a bird. A wild bird," he said absently, watching her. "Hard to tame, I bet. Suspicious of all creatures."

"Do you blame me?" she queried, trying to make it sound light and airy. "You feel the same way, don't you?"

"Yes, but nobody tames me," he said, with a taunting grin. She sat down, and helped herself from the vegetable dish. Vic sat down opposite her, and she was conscious of his gaze on her even as he ate.

The silence made her feel uneasy. "Tell me more about France, if you will," she suggested. "Was it ever pretty? You talked about the mud and the cold—"

"Sure. In the spring, the apple blossoms bloomed, and the air was like perfume, soft and nice against my cheeks. I remember one day, one of the pilots took me up to listen to the engine sound . . ." And he was off, talking about the experience, his eyes bright with excitement at the memory, the pleasure. She listened, urged him on. He was safe when he was talking. Like a panther purring.

They were still lingering over the meal when Hubert brought one of the trays back. "Said it was good," he said briefly. "Got any dessert?"

"Oh—yes, the pie!" Betsy jumped up, went to the icebox, took out the coconut pie waiting there. She cut the slices, slid them onto plates, and Hubert took them in. "Would you like some, Vic?"

"Sure, honey, looks great. Cut some for yourself," he reminded sharply, as she started to put the pie away. She made a face.

"I'm stuffed now."

"You can use a little piece."

She gave in, it was easier than fighting with him. She poured out the coffee, and they went on talking a while. She felt almost calm when they had finished, and Hubert brought out the rest of the dishes.

"I'll show Oscar his room. You're rooming with him, Vic, Gino can stay down here with Dora, if he wants." he said to the taller man, rather uncertainly.

Vic made a face. "Guess I can stand it if he can," he said with a laugh. "Is Dora awake?"

"I looked in for a minute. She's asleep," said Hubert. "The fellows want to know if you're joining them for cards."

"No," said Vic. Hubert waited, then shrugged and left.

"Which one is my bedroom?" asked Vic.

"Top of the stairs, first door on the right," she said. "Where do *you* sleep?"

She flushed, then answered. He would find out anyway. "I sleep in the one toward the front, on the right. Uncle has the bedroom opposite mine," she added with casual defensiveness.

"Close enough to hear you scream," he said, with a

grin. "Oh, quit frowning! I'm kidding, honey. I'm not going to attack you. Calm down."

"Is that a promise?" she dared to ask, in a teasing way.

"For now, sweetheart." His eyes turned narrow and calculating.

She got out the dishpan, and poured soap into it. The water was hot, fortunately. Never knew in a storm. The thunder rumbled overhead, the lightning cracked right over their heads. She shivered. "Oh, I wish I didn't mind storms so much!"

"It's natural. Storms can be dangerous. When you fear something that is dangerous, that is self-protection," said Vic, and got up when she put the first dishes in the drainer. He took the towel, and began to dry them.

"You don't have to help."

"I don't mind." He seemed deft with the dishes. Maybe he did his own housework, she thought. She wondered where he lived.

"Do you live in Havana?"

There was a silence. She glanced up at his face. It was hard, grim. "Oh—I'm sorry! I said I wasn't going to ask questions," she said hurriedly, flushing.

"I don't mind. No, I don't live anywhere. I get a room in various places. Live out of a suitcase," he said. "Someday I'll settle down, have a house. I'd like that. Haven't had a home since I was thirteen. Sometimes lately I've thought about that a lot."

"But you like excitement."

"Yeah, I like excitement." His tone lacked conviction. "What about you?"

She shook her flaxen head decidedly. "No, I hate excitement. I want peace and quiet—the rest of my life. No moving around."

"You aren't going back to the stage?"

"No. I'm no good on the stage, and it's a hard life. I don't want it anymore. I think—I think I wanted it because Lowell was there for a while, and he seemed excited about it and I thought it would be great. But it wasn't," she ended flatly.

"It's not for you. You're a homebody."

The conversation was becoming threateningly personal again. She asked him hastily about engines, and got him talking happily about how he liked to take things apart and put them together. He had worked in a garage for a time, with automobiles. He liked that.

By the time the kitchen was cleaned, the stove scrubbed, and all set up for morning, it was past ten o'clock. Betsy yawned obviously.

"I'm going to bed," she said decisively. "Come along, Bryn. We'll go outside for a minute."

"It's pouring, you'll get soaked," Vic objected. "I'll take him out. He won't go far. Come on, Bryn." He snapped his fingers, and Bryn came meekly.

Vic took him out, and they both returned with wet hair, shaking themselves vigorously. Betsy thanked Vic primly, said goodnight, and went up the stairs. When she and Bryn reached the sanctuary of her room, she found her heart pounding. In spite of his promise, she had half-feared he would follow her up there.

She closed her bedroom door after she had visited the bathroom. There was no lock on the door, she had looked for one before. Besides, any of those powerful men could break it down easily. Betsy figured she would just have to trust them. She undressed and went to bed. Bryn had already curled himself up happily on his braided rug, and was snoozing, his head in his paws.

To her surprise, she was sleepy, really tired. She turned over a couple times, and then was asleep, her face pressed to the pillow. She thought she had been asleep for a time when, groggy, uncertain, feeling a sudden terror, she wakened.

A scream ripped through the silence of the tavern. A woman's scream, loud, terrifying. Bryn jumped up, growling. Betsy slid out of bed, her bare feet cold on the floor. She sought her slippers, found her robe. Her heart was pounding heavily.

She fastened the blue robe about herself, found the door in the darkness. Betsy went out into the hallway, followed by Bryn. She knocked on her uncle's door; it opened slowly, as though it had not been fastened. But the room was dark and empty.

"Uncle? Uncle Hubert?"

But she knew he was not there. She turned, and sped down the corridor to the stairs. The door to the men's bedroom, on the left, opened; and it too was empty. She raced down the winding stairs to the lower corridor. Vic met her, his face grim.

"Don't go out there, don't, honey."

"What is it? Is Dora—I heard her scream—" She struggled against his hard arms, and managed to get to the kitchen door. She stared, her fist to her mouth, feeling sick.

Dora sat on a hard kitchen chair, tears streaming down her plump cheeks, her green eyes wide with terror, hugging her pink, frilled robe to herself. And on the floor lay Uncle Hubert—face down—pressed to the floor. Blood ran darkly red from his head, from his shoulder. He was fully dressed, in his gray suit, just as he had been that evening.

"Uncle—" Betsy choked it out. She fought free of Vic's arms, and dropped to her knees beside him. Fearfully, she touched him. He was warm. "He's alive—get a doctor—get help—"

She looked up at them in the lamplight, begging. But the faces of the men were hard, closed. Gino, unfamiliar in a pair of striped shorts, bare-legged, bare-chested, bent to Hubert, put his hand to the thin throat, shook his head. Oscar Kawecki stood in his pants and undershirt watching impassively. Vic came up to Betsy and lifted her to her feet.

"He's dead, Betsy. Someone stabbed him. Down in the cellar. Dora came out here, saw him dragging himself up the stairs. That's when she screamed."

"What—what was she doing out—here?" whispered Betsy. This was a nightmare. She would waken, and find it was a horrible dream. It could not be true.

"I come for a drink, I was looking for a bottle of brandy," Dora said defensively. "I had to have a drink, I was that dry. My God—I saw him—crawling up— then he collapsed—" She put her plump hands over her face and began to wail.

6

Betsy realized she was shaking. It was partly cold, partly terror. Uncle Hubert—killed! She stared down at his body, at the red bloodstains on his coat, on the floor. Vic held her head gently against his chest; he could feel her body trembling.

"Take it easy, honey. You aren't involved in this."

"He—was—my uncle—" Her only refuge in the world, she thought. She felt selfish, there he was lying dead, and she could only think how alone she was in this horrible cruel world.

"Goddamn," said Gino. "It would happen here. And us here for the night. Those feds will be after us like hawks." He ruffled up his hair with both hands, distractedly.

Only Oscar Kawecki, leaning against the wall, watching with his gray eyes, said nothing. Unmoved, uncaring.

Dora was weeping noisily. "Shut up, Dora," Gino ordered. "You ain't dead. Be quiet. What are we going to do?" He seemed to be addressing the question to himself.

"We'll have to get the sheriff," Betsy said automatically.

There was a sudden silence. Even Dora stared at her.

"The sheriff? Are you crazy?" snarled Gino. "We ain't going to get involved in this! We could dump him in the Sound—"

"No, no, you can't do that!" Betsy cried, horrified. "Not Uncle—you cannot—"

"The girl is right, Vic said above her head. He was still holding her closely. He wore only an undershirt and trousers, and she could feel the warmth of him, the

59

steady heat of his body. "He's been here for a time. Folks would ask questions, we would be in more trouble. We got to get the sheriff. Only the rum will have to be moved first."

Gino stood thinking about that, ignoring the body of the dead man at his feet. Didn't they care? Betsy wondered which one of them had done it, and she shook more violently. One of them must have killed her uncle—but why? Surely it would have been inconvenient for them, he was useful. So why kill him? Had one of them had a fierce argument with him after the others had gone to bed? What had happened?

The cold waves lashed against the foundations of the building, and the wind blew stronger gusts of rain against the windows, rattling the panes. Betsy heard the thin silvery chime of the clock in the taproom—one . . . two . . . three—three in the morning.

"Yeah, we got to move the stuff," said Gino finally. "We'll get Stern to move it tonight. Then we got to get out as soon as the storm lets up, be on our way."

What had Uncle Hubert been doing in the cellar at that time of night? Betsy stood there, thinking, shivering. The men were thinking also, but along other lines.

"I better see if the stuff is all there, maybe he wanted some," said Oscar Kawecki with a strange smile on his narrow face. A smile was a twitch of his lips, it never reached the cold, calculating eyes.

He went down to the cellar; they could not hear him, he moved so silently. Gino said, "Guess I'll get dressed and go for Stern. I can use Hubert's car."

Dora moved spasmodically. "What about me?"

"What about you?" Gino asked indifferently.

"I can't go on that boat again! I can't!"

"So stay here," he said callously, and called down to the cellar. "Oscar, what you doing down there? Is the stuff there?"

Oscar came back up. "The stuff is there, all the cases. But somebody's been there. Footprints on the floor, someone dripped water all over that damn engine. Poking around. Must have come up from the Sound. The stone slabs are open."

They looked at each other, silently accusing. Vic's

arms tightened around Betsy. Was Oscar lying? She wondered. Maybe he was trying to provide an alibi for them all. But nothing in the world could have made her go down to the cellar that night.

"What about him?" Gino asked as he came back from getting into his clothes. He poked gently at Hubert's body with his toe. "Should we clean him up?"

"No," said Vic decidedly. "The sheriff will have to see him. I've been thinking. This is our story. We didn't see anything, Dora didn't hear anything. She stayed in bed, right, Dora? This morning we came downstairs and found him here. That's all we know."

"We won't be here," said Gino impatiently. "As soon as the stuff is moved, we're pulling out. With Dora or without. Only you don't talk, Dora, 'cause we'll be back. Get me?"

She shrank from him, her blond head drooping. She nodded. "Sure. You know me, Gino, I won't talk."

"So go back to bed. Be quiet, get some sleep. If you want to move out with us, get dressed. We're moving out before dawn." Gino went outside, and Betsy heard the sound of the car starting, with a cough and a sputter.

"I'll start bringing the cases up to the kitchen," said Oscar. "Come on, Vic. Get your hands off the girl long enough to help." He gave Betsy a knowing grin; again it did not reach the expressionless eyes.

Dora closed her bedroom door slowly. Vic said to Betsy, urgently, "You go back to your room, get some sleep, honey. I'm not leaving you alone here, not after all this. Get some rest, I'll talk to you in the morning."

She gave him a dazed look as he let her go. "But you can't stay!" she whispered. "Gino—he won't let you—"

And besides, Vic might have done it, she added to herself. He had defied her uncle when Hubert had tried to defend Betsy. He might have quarreled with Hubert later—might have drawn that quick knife of his and stabbed him—

"We'll talk later, sweetheart. Go to bed." And he gave her a gentle push to the door. "Don't worry, I'm not running out on you!" He smoothed her cheek with a possessive hand.

Betsy went on up to bed only to lie awake, thinking. She heard cars chugging back, her uncle's, and the car of the grocer, Alva Stern. She did not hear footsteps—they would be silent, moving quietly in the night—or voices. The storm seemed to be letting up.

Presently one sputtering car left; she heard it rattle over the bridge. She turned over in bed, restlessly, cold with fear. What would they do now?

Had Vic killed her uncle? Had he quarreled with him so violently that his quick temper had flared into murder? Vic was capable of quick changes of mood, he was a dangerous man.

Or had it been Oscar Kawecki? A quiet, deadly killer, a small man with one talent—murder. He was Gino's bodyguard and helper. Had Hubert done something that Oscar felt endangered them? Was that why he had done it?

Or Gino? The man was greedy, intent on his rum-running business. Hard, ready to kill in order to protect his racket. Indifferent to the illness of his mistress, Dora. Tough and hard and cold. He could have done it easily.

Betsy was unable to calm down and sleep. Would she ever sleep again? Her thin, ageing uncle, who wanted only to make some money and be comfortable after years of roaming, caught in a web of deceit. Close-mouthed, they could have trusted him, they must have trusted him. Then why had he been killed?

She turned, heard Bryn whining happily beside her bed. His nose touched her outflung hand. She sat up abruptly, stared at the window. It was light, there was even sunshine coming in between the uneven edges of the white curtains. Morning—she must have slept.

She listened intently. Greystone was completely quiet. It was Saturday, so Florence Cunkle would not be coming today. She felt odd, being alone at Greystone. What could she do? Could she try to keep the tavern running? Surely Gino Pescara would not try to keep on dumping the rum here. Greystone would not be safe for him now.

She stepped into her slippers, pulled on the robe, went to the bathroom. She bathed hurriedly, put on a fresh dress. When she returned to the bedroom and brushed her hair, Bryn was pacing about, like an impatient child, ready to dash downstairs to his breakfast.

She patted him automatically, then they went downstairs. She entered the kitchen, flinched to see Hubert's body still there. Vic got up from his chair. She stared at him, her blue eyes wide.

"Morning, honey. You had a good sleep," he said cheerfully. "I peeped in a couple of times, but you were dead to the world." She flinched at the word "dead." "Feel better?"

Betsy stiffened. That he had dared to enter her bedroom, look at her while she slept! A wave of resentment and embarrassment swept over her. She looked down at her uncle. "You—you haven't moved him," she said slowly.

"We can't. Not until the sheriff comes," he said kindly. "You want to eat first?"

She shook her head. "No—no—I'll go now."

"I'll take you there in the car. Do you drive?" She shook her head. "Well, I'll drive you. Dora is still here. She cried, but she won't go on that boat again. I fixed the engine, and they went off early."

"Gino and—and Mr. Kawecki?"

"Yep. They're gone. I'm staying, Betsy."

Wordlessly, Betsy gazed at him. She felt despair because she was afraid of him, yet pleasure also because she had hated the thought of being alone. She felt all mixed up.

"I'm quitting the business," he said, when she did not speak. "I told them. They're not to bring any more stuff here. I want to look after you and the tavern. We can make a go of it, honey."

She swallowed. "You—you're going to stay—and—"

"Yes." He looked at her rather anxiously. "Well—we best get it over," he said, seeming disappointed in her lack of rejoicing at his statement.

They went out to the car after Betsy put on her white fox coat and her blue cloche. Vic started the car, looked at the dial. "Got to get more gas this morning," he said, prosaically.

So calm, so cheerful, and Uncle Hubert lay dead in the kitchen.

They went into town, up over the hill and down again into the valley where Saymore lay. Vic stopped at a gas pump, and got fuel, paying for it after pulling a roll of bills from his pocket.

The pump attendant looked curiously at them both. "That's Hubert Olsen's car," he stated.

"This is his niece," said Vic. He hesitated, then finished. "Hubert is dead. We came to get the sheriff. Know where he is?"

The man's jaw dropped, he hesitated before he could answer. "Dead? Old Hubert? That's queer. Well—the sheriff—he is Rob Lanahan now, since his old man died. That office in the square," and he pointed it out.

Vic thanked him gravely and drove on. "Might as well let the word out easy," he told Betsy.

"I suppose so," she whispered. Vic parked the car with a flourish, and got out to assist her. She took his hand, it was calloused, hard, and strong.

They went into the sheriff's office. One man was sitting with his feet up on the desk, studying some posters. He took his feet down, and stood up, eyeing Betsy first, then Vic.

"Howdy."

"How are you?" said Vic gravely. "We came to report a death."

"Oh? Who's that?" The man was tall and lean, in his thirties, probably, with a tanned country look, and a drawl. But the dark brown eyes were keen and narrowed. No dummy, thought Betsy.

"Hubert Olsen. This here is Elizabeth Olsen, his niece. I'm Victor Halstatt, a friend."

He motioned them to sit down. Vic told the story slowly, deliberately. Betsy thought it was so she could memorize the details, and tell the same story.

"I've been staying a couple days with the Olsens. This morning, I went down to the kitchen, and I found Hubert there, lying dead. We left him there for you to see. Dead of stab wounds, probably last night. We didn't see or hear anything," he added.

The man looked gravely at Vic. "Anybody else there? Mrs. Cunkle?"

"No, she just comes days," said Vic.

So he knew that much about the tavern, thought Betsy.

"How about you, miss, did you hear anything?"

Betsy shook her head. "There's—a lady there, staying. She's sick. A Mrs. Dora—" She hesitated, unable to remember Dora's last name.

"Dora Johnson," said Vic promptly. "She got seasick on the water. When she's better, she's going to take the train back to the city. Guess she never wants to see a boat again."

Rob Lanahan took that in, and finally drawled, "We'll get the coroner and a couple boys and go over, if that's all right. We best have the whole story together."

Mr. Lanahan found the men he wanted, and his large sedan followed the little Ford across the valley, up over the hill, down and across the bridge, parking in the area beside the tavern, near where the tumbledown stables stood.

They went into the kitchen, to find all silent. Hubert lay stiff and cold.

"Reckon the lady will want to leave us," said the coroner, getting down briskly, and opening a bag.

Vic nodded, and took Betsy to the taproom. "Now, don't fret, I'll take care of everything," he said in a low tone.

She nodded. "Thank . . . you," she whispered.

He squeezed her arm, then left her. She sat in a tall-backed chair near the fire with her hands in her lap, not thinking much, in a sort of daze, while the men walked about, down to the cellar, talking a little, shuffling about. Bryn found her, and put his head in her lap, comfortingly. She stroked his silky soft head, and put her head down against his for a moment. "Oh, Bryn, it's such a mess," she murmured.

Bryn whined and licked her face. The sheriff returned presently, with three men and Vic trailing them.

"We just have a few questions for you, ma'am," said the sheriff, and sat opposite her.

Vic leaned against the mantelpiece, and gave her a long, cold warning look. She stiffened, and braced herself. She had to tell the story right, or Vic would be furious. His fury would be terrible, she thought, with another tremor of fear.

"Now, Miss Olsen, the deceased was your uncle?" The gentle drawl was deceptive, the sheriff had drawn out a notebook and was meticulously writing in it as he spoke.

"Yes, he was my uncle. The older brother of my father," Betsy said carefully.

"And your father—he is—"

"Dead—when I was eleven."

"Your mother?"

"She died when I was fifteen."

Mr. Lanahan asked about other matters, where she had lived, what she did, why she had come. She answered slowly, choosing her words with care.

"And your uncle was your last remaining relative in the world?"

"Yes, sir. That was why I came. He wrote once in a while. I knew he had come to Greystone. I thought—thought he might let me help with—the cooking and cleaning—" She put her hand to her throat.

"Did he speak of his business to you?" The question came as smoothly as the others.

She tried not to look toward Vic. She pressed her hands together. "The tavern—yes. It had gone down, he had few overnight guests. It was—agreed—that if guests came on the weekend, I would cook and clean for them. During the week I cleaned and did the laundry." She had a strong feeling this was not the answer the sheriff wanted, and, lids lowered on her blue eyes, waited for his comment.

"Yet he let you stay—with those few guests?"

"Yes. He was—kind, gentle. Oh, I don't see how anyone could have killed him." Involuntarily, her hands went to her face.

"Did he speak of any enemies?"

She shook her head. "He . . . had none, that I knew of. How could he? He was a mild, gentle man." Yet even as she spoke, she recalled how Hubert had tried to stand up for her with Vic.

"Um—yes, he was. Well, Miss Olsen, this is a sad and difficult time for you. But there is one ray of sunshine." The sheriff looked toward her with rather sympathetic gaze. "I happen to know he made out a will about a year ago, left everything to you, his sole remaining relative. I believe he has some money in the bank, and of course there is his lease of the tavern. He paid a year in advance for that."

"He—made a will—left all to me? Oh, how kind." Betsy did not try to suppress her tears, she was incredulous and deeply touched. "How kind of him—I thought he didn't really care—he was kind—I felt so alone in the world. If I had known, I would have come before, and—and helped more."

"He was fond of you," said Mr. Lanahan, folding up his notebook, setting it precisely in his pocket. "I was there when his will was witnessed. He spoke of you. He said you were like your mother."

She nodded, and wiped her eyes with her sleeve. Vic came over, offered her a handkerchief. She took it, wiped her eyes with a murmur of gratitude.

"You're staying?" asked Mr. Lanahan.

"Yes, I am," said Vic with a touch of defiance. "She needs a man about. We haven't known each other long—but I'm going to look after her."

Betsy stared up at him helplessly, the blue eyes misted with tears. The men in the room gazed curiously from one to the other. The sheriff got up, and so did they.

"Well, we'll take care of—your uncle. The coroner will have to make a thorough investigation. We will inform you of the results. The funeral—"

"I'll take care of all that," said Vic definitely. "If you'll let me know when you are through—that is, I'll make arrangements for the funeral. It is Jones Mortuary, isn't it, in Saymore?"

The coroner, an older graying man, coughed slightly. "Yes, that's right. I shall probably complete . . . the investigations by Monday. You could have the funeral on Tuesday or Wednesday. I expect folks will want to pay their respects."

The sheriff said something conventional, yet sincere, about how sorry he was, and the other men murmured condolences. Then the sheriff said, "You'll be careful, Miss Olsen? And let me know if anything odd occurs."

"Odd?" she said, thinking about the funeral, when Uncle Hubert would be put into the cold earth.

"I mean—the person who attacked him may return."

"I'll be here," said Vic, his hands on his hips, his chin stuck out. "That's why I'm staying. She is under my protection, and you might pass the word about. If anyone tries to hurt her, he'll have me to answer to."

The sheriff eyed his lean muscular form, the hard face, and nodded. "I'll pass the word," he said drily. "It may help. Well, if either of you hears anything, you know where to find me. My respects, Miss Olsen," and he went out into the hallway, then to the kitchen.

Vic followed them out, and Betsy heard the cars pulling away. Then silence flowed through the old building, a listening, waiting silence, as though—as though someone waited in the shadows—someone ominous. . . .

Betsy jumped up. She could not just sit and brood all day. She would go crazy. "Come on, Bryn," she said, and the spaniel trotted obediently after her to the kitchen. She stopped abruptly.

Vic stood there. A steaming kettle was on the stove, and he was working at the skillet, a towel tied about his middle.

At the expression on her face he said belligerently, "You have to eat, Betsy. Life has to go on."

She glanced at the dark spots on the floor; the men hadn't been able to scrub away the bloodstains completely. She averted her eyes quickly.

"Yes, yes, it has to, I guess," she said drearily. What would become of her? She would fear every day, every night, the rest of her life, however long that might be.

"You sit down, I'll have breakfast ready soon." She sat obediently, and Bryn crept to her slippers and laid himself down across them.

She drank some coffee, ate a little of the eggs and ham, a slice of toast. "Dora?" she murmured.

"She is asleep again. I'll take something in later. We have to talk, Betsy."

She braced herself. The dark face across the table from her was lean, alert, eager. "All right."

"I want to stay here," he said persuasively. "Listen. We could make something good of this. A restaurant real again, maybe. We can build up the business—"

"I'm—I can't plan yet," she said weakly. "Vic, I can't even think! Don't push me, please!" It was a desperate cry, and he reached out and caught her fingers across the table, and squeezed them.

"Take it easy. It'll be all right, sweetheart. Just know I'm here, and I won't ever let you down."

The day went on, an ominous day, with the reminders of the blood on the floor. Dora wakened, fretfully asked for some tea, shuddered, and turned green when Betsy told her what had happened

"Don't tell me anything. God, I can't wait to go! Did Gino say anything about my railroad fare?"

"No, I don't think so, but I'll ask Vic."

Vic shrugged when asked. "Don't think Gino was considering anything except saving his hide," he said with calm brutality. "Tell her not to worry. She can stay here until she feels better."

Betsy sighed. "I feel—I'm imposing on you, Vic," she began carefully. "I—I don't want to lean on you. It isn't your concern, though you have been very good—"

"What are you talking about, honey?" he asked gently. "I want to stay, it was my idea. I'm tired of drifting, of running before the wind, trying to escape from the law, chasing after gold dust which turns to tinsel. You're the girl I've been looking for all my life, don't you know that?"

This was worse than she had thought. That he should imagine himself in love with her . . .

She gazed at him helplessly, the wide blue eyes filling with tears of utter frustration. He misunderstood, caught his breath.

"Oh—honey—" he whispered, and drew her to him gently. The hard lean body pressed to hers, he tilted her chin when she would have hidden her face against his chest. "Darling—oh, sweet—" His lips found hers, parted them, pressed a warm masterful kiss on them, urging her to respond. But Betsy could not, she felt limp and weak and helpless.

He nuzzled his face against her soft throat, kissed the

vulnerable place under her ear, brushed against her pale cheeks, returned to her mouth. His kiss was harder, more demanding. She could not answer. She was afraid— afraid—as much afraid of the drumming of blood through her body, the traitorous weakness that made her long to lean on a man's strength—any man, even this tough hard man, this man so quick with his fists and his knife!

She closed her eyes. He brushed teasing kisses against the closed lids, against her forehead, he smoothed back her short flaxen hair, held the nape of her neck with his palm. He could crush her in his hands, he was so hard and strong. She sighed. What could she do? She had better string along with him, un- til she could get away. But where could she go, how escape?

The drumming of hard fingers on the back door shocked them both. She went stiff, drew back. Had Gino returned? Or Oscar Kawecki? Or the sheriff?

"Damnation," Vic said, and let her go reluctantly. He went to the back door. "Yes? What is it?"

The tall, handsome red-haired man gazed at him with surprise and a certain wariness. "I'm Bradford Schuy- ler, a friend of Hubert Olsen. I just heard the sad news."

Vic stood back slowly. "Come in. I'm Vic Halstatt."

The men did not shake hands, but circled each other as though strange dogs, Betsy thought a little hysteri- cally. Bryn gave a short bark, stood to watch them both as she did. Mr. Schuyler turned to Betsy.

"My condolences, Betsy," he said, quietly, intimately, as though he had met her often. "I am so very sorry. So soon after your arrival, too! I can't tell you how I re- gert this! How did it happen?"

She caught her breath and looked at Vic, who recited a brief version of the agreed-upon story. He did not ask the man to sit down. Betsy did not, either. She kept thinking how the man had warned her not to stay. He knew about the rumrunning. What if he talked, guessed too much?

Bradford Schuyler shook his head again and again, in sad disbelief. "To think he died so shockingly. Such a kind, good man. I still can't believe it. Terrible thing."

"Well, it was good of you to stop in," said Vic rudely. "Of course, Miss Olsen is very tired and shocked. We can't ask you to stay."

Mr. Schuyler came over to Betsy, took her hand, though she did not want to give it. "Miss Olsen, if there is anything I can do, you can reach me in Saymore. I have an office over the bank. Please do call on me, for anything at all. It would be pleasure to assist you. Your uncle and I were great friends."

"Thank you, Mr. Schuyler." She was nervously aware of Vic's scowl as the big hand continued to hold her slim one. She drew it away abruptly. "It was good of you to stop in," she repeated Vic's words automatically. "It—it was a very—shocking thing."

The light-green eyes looked down at her with deep sympathy, and more—an admiration she could not help but notice. He briefly inspected her head, her slim shoulders, the soft drape of the blue dress over her slender form. Back to her eyes, into which he gazed—a little too long.

Vic opened the back door. "I am sure you will understand we have plenty to do," he drawled, in a deadly fashion.

"Of course, I understand completely. When you are over the shock of it, we can talk business," he said gravely to Betsy. "I can understand you will wish to leave the tavern. It is no place for a lady like yourself. Good-bye for now. I will, of course, attend the funeral, as Hubert's other friends will wish to do."

He had no sooner left, in a handsome long silvery-gray automobile, then Vic burst out jealously, "Now who the hell is that man? Where did you meet him? How long have you known him?"

Betsy started in alarm. "Goodness, Vic. I met him only once soon after I came. He is a friend of Uncle Hubert. We just talked—"

"The way he sounded, you were great friends!"

"That is just his manner, I think," she said uneasily. She was worried by his scowl, his flashing eyes. He was too quick to anger, too tempestuous and possessive.

"Well, I don't like his manner! Holding your hand like that! And you didn't dislike it!"

"Oh, Vic." She sat down on a kitchen chair, and put her head in her hands. She felt too tired and dispirited to fight him.

"Oh, God, honey, I'm sorry." A light touch stroked her hair. "Don't mind me, I get crazy sometimes. Come on, cheer up. Want a cup of tea?" His tone was more calm, but she could not forget the blaze of sheer fury that had preceded it. He could be a violent man, with little provocation.

7

Sunday was quiet, as though Greystone held its breath, and pale wraiths waited in the shadows. Betsy moved about the place, with Bryn a comforting presence at her heels. She walked outdoors for a time, until the cold wind drove her back inside.

Vic had unearthed a tool kit, and he whistled as he repaired a broken window, fitting glass neatly into the frames. He poked around, decided the roof needed repair, which he would do when the wind died down. He stood with his hands on his hips, eyeing the once private dining room disapprovingly.

"Terrible mess," he said to Betsy.

For once she agreed with him completely. "Oh, yes, it is dreadful. It was just let go. Such a shame," she said wistfully. "If I stay, I could fix it up with new curtains—"

"If you stay?" he caught her up sharply. "Aren't you going to stay here?" He swung around to face her.

"Well—I just don't know what is going to happen," she evaded, flushing. "I mean, the sheriff said Uncle left everything to me, but I haven't seen the will. And I don't know if the man who owns the tavern will let me run it."

"Hmm, I can run it," he said aggressively, a shade wistfully. When she made no response, Vic shrugged and paced about the parlor, then abruptly went down to the cellar.

Just when Betsy wondered what he was doing down there, he came back up with a suitcase and went upstairs. She did not follow, clasping her cold hands tightly as she sat at the kitchen table. "Oh, Bryn," she murmured with a sigh. He whined, looking up at her with large understanding eyes as she stroked his head.

Vic clattered downstairs again. "I decided to use your uncle's room," he said defiantly. "That way I can keep an eye on you."

She could feel the blood draining from her head, it made her dizzy. Did he mean to take everything for granted? Did he mean to force her into an affair, for her own protection? Was that how she would pay him for . . .

Abruptly Vic went back down to the cellar again. Her elbows on the table, Betsy cradled her head in her hands, and fought a silent conflict. She had done it before, had had a couple affairs with producers in order to get parts. After Lowell had died, she had not cared about anything. A few affairs—what did they matter, Betsy reflected bitterly. But the thought of this man holding her intimately, knowing her, possessing her—somehow this was different. She feared him.

Betsy knew she would never feel secure again. Never. There was no love in it for her, no warmth, no safety. Why did she bother to keep on going?

What must she do to continue to remain alive in this hateful cruel world? Was it worth the price? Why not just die, slide down into the cold waters of the Sound, let them close over her head, enfold her. It would not last long, and the agony that was her life would be over.

Bryn whined. She raised her head, and was sitting quietly at the table when Vic came up. He carried a large box of curious materials. Betsy was intrigued in spite of her churning fears when he opened the box, and began to dump out strange little parts.

Vic's face had become light and eager again. He sat down at the table, and like a lively boy began to explain: "This is a crystal set. I bought it in Miami, I can put it together. Thought I'd do it on the way back to Havana this trip, keep busy, the long trip back is so quiet. But this will be fun for us both. You ever have a radio?"

"No. Is that what it is?" She eyed it with curiosity, though dubiously. "A friend of mine had one in his apartment, but it was different. It was huge, and had batteries—"

"Friend of yours? Did you live with him?" Vic snapped, his face darkening as his blue eyes narrowed.

Betsy stared, flushed. "No, of course not," she said quietly. "He was an actor who tried to help me get work. He had inherited money and didn't have to act. He was good to us all. When—when we were down on our luck, sometimes he had a feast for us all, invited us over. He was . . . nice."

"Oh." Vic relaxed and turned his attention back to the radio. He had several parts that looked like telephone receivers. He began to wire some of the sections together, moving slowly, reflectively. Work like this really seemed to appeal to him. He worked on it for about an hour, then handed a receiver to Betsy. "There, now, listen to that."

Warily she put it to her ear, then started violently. "That's music!" she said, surprised.

He grinned his charming grin at her.

"Yep. Music. We can get lots of stations here on the coast. Want to hear a ship at sea?"

He adjusted some dials, and immediately Betsy heard the sharp crackle of signals. She winced, took the receiver away from her ear and handed it back to him. "Oh, that's loud—"

He listened, rapt, intense. "Isn't it great? To pick up the air waves like that." He turned to some music, insisted on her listening once again. He played quite happily with it for a time, and they heard a news station, clear from New York City, then some music on a Newark, New Jersey, station.

To tease Bryn, Vic put one of the receivers to the dog's ear. Bryn barked in surprise, and tried to snap at it. Vic burst out laughing.

Dora opened her door and came out, wrapping her pink fluffy negligee about her. "What's going on, what are you shouting about?" she asked crossly.

"Vic made up a crystal set. He was showing it to Bryn," Betsy explained, her face still alight with laughter at the way Vic was playing with Bryn. Bryn growled in mock anger as Vic teased him with the set once again.

"The way you act, you'd think everything was sweet

and lovely," snapped Dora. She came to the table, finally sat down. "God, I feel horrible."

"I'll fix you some hot tea," Betsy said, rising.

"You don't have to wait on her," Vic told Betsy shortly, as he shot Dora a look of dislike. "She can get her own stuff."

"I know how, but I'm sick," whined Dora. "God, honey, can't you get me some brandy?"

"I think you better have some tea," Betsy said gently. "Your stomach will settle better. I'll fix some toast and egg."

Dora seemed to turn green as her hand flew to her mouth. "I can't eat—don't ask me to eat—"

Nevertheless, when Betsy had prepared the tea, Dora drank it cautiously, and ate some of the egg and toast. Vic had gone away, Bryn at his heels, to see what else needed fixing.

Dora stayed to complain about how Gino treated her, and wonder how soon he would send her the money to get home on the train. Home was evidently Florida, and she longed for it. Nothing would persuade her to ride on a boat again. They were horrible, smelly, wretched things that swayed every which way, and made one deathly ill.

Finally she returned to her room to sleep again. Betsy was glad to be alone, to think, and try to plan. She could not remain here alone with Vic. Surely he would see that it was unconventional, that she could not do so. She could hear him whistling in the front parlor as he yanked down the dusty draperies and Bryn barked in protest at the cloud of white kittens he raised.

Dinner was no problem, as there were plenty of things to choose from. Vic had a good appetite, and he encouraged Betsy to eat. Then he took Bryn for a walk, and ended up near the car. Betsy saw him peering into it, opening the hood, and working away contentedly for a while. Anything mechanical he seemed to enjoy immensely.

She dreaded the night, but Vic went to bed in her uncle's room with no more than a pleasant goodnight to her and Bryn. She shut the door and lay awake worrying for a time, but when all was silent, she finally slept.

Monday was a brightly sunny day. Betsy washed the dusty curtains, and was dismayed when they fell apart in her hands and she had to rip them up for rags. Vic consoled her.

"We'll get some more fabric from the stores, something pretty. Maybe blue like your eyes. You can sew, can't you?"

"Yes, I could make some new ones." She did not add, If it seemed worthwhile to sew any, for what if they did not stay?

The sheriff dropped by in the afternoon. It was all right to go ahead with the funeral on Wednesday. He had spoken to the preacher. Everyone sent condolences. People were sending flowers to the mortuary. A plot in the cemetery behind the church was being arranged for. The lawyer would contact her about the will. Florence Cunkle would come if she was needed, Betsy had only to send word.

"Old Ned Palmer wants to see you, but he'll wait until a decent interval," Rob Lanahan said. "He's your landlord, you know." His soft voice was calm and drawling, he was polite. Only his eyes were sharp, studying them both.

"Oh, yes, I must talk to him—only I have to decide what to do," Betsy said nervously.

"We're staying," Vic said, giving her a hard look. She twisted her hands together. The sheriff did not miss the gesture.

That night when Betsy was asleep, she heard sounds, and wakened in terror, to the soft thud of cases, the sound of voices muffled down in the cellar. She sat up straight in bed, holding her hands to her slight breasts.

She dressed rapidly, all thumbs. Bryn had roused, and was growling anxiously. She hushed him, fastened her shoes, and went out.

Vic's door was open, he was not in the bedroom. She hurried downstairs to the kitchen. A lamp was lit on the kitchen table, the cellar door was open.

Dora's door was open, and she said querulously, "Is it Gino? Tell him to come up!"

Betsy had her hand to her throat. Her heart was thumping loudly, and she paid no attention to the sick woman. She could hear Vic arguing with Gino downstairs. She dared not go down.

Yet she wanted to know what was going on. Finally she went to the cellar stairs, hesitated, then went down a third of the way, until she could see three forms hovering around cases in the middle of the cellar.

Candles were lit, and stuck in wax on the wooden shelves of the pantry. In the dim light she made out Gino and Oscar and Vic. Oscar was dragging up still another case, pulling it up on a rope from the motor launch below. She could hear the throbbing of the motor as it turned over.

"Goddammit," said Vic, enraged. "I told you not to bring any more hot stuff here! You got to take it back."

"Can't. The feds are hot on our tail," said Gino, refusing to be upset. "You just keep it here, pass it on. No trouble. You get paid the same as Hubert. Which is generous, considering you walked out on me without notice!"

"How close are they?" Vic snapped, his hand ruffling his dark hair. He had a pair of blue pants over his pajamas.

"Close enough. They followed up from New York harbor."

Vic groaned. "You damn fools! Why didn't you dump it overboard?"

"Twenty cases of Madeira? You mad? And the brandy is worth a fortune." Gino lowered his tone persuasively, she could not hear the words. A bunch of bills were stuck out to Vic, he shook his head, but Gino laughed, and stuffed them into his pajama top. Vic seemed angry, but Gino was calm.

"Come on, we got to get away," Oscar urged, and jumped down into the launch.

"Wait—Dora wants to see you!" Betsy called from the stairs.

Gino paused, his dark face upturned to her. "So the little lady is about," he said teasingly. "Tell that dumb Dora I don't care what she does. She was the one wanted to come, I told her not to. This is one fix she can get herself out of. Tell her I'll see her next trip to Miami!" And he laughed, and jumped down into the launch.

Vic was muttering to himself, his hands on his hips. "No time to get Alva," he said. "God damn, they made us a mess! We can't get caught with this stuff."

"That's your problem," said Gino's muffled voice from the boat. "Oscar, can't you handle this damn tub?"

"Listen, don't bring any more liquor!" Vic ordered him, bending to talk through the slabs in the cellar floor. "I won't have it! We're going to run a clean place—"

"You ordering me around? I know you, Vic, don't you try anything on us! The merry voice was suddenly cold and deadly. "You're in this as deep as we are, don't you forget it! No singing, or the feds will have you in prison as fast as us—faster! We'll be in Havana, and they can't touch us. Remember that!"

"Don't bring any more—God damn you!" Vic shouted as the motor roared to life.

He was left staring down morosely at the cases. "Damn, the feds are close behind, and suspicious! What the hell am I going to do with this?"

"Can't you dump it in the Sound?" Betsy asked from the stairs.

He shrugged. "Wish I could. Well, I'm going to load it in the rowboat, and take it as far as possible." He bent, tugged the rowboat into position with a rope below the slab nearest the cases.

Betsy watched in silence as Vic lifted the heavy cases. Impulsively, she went on down the stairs, and began to help him.

"No, they're too heavy, Betsy. You go back to bed," he urged her.

"You might have to hurry, Vic," she replied in a low voice. "If the feds come and the stuff is still here—"

"Hold the rope then, hold it steady, and I'll dump the cases down."

Betsy held the rope while Vic panted under the weight of the cases, sweat streaming down his face. Much as she feared him, Betsy was sorry for him. He had been left with this, he hadn't wanted it. And he was in trouble with Gino because he had dared to stay with her.

She fastened the boat securely on a metal rod near the lever which controlled the stone slabs. Silently she came back, and began to lift and tug the cases closer to the opening in the slabs. The heavy wooden cases hurt her small tender hands. Grimly she persisted.

Vic finally jumped down into the boat, and took the cases as she half-lifted, half-tipped the heavy wooden crates over the edge of the slabs. He took them on his hard shoulder, lowered them into the boat. Finally the boat was full, sagging deepy into the cold waters.

She was panting, weary, with sweat streaming down her face and body. Her heart was beating heavily, hurting her chest. She finally caught her breath sufficiently to say, "What now?"

"Got to dump the cases somewhere. Maybe along the beach. I might find a deserted place, where I can cover them up with branches. Listen, honey, would you go up to my bedroom, bring down my black sweater, and a coat and cap?"

"Sure, Vic, right away." Still worried about him, she was glad to have something to do for him. Drenched wet with sweat, he was going out into the cold October night to work hard again.

She raced upstairs. Dora whined, "Where's Gino?" but Betsy did not pause to answer. She went into Vic's room, groped around in the dark of his wardrobe for the sweater and coat, found his cap on the dresser. On the way down again, she snatched her coat from the rack in the hallway. She could not let him go alone.

Through the open slabs, Betsy lowered the sweater and coat to him, then his cap. "Good girl," he said quietly. "Okay, honey, wish me luck."

Betsy looked down at the boat sunk dangerously low in the water and Vic sitting on a case of that crazy moonshine with his hair damp around shining face, and shoved her arms into the coat. She found a scarf in her coat pocket and fastened it around her head with cold shaking hands. "I'm coming with you, Vic. Help me down."

She leaned down, and after a moment of surprise, he reached up, held her waist, and lifted her down into the boat with him.

"You can't come, honey," he said, but he hugged her to him.

"Yes, you have to have some help. There's the feds—they might . . . Come on, we have to hurry!"

His lips brushed her cheek warmly. "You'll do, sweetheart," he said warmly. "Now, you sit down on the cases, and try to keep warm. I can handle the oars myself."

Betsy sat down unsteadily on the cases, scarcely able to see Vic over them as he pushed off. He steadied the boat and they slid soundlessly out from under the stone foundations of the building.

Then they were out in the open, and the moon was full. "Damn moon, bright as hell," Vic muttered.

She glanced up at it. A romantic moon-filled starlit night, and for their purposes it could not be worse. The waters of the Sound were so brightly lit, Betsy knew they could be seen for a half a mile or more. She could even see the beaches along the Sound.

Vic was rowing slowly, lifting the oars carefully in order to make as little sound as possible. His dark gaze kept searching along the shoreline.

Several miles up, Vic turned the boat in toward shore, but moved parallel to it for a time, peering at the shoreline intently. Then he whispered with satisfaction. "That's it, I noticed it the other day. It's a line of trees and there are no houses beyond."

He swung in more sharply and glided the boat toward a small, dry, sandy spot. Beyond and above them trees spread thick dark shadows along the sand. Low brambly bushes closer to the shore would shelter the cases. Vic pulled the boat up as far as he could, then hopped out. Betsy followed him, her feet sinking into the soft dry sand.

It was even heavier work, lifting up the wooden cases of liquor and carrying them twenty yards up the beach, to dump them under the thick bushes. Vic carried twice as many as she did, but Betsy could feel her heart thumping till it was about bursting her lungs. She was still not strong and had little energy left to draw on.

When Betsy felt she could not lift another case, she stared in disbelief at how many cases there were and silently lifted another. She moved mechanically, heavily, along the beach. When she dumped down the last case, Betsy helped Vic collect dry brush to cover the cases, smoothing the sand where it was disturbed.

"That's the last," Vic said. "I'll sweep a brush after us on the way down to the beach, wipe out our footprints." He beckoned her to go before him down the beach to the rowboat. Then he backed down to the beach, sweeping a branch back and forth before him, so that their tracks were now smooth sweeps of sand.

Her hands were stinging and cut from the brambles. She was trembling uncontrollably as she half-stumbled, half-fell into the rowboat. Vic followed, not realizing Betsy was practically unconscious with exhaustion. He seemed fresh as before, picking up the oars and shoving them out further into the Sound.

Relieved of its load, the rowboat bobbed up and down on the waves of the Sound while Betsy clung weakly to its sides, realizing how easy it was to get seasick. In her state of exhaustion, she felt as though she would never breathe normally, nor ever walk again. As Vic rowed quietly and quickly back, she paid no heed to the lovely moonlight or the soft breeze that blew wisps of her wheaten-colored hair about, making them look like tendrils of the moon. All she thought about was whether her arms would ever stop aching.

"We'll be home soon, honey. Thank you for being such a soldier and helping me out."

The pride in Vic's voice lifted her spirits for a moment. Betsy felt a stirring of an emotion, but she was too tired to think about it.

They reached the tavern at last. Betsy wondered how she would make it from the boat to land. When they reached the cellar, Vic leaped up, rope in hand, and tied the boat securely to the old, sturdy foundations. Then he reached down. "Come on, honey, give me your hands."

She managed to raise her heavy arms as Vic lifted

her up easily, his strength making mockery of her own. He set her gently down on the cellar floor.

"I'll be right back. I want to get a broom and sweep up the chips of wood. Then we'll be all ready if the feds do come."

As Vic turned to fetch the broom, Betsy knew she could not even walk one step. She watched him walk up the cellar stairs so easily and almost hated him. The candle flames flickered before her eyes. She was worn to the bone, paralyzed. Even her brain was numb.

She tried to take one step away from the wall she was leaning against. As she moved forward, her legs began buckling under. Betsy watched Vic run up the last steps, and tried to cry out, but no sound would come. She reached out blindly for the nearest candle. It was going dim . . . dim . . .

Sighing, Betsy collapsed on the floor of the cold, dark cellar.

8

Betsy felt herself awakening from a dark, formless dream. As her mind focused, she was aware of a rough cheek against her own.

"Betsy, honey, honey, wake up—oh, sweetheart, wake up—come on, honey—"

She had to answer. Her body ached from head to toe, she moaned.

Vic's voice was relieved. "Honey, you awake now? God, what happened?"

She mumbled something. He leaned over her, picked her up in his arms, then carried her to the cellar stairs. She felt like a child, he moved so easily with her.

He carried her up the stairs and then to the kitchen, pausing to survey her face anxiously. She blinked dazedly up at him, in the dim light of the kitchen lamp.

"You're all worn out. God, what a fool I was. I'll get you up to bed, and fix you up." He carried her up to the second floor, along the hallway, to the bedroom. Bryn got up from his rag carpet to circle them worriedly.

Vic sat her down on the edge of the bed, fumbled at the buttons of her coat, slid it off her limp arms. He unfastened the scarf with gentle fingers, took it off, ran his hands through her hair.

"You're wet to the bone, honey."

She nodded, her huge eyes fixed solemnly on his face. He had paused to light the oil lamp on the dresser, and everything seemed to waver before her.

"Just . . . tired . ." she said in a thread of a voice.

Her nightdress lay on the bed. "Honey, I'm going to

strip you, dry you. You can't stay in these clothes." He hesitated, but she could not even voice a protest.

He took off her shoes, stripped off her stockings. Then he stood her up gently, slipped off her dress, her petticoat and underclothing. Betsy was too cold to be embarrassed, she felt like a block of ice. He grabbed a towel, rubbed her briskly, then slid the warm nightdress over her head.

"Now, into bed with you," he said. She obeyed, sliding under the bedcovers with a feeling of intense relief. He took the towel to her hair and rubbed it dry with gentle motions. For such a tough guy, he could be very nice and sweet, Betsy thought wearily.

Once in bed, Betsy began to shiver so uncontrollably that the bedcovers trembled. Vic frowned.

"You're too weak to have done all that," he muttered to himself. "God, I should be shot! Letting you lift all those cases. You're a bundle of nerves." He stroked her shoulders gently, she could not stop shaking.

"I'll go get you some brandy."

She shook her head weakly. "Not—brandy—not good—for me—doctor said . . ."

"Hot tea, then. With plenty of sugar." He brightened up. "That was my mom's remedy. I'll go fix it. Bryn, you stay here!"

The dog flopped down obediently on the carpet beside the bed. Vic went out silently. He had discarded his boots, and he moved like a shadow in his stockinged feet. Betsy closed her eyes. The night had been a wild horrible dream, ending with her collapsing on the cellar floor. She could still feel the cold dampness under her body. She shivered convulsively.

In a few minutes, Vic returned with a tray. He set it down on the small rosewood table beside the huge bed and poured out a little tea, testing to see if it had brewed enough. Satisfied, he added liberal amounts of sugar and cream to the steaming cup, then held it to her lips. "Come on, honey, drink up."

She had trouble sitting up. Finally he sat down on the edge of the bed, and held her shoulders against himself and stroked her hair. When she was more calm, he held the cup to her lips again. She managed to drink a few sips. The hot liquid slid down her icy throat, warming her.

"Oh . . . better . . ." she murmured.

"Is that good, honey?" He put his cheek to her hair, and gently held her as she drank. The trembling began again, shook her, then slowly died down.

He had brought up some sweet sugar cookies she had made that day. He urged her to eat one or two. "You need the sugar for energy. Guess you got drained to the limit. God damn me for a stupid fool!"

"No—I—wanted to—help—"

"That damn Gino. I'll fix his clock if he tries to pull that again," Vic said, and the rage in his tone made her stiffen. He sounded so deadly and grim.

She ate one cookie, then a second, and he poured another cup of tea. "You—drink—some—" she urged. "You—got so—wet—from work . . ."

He urged her to drink half the cup, then he drank down the rest. "Ah, good," he said with satisfaction. He let her slip down in bed, and drew up the covers to her chin. "Feel better now, darling?"

She nodded, her lids drooping.

"You—take care—of yourself—too, Vic . . ." she managed to mutter wearily.

"Sure, honey. You relax. Bryn, you stay with her."

The dog whined, and lay down again, large eyes fixed on Vic as he left the room. She could hear him in his bedroom, which had been her uncle's. He moved about, she heard the wardrobe door open and close. He went to the bathroom, she heard the taps running. She hoped he would have a hot bath, and get warm. He could catch a bad cold, being out like that and soaking wet from working. The night air was so chilly.

Thinking of it, and the silent figures working in the cellar—and her uncle crawling up the stairs, bleeding, dying on the kitchen floor—Betsy began to tremble again. The bed shook with her tremors. She could not seem to control them. Bryn began to whimper, and got up to roam about the room, whining and barking in alarm.

Vic came running. "What's the matter?" he asked sharply. He walked into her room wearing blue-striped pajamas with long sleeves. His hair was wet from his bath, he was rubbing it with a towel. "You shaking again, honey?"

"Yes—can't—stop— The bed—is so—cold."

"There aren't any hot-water bottles around, I looked. Damn it, you can't lie there like that." He brought in more blankets from his room and put them over her. They made her feel stifled, yet still cold.

She was thinking of her uncle, the blood running down him, blood all over his head and back. He had been stabbed in the back, she thought. Blood . . . blood . . .

Vic could be hard and cruel. He might have killed her uncle in a moment of fierce anger. He seemed to have no control over himself when he was angry. Maybe they had fought, and Vic had killed him. Then, remorseful, he had done what he could to atone. He had decided to remain and look after Betsy, since her uncle could not any longer. Yes, that would be like him, she decided feverishly.

"Damn me for a fool, that I let you go out with me," Vic muttered worriedly. "Be quiet, Bryn! Settle down there!" At his unusually sharp tone, the dog settled meekly down on his rag carpet before the window. But his head was still raised, and the large mournful eyes peered anxiously toward his mistress.

Now she was hot and perspiring, shaking as though with malaria. She remembered the days and nights of pneumonia. It felt like that, intensified. Only, then, she had not been able to breathe. Her throat had closed up, she had gasped for air.

She tossed and turned. Vic watched her, his mouth tight.

"Look, honey, are you upset about all this?" he asked gently.

Upset! She wanted to laugh hysterically. Her uncle had been murdered, the rumrunners had returned to Greystone, they might be caught by federal officers and taken to prison—and Vic wanted to know if she was upset!

"I'll—be—all—right . . ." She tried to turn over on

her side, but her body ached so she could not even move."

Vic sighed. "I'm going to sleep with you," he said, with an odd look at her. "I can keep you warm at least."

Betsy could not speak, her throat was now closed up completely, with nerves, with fear. She did not want this hard man close to her, but knew she could not fight him. He was too strong, he could control her with one hand.

Vic blew out the lamp and climbed into bed with her. "Too many covers," he said, and threw back some of them. Then very gently, he took her into his arms. He patted her head down onto his shoulder, as though she were a small child. "There, now, love, settle down, and be quiet."

Stiffly, reluctantly, she put her head down. Would he try anything? Oh, how could he, when she was so weary. Betsy deeply resented his taking advantage of her weakness. However, as she lay there, he just held her, quietly, close against his warm taut body.

His warmth seeped through to her, forcing out the cold and fear. She relaxed against him, and he patted her shoulders soothingly. The darkness and the warmth and Bryn's light snoring made her begin to calm down at last.

She sighed, pressed her cheek to his chest. He was a hard man, his chest felt like iron. She thought of how he had tossed those cases about, as though they were building blocks. He had panted and perspired, yes, but his arms had lifted them up, he had carried them up the beach, walking in the shifting sands like a pirate.

Pirate. Hadn't there been a pirate about in the old days? Betsy vaguely remembered the story of a Spanish nobleman, coming into Greystone Tavern in the old days. Mrs. Cunkle had told her chattily one day how a Spanish ship, towing a colonial vessel it had captured, had sailed into Long Island Sound and how, seeing it, an American ship attacked it and bottled it up near the islet on which Greystone sat. The Spaniards had lost, and all but one got ashore immediately—except for a nobleman who came up into the tavern, probably through the slabs in the cellar floor. He had collapsed and died, Mrs. Cunkle said, on the front steps. But the other Spaniards, put in Saymore jail, said he'd been carrying precious jewels and gold . . .

What else had she said? Vaguely Betsy groped in her memory. Contented by the warmth, her shaking stopped, she dreamed idly as she waited for sleep to overtake. Pirates—jewels . . . It was like a story in a children's book. She could just see a dark Spaniard crawling up into Greystone, wounded—blood on him—like on Uncle Hubert . . .

She shuddered again. Vic patted her back gently, leaned over and kissed her cheek. His lips were warm and soothing. Not demanding, not passionate. Just careful and loving and gentle.

Vic—his kisses. Lowell Reece had been so different. He had been gentle with her at first, then when he learned she returned his love, he had been passionate, fiery. He had wanted her so much—and was going to war and might not return.

So they had loved together and slept together—again and again—two young lonely people, drawn together by urgent desire and the agony of parting. But then he had gone, kissing her eyelids as he left her at dawn—never to return to her loving arms.

She slept, with Vic's lips on her cheek, her body close to his. Her dreams were confused, of a pirate in a crude little flying machine, dropping jewels on her head. Vic laughing, throwing back his head as he drank from a bottle. "Yo, ho, ho, and a bottle of rum," he was singing. Uncle Hubert in a sort of gray mist, stretching out his bloody hands to her, imploring, then turning his hands, pushing—"Go away, Betsy, don't stay, it is not safe—no, not safe, not safe . . ."

She wakened once, turned over uneasily. What had made her stir? Bryn's bark? Yes, he was barking softly, padding to the door. There was a shadow standing there, with the light behind her from the hall window. Betsy blinked. She was held closely in Vic's arms and could not get up.

It was dawn. She could see the color of the woman's hair, blond, and the color of the negligee, pink. Dora

Johnson stood there, staring at them. Then, quietly, she slipped away. Bryn gave another disapproving snarl, then came over to Betsy and pushed his nose into her outstretched palm. He licked her, yawned, and padded back to his bed, satisfied. He had defended her.

Dora Johnson had seen her lying there in Vic's arms, both of them fast asleep. Betsy's face burned in the dimness. The woman had guessed, had come upstairs to see if her suspicions were true. What would she do with the knowledge? Gino would not care, he probably thought they had come together the first night. He knew Vic couldn't keep his eyes off Betsy.

Vic had wanted her from the first. Now everyone would know about their affair. Betsy turned over. She could just make out Vic's sleeping face. It was relaxed, younger in the grip of sleep. His mouth was sensuous, the lower lip quite full and curved. His chin was hard, but there was a cleft near its end. She strangely wanted to touch that little indentation, it was rather endearing. She studied his face curiously. Straight eyebrows, long dark lashes, the curly red-gold hair tangled, one curl near his ear that seemed to tickle him, for he stirred restlessly, and pushed it back with a shoulder shrug.

Betsy stretched cautiously, trying not to waken him. He must be weary also. Her bones ached, her legs and arms were stiff as boards. But she could move. She had a little more energy than last night when she had collapsed.

When Vic moved, she shut her eyes and pretended to sleep, drawing long even breaths. She felt his gaze on her, felt the gentle touch when he brushed her hair back from her forehead. Then he moved, drew away from her. She could scarcely keep back the sigh of relief. He got out of bed on his side, and Bryn gave a sleepy bark of disapproval.

"Be quite, you fool pup," Vic whispered. "You want to wake *her* up. Shut up and guard. Guard, Bryn!"

Bryn whined, and Vic must have patted him, because his tail went thump, thump on the floor. Then Vic went out quietly, closing the door softly behind him.

Restless now, Betsy lay awake for a time. She wanted to know what Vic would do about the cases of moonshine. Would the federal officers come? Maybe she should go down to the cellar and make sure there were no signs of the cases left. Had Vic remembered to sweep the cellar floor?

Finally she could stand the suspense no longer. Betsy slid out of bed and into her slippers. Put on her robe, and listened. Vic was moving about his bedroom. She waited, holding her breath. Finally he moved away, down the hallway. She heard his booted feet on the stairs. Then she went to the door, opened it cautiously.

She heard him downstairs. The bathroom door stood open. She went to it, and washed up quickly. Then she came back, and got dressed; her arms were stiff and clumsy, but they worked. She felt better as she exercised quickly, a few swings from head to toe, some arm twirls and knee bends. She was out of condition. Her dancing teacher would have scolded her. She would never make the chorus line like this. She smiled faintly. New York and Broadway chorus lines seemed intensely remote, here in this wilderness, on this island in Long Island Sound.

Bryn was eager to go. She patted him, brushed her wheat-blond hair, and sighed. "All right, boy, let's go and see what this day brings forth."

It could not possibly be as bad as the previous ones, she thought.

9

Vic was sitting dejectedly at the kitchen table, his hands cupping a mug of coffee. At her entrance, he glanced in her direction, then jumped up, his face transformed.

Betsy—you up? I thought you would be ill in bed," he said anxiously. He glanced over her trim white blouse with the wide frill of chiffon at the throat and wrists, the slim dark-blue skirt. "Are you sure you feel well enough? I've been cursing myself for letting you go out last night."

"No, no, I'm sure I shall be all right. I'm just a bit stiff this morning. I—I am sorry I collasped last night. You were very kind to me," she added shyly, flushing as she thought of the night in his arms. He had been more kind than she had anticipated, not taking advantage of her extreme weakness.

"It was the least I could do. Sit down, sit down. Let me get you what you want. Tea? or coffee? And how about some eggs?"

Vic insisted on seating her at the table, then whipped up scrambled eggs and ham. Triumphantly, he served up a fine breakfast indeed.

She gave him a smile of gratitude, and it seemed to please him immensely. He sat down opposite her, and attacked his own breakfast enthusiastically. "Taste good, honey?"

"Um, you're a good cook."

"You have to learn when you live alone, or starve," he said, a shadow crossing his face momentarily. She noted the sun-lightened hairs on his wrist, the lean strong hand, the smooth fit of the dark sweater across his hard chest. The blond curls had been brushed, but already a few of them were straying.

"I was wondering," Betsy said timidly. "What are you—are we—going to do about that . . . load?"

"I've been thinking. I swept the cellar floor, by the way. The feds are sure to come. They know this was the dump by now. And they were chasing the cruiser last night. I don't think I'll try to pick up the stuff just now, or notify Alva," he said in a low tone, leaning close to her ear. She reached down, gave Bryn a bit of ham, which he snapped up.

"What—then? Won't it be dangerous to leave?"

"I want to watch, see if the feds are around. They may have located the dump and are guarding it, waiting to see who picks it up. They may want to find out who the contact is. Alva would be walking into a trap."

Betsy wondered how Alva disposed of that much liquor without being caught, but then decided she'd really rather not know.

"Do you think so? Then they—they'll close in—we might go to prison—" She laid down her fork, clenched her hands together. "Oh, Vic, I wish I had never come here!"

"Don't panic!" he said sharply. "They won't find the stuff here, and damn it, I won't let Gino bring any more. We're starting fresh, hear me?"

She bit her lips to stop their trembling. She curled her fingers around the mug of hot coffee, and then lifted it to her lips. The hot fragrant coffee hit her stomach, and warmed her. He was watching her closely. "All right, Vic, I'll try to stay calm. But, surely Uncle knew . . . he would be found out sometime."

"That may be why he died," said Vic slowly. "I've been trying to figure it out. I don't think Gino did it. Did you think so?"

She started violently. "No—" She could not tell him she had suspected *him*! "I wondered—Oscar Kawecki seems such a cold man—violent—I wondered . . ."

"He might have. If he thought Hubert would betray us. I don't know. All I know is I won't have them coming around anymore. That's final."

Betsy was silent. She hoped Vic could persuade them

to stay away. She didn't know if he could. Gino was calmly determined to keep Greystone Tavern as his rum dump. Greystone Rum. The cases and cases—it made her shoulders ache just to think of them.

"Well, I'm going out fishing this morning," said Vic, draining his cup and setting it down. He got out a package of cigarettes, offered her one. She shook her head. "We can use some fish, if I get some. And it's an excuse to row over where I can watch the dump and see if anybody's about. If it's safe, I'll go for Alva later today, get some groceries, and tip him off. He can collect it tonight."

"That would be a relief," she said slowly. "But won't it be dangerous for you—?"

"To go fishing? No law against fishing," he said, with a grin carving lines in his tanned cheeks. His eyes sparkled with daring. Yes, he liked excitement as most men did. While all she wanted was peace and quiet—would she ever find someone to share that with?

Betsy assured him she could do the dishes, start some lunch, and take care of Dora. The woman's door was shut, they had heard no sound from her. She was probably used to sleeping late. Betsy thought of that silent shadow at her bedroom door, and wondered if Dora intended to make use of her knowledge, or how.

Vic went out, clad in boots, black sweater, black pants, a thick blue fisherman's sweater over the other. A black cap on his head, Uncle Hubert's fishing pole in his hand. He went down the stairs to the cellar, she heard him untying the boat, humming to himself, heard him jump down into the boat. She got up and went to the front parlor, Bryn padding after her.

She watched from the windows, and soon he came into view, rowing vigorously out into the sunlit Sound. It was a bright clear day, the sky as blue as summer, for all the October wind. Waves ruffled in small white caps. Vic's back was straight, his head lifted to the wind, his arms rowing strongly. He was soon a small figure in the distance. She turned away, and went back to the kitchen. She would dust.

She went for a cloth, a mop, and dustpan, and set to work. It felt good to do something practical and useful, and she began to hum as she worked. Maybe things would turn out well. Vic seemed to know what he was doing.

She carried out one panful of dust, dumped it in the wastebasket, went back to dusting. The thick layers were discouraging. The room must not have been touched for years. She finally wet the mop, and began to scrub around the floorboards under the windows.

Suddenly Betsy heard footsteps from the cellar. Bryn stiffened, gave a yelp, and started for the kitchen. Betsy followed, clutching her wet rags. Surely it wasn't Vic back already. Could Gino have returned?

Maybe Gino would pick up the cases and take them away. Hopefully, she went out to the hall and opened the door to the cellar, and peered down. All was dark.

"Betsy? Bring a lamp!"

It was Vic, in urgent, muffled tones. "Oh—yes— right away, Vic!"

She lit one of the coal oil lamps set on the kitchen ledge, and hurried down the stairs, Bryn padding after her, grunting. She gasped when she saw Vic. He was bending over someone who lay limp on the cellar floor. For one horrible moment, she thought the man was dead.

Then he moved, groaned. Vic soothed him, "Take it easy. You're okay, man. Hold the lamp closer, Betsy. Got to see how bad he is."

"Who—who is it?" Betsy quavered, holding the lamp closer with shaking hands.

"Jim Burton," he said curtly. Betsy could see the pale face of the law officer, the lank brown hair dripping water on the cellar floor, the dark wet clothes, the darker spot on the shoulder. "He's been shot."

She stifled a cry. Bryn was snarling uneasily, circling the two men. "Who . . . did it?" she whispered, wondering if Vic had. She didn't remember seeing Vic carry a gun, but she would be willing to bet he had one.

"Don't know. But I can guess. He was near the cases. Lying half in, half out the water, shot and unconscious. Guess the guy who did it was scared off, or he would have stayed to finish the job." Vic had pulled back the shoulder of the dark jacket, and yanked aside the shirt to examine the wound, which pulsed and throbbed, as dark blood flowed over the pale flesh.

Betsy felt sick. It was a scene repeated, her uncle lying on the kitchen floor, blood flowing, darkening white flesh. Another man dying . . .

"I'll carry him up to the kitchen, can't see here. I'll have to get Robert Ming," Vic said

"You can't carry him—he's too heavy."

"Yes, I can. Go ahead of me, hold the lamp, that's a honey." He motioned her ahead of him impatiently, then bent down and lifted the man, hoisting him over his hard shoulder, so the man lay face down over Vic's back. Then slowly, with some effort, he carried him to the stairs. Betsy hurried up ahead of them, snapping her fingers for Bryn to stay out of the way of Vic's feet.

Vic grunted with effort. The young law officer was no lightweight, like Betsy. He was lean, but he was tall and big-boned. Vic managed to get him up the narrow stairs into the kitchen, and then let him slide to the floor. He stared down at the unconcious man, wiped the drops of sweat off his forehead with his wrist. His face was older-looking, grim and anxious.

"What . . . can I do?"

"Get a couple blankets and a pillow. I'll get him settled, then go for Ming and a doctor, if I can find one."

Betsy sped to the closet for the blankets, opened the hall chest, found two, and a pillow and case. She ran back, in time to see Vic bathing the wound gently with cold water, pressing a thick pad on the pulsing gap. "The bleeding is stopping, thank God. There's a bullet right through him, holes on both sides of his chest," Vic said briskly. "Should be a clean wound. It gets nasty if the bullet hits the bones, and stays inside," he explained to a white-faced Betsy.

She spread out one blanket, Vic moved the man to it, and gently slid the pillow under the limp head. Then he covered Jim Burton with the second blanket. Betsy fetched a towel and wiped the salt water from the thick dark hair.

"He's quiet. You stay by him, while I go. Won't be long. You aren't afraid, are you?" he added as an afterthought.

Betsy looked up at him in exasperation from where she knelt by the wounded law officer. "Of course I am!" she snapped. "Do you think I'm cold as ice?"

He gave her a boyish grin. "Glad to hear you aren't, honey," he said impudently. He looked for the car keys, jingled them, went out to the car. Bryn settled down beside Betsy, whining a little as the wounded man moved slightly.

It seemed an eternity, but it was just over an hour before Vic returned. With him was Robert Ming, his face scowling. When he saw his young officer lying limp on the floor, he gave an exclamation, and dropped down beside him.

"Did you get the doctor?" Betsy murmured to Vic.

He shook his head. "Out of town, I left word. He'll see young Burton at the place where they are staying, his wife said."

"Tell me again where you found him," Ming said curtly, his fingers on the wrist of the limp officer.

"Along the Sound, I went out fishing early—"

"You can save the lies. I know a cache was dumped last night! Where was he?"

Vic stiffened at the arrogant tone, but kept his voice even. "Like I—told—you—I went fishing early. I was out near a grove of trees, saw a dark figure lying half in the water. I went closer, discovered he had been shot. I hauled him into the boat, brought him back here."

Ming had removed the top blanket to examine the wound. As he lifted the pad of thick clotted blood, his face grew more grim. Betsy stared down at the dark head of the older officer. He was keen. He knew what was going on. Would he arrest them?

"His clothes are wet," he said abruptly.

"Found him in the Sound," Vic said gently.

"You could have shot him down in the cellar, dripped water on him—"

"Brought him upstairs, gone for you and the doctor, bound him up? Think again, Mr. T-man."

Ming looked grimly up at the equally grim face of Vic Halstatt. "I'm not satisfied with your story. Tell me again what happened."

"Once more," Vic said flippantly, sitting down on a

kitchen chair. His face was weary, the lines dark under his eyes. He told the story of going out for fish, and finding the body of young Jim Burton.

"And tell me where it was."

"I think you should get him to a doctor," Betsy said with spirit. She pointed to the limp young man at their feet. "Are you both going to argue and argue, while he needs medical help? He's still bleeding!"

Ming stood up, turned to her, eyed her from wheat-blond hair to her neat white blouse and trim skirt, to her slim feet in the little black slippers. "And where were you last night, young lady?"

Vic got up. Betsy was slowly turning red, she could feel the blood rushing to her head. She put one hand to her cheek, it was fiery hot already. "I was in bed," she said, in a small voice, glancing involuntarily at Vic's dark scowl.

"Hum. You were?" Ming said, calming down. He sighed. "Yes, you probably were. Anybody else here?"

"Mrs. Johnson. She's in the first-floor bedroom. I don't think she's awake yet."

Betsy was still saying the words when Ming went lightly to the hallway, to Dora's door. He opened it silently, peered inside, closed it gently. "Well, I never!" Betsy gasped indignantly, as he returned.

"Yes, she's still asleep, snoring, with a pink mobcap on." He grinned at her furious face. "At least you can prove that. I saw it myself. It's just you and Mr. Halstatt here. I want to know all about last evening, what you did, where you went—"

"Gonna leave him lying there while you converse?" Vic queried gently. Burton was stirring, his eyelids fluttering uneasily.

Ming gave him a quick, but nevertheless anxiously compassionate look. "No, damm it, I'll have to take care of him first," he growled. "But I'll be back, you can bet on that! You're playing with fire, both of you, thinking you can decieve the law forever! I'll find out the truth one day, and you'll pay for it, all the way!"

"I can hardly wait," Vic said smoothly, his hands stuck in his belt, outstaring Ming.

Ming gave him another hard look, then nodded

slowly. "We'll both wait," he said ominously. "Now, help me get him out to my car."

Vic shrugged. Then he bent, and lifted Burton up over his shoulder again. "Lead the way, T-man," he said, in a thinly veiled taunt.

Ming seemed as though he would protest, seeing the way Vic lifted the man. "All right, take it easy with him, or I'll have your hide."

He opened the kitchen door for him, followed him out, and Betsy watched from the kitchen window as they settled Jim Burton into the back seat of the black sedan. A blanket was laid on him, then Ming got into the driver's seat. The men continued to talk, but she could not hear what they said. Finally Vic stood back, his hands on his hips, his dark face closed and cold. Ming cranked the engine and drove off.

Vic watched him go, then came back inside. Betsy turned to face him. "What—what did he say?"

"Repeated himself," Vic said with a shrug. He took off his heavy blue sweater, and sat down in a chair. "Well, all he can prove is that we rescued his T-man for him. And that should not send us to jail, should it, honey?"

She did not smile in response to his light question. "Oh, Vic," she said under her breath. "I'm afraid. What if the cases are found?"

"Let them. They can't trace them to us. God damn that Gino, I told him not to leave them! Burton was probably watching, and Alva or someone tried to pick them up. Funny, I didn't think Alva would try to shoot his way out of trouble, though." He scowled down at the table, leaning on his elbows. His lean figure in the black garments that emphasized his strength seemed like a coiled spring, like a panther, ready to pounce.

He rubbed his hands through his thick red-gold curls. "Damn, I'm sleepy."

"Why don't you get some rest? Go up to bed, I'll call you when lunch is ready." She forced herself to sound calm.

"No. I think—I think I'll go tell Alva. I'll get us some groceries—make out a list, will you, Betsy? He can get the stuff at his own risk. Besides, I want to see his face when I tell him about Burton," Vic added grimly. He glanced at the small clock in the kitchen wall. "Should be open for business in half an hour. I'll get going. Are you afraid to stay alone?"

She was afraid, desperately afraid, but not of being alone. She was afraid of all the tough men in the world, who thought little of stabbing each other, or shooting, or drowning—all the men who wanted money so much, were so greedy for money and liquor and power, that they didn't care who got in their way. Quiet Uncle Hubert, murdered, stabbed to death, because he was in the wrong place at the wrong time, she thought wearily.

Awaiting her answer, Vic studied her face keenly. "You are afraid, aren't you, sweetheart?" he asked gently. "Listen, I'll do my best to protect you. You believe that, don't you?"

She drew a shaky breath. "I . . . believe you will, Vic," she told him, and to her surprise she found she meant it. He did like her a lot, and he was quite capable of protecting her, if anyone could. "I am grateful—"

"Hell, I don't want gratitude," he said, the chair legs scraping as he got up abruptly. "I'll be on my way. Make out a list while I go upstairs a minute, will you?"

She found a scrap of paper, and wrote hastily. When he returned, she handed him the paper. "Just a few things, some eggs and spices and sugar."

"Sugar and spice and everything nice." He seemed to have regained his temper. He bent and teasingly traced a kiss along the back of her neck, at the edge of the feathery bob. "That's what my girl is made of."

He went out before she could answer. Bryn whined in disappointment, and watched him at the kitchen door. Betsy sat still, feeling the funny little thrill that had flicked through her at his caress. She couldn't be falling in love with him. Not a man like Vic. A gangster, in trouble with the law, on the run, craving excitement—as Lowell had.

She couldn't possibly love a man like that ever again. If she ever loved again, she would want a quiet gentle man, a peaceful man—not someone like Vic, laughing with pleasure at danger, cold with menace as he faced Oscar Kawecki, expertly flicking a knife, wielding a gun if he needed to. Capable of any violence to get his way. But murder? Would he commit murder? If someone got in his way?

As she sat at the table puzzling over that, a fly made lazy by sunlight and late autumn buzzed in the window. Bryn snored at her feet. She reviewed the facts over and over again, as Robert Ming probably was doing.

Would Vic Halstatt have shot a man in the shoulder, dragged him into the cold waters, then changed his mind and gone to great trouble and effort to bring him back in the boat, haul him up into the cellar, treat his wound, get the officer for him, try to help him? It didn't make sense.

Then someone else must have shot Jim Burton. If so, who had? Alva Stern? But the grocer had not been notified yet about the cache. He didn't know where the haul was. Unless he had seen the cruiser offshore, had heard somehow the cache was there, or followed them over to the trees with spyglasses. She wondered where the grocer lived. In the village of Saymore? It was over the hill, in the direction opposite the point on the shore where Vic had decided to leave the precious Madeira and brandy.

But someone must have seen them, to have gone to the cache. And Jim Burton must have followed him, or gone ahead of him. She frowned, puzzled. Would they have heard the shot, or was the wind too high last night? And how long ago had Jim Burton been shot?

All she could think was that Vic had probably not done it. It was too illogical that Vic would have shot a man, then rescued him. It just didn't make sense. Wearily Betsy realized that the longer she stayed at this dismal tavern, everything was making less and less sense.

10

Vic returned within an hour with a small box of groceries. He dumped it on the kitchen table. Betsy looked at his face. It was grim.

She started to unpack the box, but he stopped her with a gesture. "Get your coat and scarf, we're going out."

She began a protest, then stopped. She ran upstairs, got her clutch and a scarf, came down, grabbed her white fur coat from the hall rack. Vic helped her into it, then snapped for Bryn.

Bryn hopped into the back of the car as though he were enjoying the prospect of a ride. With Betsy seated beside him, Vic backed up, and over the bridge. He took the narrow road up the hill, and then down toward Saymore. The automobile chugged along at a great rate.

"Why?" she whispered, as though someone could hear.

"Alva is going after the cache. Burton is being taken care of, Ming is coming back to talk to us. I want us to be away from the tavern for a while. Give us a chance to get our stories straight."

His tone was cold and hard, his face had lean taunt planes in the October sunlight that streamed through the window of the car.

"What—what will we do—in town?" Her cold hands clasped each other so hard her fingernails dug into her flesh.

"First we're going to the mortuary, finish arrangements for the funeral," he said quietly, then reached out and patted her clenched hands. "Take it easy. I've got it under control. The funeral is tomorrow, we'll order flowers. Then we'll go buy you a dress."

"I don't need a dress," she said automatically.

He flashed a grin at her. "I want to buy you a dress," he repeated. "You going to fix up the front parlor? Shall I buy some curtain material, and order them made?"

"I—I thought I . . . could . . . make up some curtains. A simple pattern," she added, pressing her fingers to her forehead. A headache was starting, right at the temples. Pressure.

"You want to? Like to sew?"

"Yes. I usually make most of my own clothes," she told him, more naturally. "I enjoy sewing."

"Fine. We'll get some curtain material, you choose it. Want a sewing box?"

"No—no, there's a nice one at the tavern, it must have belonged to someone, long ago."

"I bet the old place has quite a history," Vic said as they turned into Saymore's main street. He turned the wheel of the automobile, and quite easily he slid it into a curbside parking place. Opposite was the town green, and she was aware of children playing there, small ones, with mothers walking slowly, or talking together. They looked over curiously at the car, and at her, as she and Vic got out.

Vic led her to the funeral parlor, and opened the door for her. As they went in, she was hit by the odor of the place, the smell of stale flowers, the smell of preservatives. It made her half sick, as it called to mind her father's death, then her mother's. Too many memories, she thought, her head throbbing.

An older man came to them, half-bowed, studied their faces, shook hands. He had a big soft hand, plump and white. Not like Vic's hand, which was calloused and brown.

They talked about arrangements, and the man led them in to see the open casket. Pink-cheeked, peaceful-looking, Uncle Hubert looked almost natural.

"He looks the way he did—years ago," Betsy said softly. She thanked the man, and he seemed gratified. Vic spoke of the flowers.

"No need to get more," he said. "My, just look about you. Half the town sent flowers."

"I'd like a little bouquet, for his hand," Betsy said on impulse. "He—he liked it—when he saw Dad's—"

"I'll arrange for it, Miss Olsen," the man said gently. They discussed the flowers, Betsy took one more look at her uncle, lying there so still and peaceful in the pink-lined coffin. Then they left.

Vic had his arm about her as they went out. He could feel her unsteadiness.

"Too much for you?" he asked quietly.

She put her hand to her head. "It's—so confusing. I think I have a headache."

"We'll walk a bit," he said softly, and kept his arm about her. They walked across the town square, slowly, enjoying the cool autumn wind in their faces. The sky was blue as in June, with a few clusters of wind-drifted white clouds. The white church with its tall steeple cut cleanly across the sky, the red-brick homes with red tiles and white woodwork, the old whitewashed frame houses, the lampposts all in neat lines around the square—it all seemed so comfortable and welcoming. Even the tiny moving-picture theater, where a Cecil B. DeMille film, *Feet of Clay,* was now playing—Rod LaRoque its star. Coming attractions announced a Gloria Swanson picture and DeMille's *Triumph,* with Leatrice Joy.

"Oh, I wish I could live here forever," Betsy exclaimed involuntarily. "It's so different from the city. So quiet, and peaceful."

"Why not?" Vic asked. "Why not live here? We can run the tavern—"

But immediately she remembered, a shiver running down her spine as her heart plunged down again. What a mess—the rumrunners, the cache of rum waiting to be discovered, the officer who would question them relentlessly, and perhaps the murderer of Uncle Hubert returning . . .

It was terrifying. Betsy wanted to leave, to run away from the old stone tavern. But where could she go? She had no place, no one to run to. Suddenly there was no escape.

"We could run it as a restaurant," Vic was still saying, his lean arm like iron about her slim waist. They paced along slowly, she pulled the white fur collar up about her bare throat. "You could fix up the front parlor, I'll repair the roof, and fix things up. You could do the cooking with Mrs. Cunkle, supervise her. I'll do whatever you want, Betsy." Vic sounded urgent and hungry for her approval. "You like the idea, don't you?"

"I—I can't think right now, Vic. When Mr. Ming comes—he'll question—"

Vic made an impatient move with his hand, chopping off the sentence. "Not to worry! Listen. You don't know anything, you were ill, went to bed early. I was looking after you. That's all true, only we'll say it was earlier, say you went to bed about ten o'clock." He made up the story rapidly, repeated it for her. She nodded obediently, muttering after him, like an actress learning her part, he thought.

"When they had the story settled between them, he turned her back up the little side street they had wandered down.

"You were an actress for—how long?"

"Oh, I had parts when I was eighteen—we played on the road a lot," she said absently. "It seems so long ago! I understudied a part on Broadway, in *Rain*. Do you know that play?"

"God, I saw it! And you must have been backstage! Think of that, we might have met!" He squeezed her exuberantly. "What else were you in?"

"I did some road shows. We were going to do *Rain* on the road, only I got sick, my girl friend got the part. Then I understudied in *Loyalties*; that was a British play. The accent was difficult, but it's an interesting play, by Galsworthy. And I was in *Liliom*. That was a sad one. But pretty."

He listened, absorbed, asked questions about the theater. "I saw *The Emperor Jones*—wow, that was something. And *R.U.R.* Gosh, that was scary, thinking of all the world peopled by robots!"

"I know," she said, more naturally now. They could talk the same language. "Did you go to plays whenever you came to New York?"

"Sure. Musicals, too. I like musicals. Did you sing in them?"

"Some. Usually in the chorus. My voice was too weak for leads."

"You have a beautiful voice," he said admiringly.

She glowed at his admiration. It had been such a long lonely way she had been trodding by herself. Men had paid attention to her, but they had wanted only one thing and she had been wary of giving it unless she had to. But Vic wanted that also, didn't he? Sex, that was what men wanted. Yet somehow she had the feeling that Vic wanted more than that, that he was interested in her mind, her emotions, how she felt, what she wanted in life. He felt . . . protective, gentle, as though he would defend her fiercely from anyone.

"Here we are," Vic said, halting her at a door. It was a large dry-goods store. In the window was a blue-and-white checked dress. "Like it?" he asked.

"Oh, it is pretty!" The style was nice, hem at mid-calf, rather daring for a small town. The white collar was round and demure, the waist was nipped in, nowhere as straight as on the dresses being worn in New York. Not boyish, but feminine and pretty, with a full skirt.

They went in, she tried it on behind a screen. The saleswoman was admiring, Vic's eyes glowed. It fit perfectly, except for just a little tuck needed at the waist.

"Maybe you'll gain weight," Vic said. "Once you start eating properly! I hope so, anyway. Want it?"

When she nodded, he promptly reached into his pocket and peeled off some notes. She thought of Gino handing those notes to Vic, and felt a little sick. She turned away as he paid for the dress, and she went to change.

"Now we'll look at some curtain material," Vic said.

The saleswoman went behind the long counter, looked at the bolts of material on the shelves dubiously. "Well—we have some nice chintz, or some satin. What would you like?"

"Something we can wash," Betsy said, reappearing in her blouse and skirt. She came over to study the bolts. The woman took down several, and Betsy fingered them.

There was a blue plaid, but it was not the right color

for the old private dining room. She looked at a brown, but it was too dull and drab. It was Vic who noticed the striped bolt, and the woman took it down and spread it out.

"There, that is a pretty one, you have a nice eye, sir," Betsy said seriously.

Vic gave Betsy a wicked look, and a wink. "Sure I have," he said. "I can recognize beauty a mile off."

The woman looked at him dubiously, but was too absorbed in her task to listen. "You see, it's a nice stripe, with red and brown and dark orange in it, look nice at the windows, it would. And you can wash it by hand. Thick feel, isn't that nice?"

Betsy was already feeling the fabric, it felt almost like a thick tweed, with a nice texture of satiny threads mingled with cotton. "I like it," she said finally. "And I think it would make up pretty."

"How much do you need?" asked the woman, bouncing the bolt open further. Betsy was stuck, she had not even thought to measure the windows.

Vic had, to her astonishment! He pulled out a crumpled piece of paper, and said, "I measured all the windows in the private dining room. How do you figure the curtains from there?"

They put their heads together, figured that for the draperies to hang straight with pleats they would need three times the width of the windows. It seemed a frightful amount of material, but Vic insisted. "We won't buy draperies or white curtains, just have this at the windows. Easier to handle."

"You planning on fixing up the tavern?" the woman asked brightly as she measured and began to cut. She gave them a curious look. "Mr. Olsen, he just didn't seem to care much about having much business."

"Well, we do," said Vic, leaning against the counter, and watching her scissors snipping carefully along the fabric. "We're going to fix it up, and have specials on the dinners. You might spread the word, if you will. Not so much on overnights, but we'll be serving luncheons and dinners regularly except Sunday."

She gave him an approving look that lingered on his dark good looks. "That's fine. I don't approve of things being open on Sundays. Though I must say, for travelers it is convenient."

Betsy opened her mouth to object, then shut it again. Vic was certainly taking plenty for granted. Yet, wasn't she also by using Vic's money to buy curtains, and letting him buy her a dress?

They took their time, bought thread, new small scissors, paused to get some magazines and a newspaper. Vic bought some pipe tobacco and a couple of mystery novels. She wondered why he would want to *read* one, there was mystery enough at Greystone. He paused to chat with the man in the bookstore about opening the tavern to parties and groups of citizens. The man suggested that the local musicians' club might be interested in coming once a month for the day, and Vic said he would check with them.

"Doesn't hurt to get some business started," he said with satisfaction as they finally started back toward the car. Bryn had been asleep in the back seat. He yipped a welcome and licked Betsy's ear as they got in, nosed curiously at the packages they set on the seat in back.

Vic was talking animatedly about building up business as they headed down the hill and rattled up the road and across the bridge. Then he stopped talking abruptly, his mouth hardening. "Got company," he said briefly.

She recognized the big sedan of the law officer, Mr. Ming. And as they pulled in to park, he came around the side of the tavern, hands behind his back, as though he had been strolling around.

"Expected you back an hour ago," he said coldly.

"We had errands to do. Excuse me, got to take the stuff inside," Vic said, very busily shoving and pushing the packages around. Betsy accepted the smallest one, and shooed Bryn ahead of her into the kitchen.

Dora Johnson was sitting at the kitchen table, dressed, for once, in a purple crêpe dress with pink scarf at the neck. She gave Betsy an outraged look.

"Where have you been? I've been alone for hours!"

"We had some errands to do. I expect you're hungry. I'll start lunch right away. My land, it's past two o'clock!"

"It sure is. And that man out there, he came poking his nose right into my bedroom," Dora said bitterly. "Might know the law officer has to poke his nose everywhere! Gave me the start of my life, when I woke up to see that great nose poking in the door."

Robert Ming was coming in the back, holding the screen door for Vic. Betsy couldn't keep from looking at him, then, overcome, she darted out into the hallway, took off her coat and hung it up. She ran upstairs to put away her clutch and scarf, took a couple minutes to brush her hair and visit the bathroom, then, her giggles having subsided, she went downstairs once more.

Vic took Ming into the taproom, "so we won't disturb Miss Olsen while she fixes luncheon for us," he said, very politely, notifying the officer that the investigation was interfering with their normal life. Dora sat there, grumbling and yawning, sniffing with pleasure as the fragrant odors of steak began to creep through the tavern. It drew the men away from their sharp arguing in the taproom. Vic looked bland, Ming looked disgusted.

"We'll be around again," Ming said sharply, and went out with a curt "Good day" to the others.

"See you," said Vic, and gave Betsy a wink. He rubbed his hands with satisfaction. "Got to wash up. You about ready with luncheon, honey?"

"Honey," muttered Dora to herself. Vic gave her a scowl, and she flushed and shut up.

Vic went upstairs. Dora sat silently as Betsy set the table rapidly and cut up a fresh cucumber and some raw cauliflower into an attractive arrangement on a blue plate. "The vegetables are about done for the year," Betsy said, just to say something.

"Um. I like potatoes myself."

"I'll fix some tonight. How do you like them?"

"Mashed, with lots of thick gravy," Dora said greedily, licking her lips unconsciously. "You got any chicken? There's nothing better than chicken gravy."

"We'll have it tonight."

Dora brightened up. When Vic returned, she was talking about nightclubs and speakeasies in New York, how she had sung for some famous gangsters and been praised. "They sent a bottle of champagne backstage for me," she said proudly.

She chattered on through the meal. Vic seemed irritated, but he did not bawl her out or shut her up. Betsy was glad of that. She hated discord.

They got through the rest of the day. Betsy measured the curtains and material and, with Vic's help, cut it carefully. They laid it on the long table in the taproom.

"Enough for today," Vic said when they were finished. "You can sew them up another time. You work too hard."

She gave him a smile that was unconsciously wistful. "Oh, Vic, it's so nice to have a place to do for. After living in small uncomfortable rooms, with drab furniture, shabby things, it's so—so nice to spread out, and plan. Don't you think so?"

His face lit up. "It sure is. The way I feel, too. I haven't had a real home for a good many years. I hate drifting."

"I thought you would like it. The excitement, I mean." She folded the curtains carefully, avoiding looking at him.

"You can have enough of excitement. I want to settle down." He seemed sure of that. She wondered, as she prepared the dinner, cut the chicken pieces, fried them golden brown, mashed the potatoes. Was Vic really tired of excitement? Or did he just want a change for a time? He was reckless, charming. He could put on an act, too, as well as any actor. Look at the way he calmly deceived the Treasury man. She drew a deep sigh. Only the routine work got her through the days. If she had time to think, she would get scared all over again.

Dora Johnson went to bed early, complaining there was nothing else to do in this place. She had a bottle with her, Betsy could smell the liquor clear out in the hallway.

"She'll be on her way, as soon as Gino forwards the money," Vic said, with a scowl. "She's a pain. The sooner she's gone, the better. I'd give her the money myself, only I know I'd never see it again."

They sat in the taproom, Vic reading the newspaper, Betsy leafing through the magazines, pausing at the pictures of fashion news. "I think skirts are going up," she commented.

"That won't make me mad," Vic said, forgetting his gripe.

"Look at that one." She held up the magazine to a picture of an evening gown, of a figured lamé, with straps for holding it up, a flat bosom, no waist, the hem halfway to the knees.

"No girl in the world looks like that," Vic commented critically. "Flat as a board."

"Vic, I meant the dress!" she giggled, her eyes flashing into blue sparkles.

"Okay, honey, on you it would look good," he said softly, and laughed as she blushed. "But you have more to add to it than that dame. Look at the next one."

It was white crêpe brocaded in gold, with a long gold stripe crosswise across the bosom over one shoulder, the other shoulder bare. Betsy giggled again. "I can see me in some evening place in Saymore!"

"I'll take you out dancing some night," he promised. "You'll knock 'em dead. Like to dance?"

"Oh, yes, I love to."

"I'm not that great, but I'll try."

She settled back again with her magazine, this time looking at the pictures from Vic's viewpoint, a little smile curling her lips. He kept glancing at her from over his paper. Bryn whined, yawned.

"I'll take him out. He's sleepy," said Vic.

"So am I. I think I'll go up to bed."

"Okay. Good night."

She went upstairs, and presently Bryn padded up, curled around his rug, settled down with a great yawn, his silky coat fluttery from the wind. Betsy undressed, went to the bathroom, brushed her teeth and returned to her room. She took off her cotton robe, slipped into bed, blew out the lamp, and settled back. It had been a pleasant evening, almost ordinary and undemanding.

The door opened a crack, then more. Betsy stiffened. Vic came in in his pajamas, standing in the darkness like some Nordic god.

"Betsy."

"W-what?"

"I want to make love to you."

Just like that. Betsy was silent, her breath caught in a gasp.

When she said nothing, Vic came closer, then slid into bed beside her. She was stiff as he took her in his arms.

"Last night," he said, his voice muffled against her ear. "It was the hardest thing in the world just to hold you, and not take you honey. I want you, Betsy. I want you bad."

His arms were trembling, his tone urgent. Betsy knew she owed him a great deal, perhaps as much as any producer she had ever slept with, almost as much as Lowell— She feared him, but he had been good to her, protective, kind. The thoughts were running around her head like frightened mice, even as his arms tightened about her. He turned her to him, so they lay on their sides facing each other.

"Betsy," he said huskily. His lips touched her cheek, moved over her ear, down to her throat. It had been a long time since a man had touched her like that. "You're so silky-soft, you're so sweet. I never met anyone like you. You're loving and giving, and I want that so much. Oh, God, I want it."

Betsy relaxed in his arms, trying to forget the way he he had whipped out a knife so fast, and the deadly way he handled Oscar Kawecki and defied her uncle. She must forget—she must . . . She curled her arms about his neck, and came closer. He drew in his breath, and his mouth met hers, urgently, in a caress that went on and on.

One of his hands moved down to stroke her thigh. She stiffened. "Are you scared?" he murmured softly against her cheek.

"I've been scared for—months. I run and run and get nowhere." In the darkness it became easy to talk to him. "When I was sick last winter, and lay in bed—and didn't see anybody for a week—and was hungry—oh, Vic, I thought I would die there and nobody would even know I was dead!"

"Oh, honey, honey," he whispered, his touch now soothing and comforting.

"Then I came here. Uncle didn't want to take me in, but I begged him. Then—then Gino came—and Oscar Krauss, and I was scared to death—when he died—oh, Vic, I'll never be safe again."

"Sure you will, sure you will," he said, with assurance, caressing her, her hair, her cheeks. "Honey, I'm going to take care of you. Believe that, with all your heart. I love you, I'm crazy about you. I'm going to look after you, and you'll never have to be frightened and alone again. I mean it, honey." He tilted her chin and kissed her again, his hard mouth softening against her lips.

She wanted to believe him, she wanted to lean on him. She wanted to give to him, and receive from him. If she could only believe in him, be able to trust him . . .

His hands were gently caressing, soothing, as he smoothed them over her waist and hips. He caressed her breasts through the cotton nightdress, then gently he took it off and removed his pajamas also.

His naked hard body lay against hers and Betsy could feel his desire awakening hers. His caresses became more certain, and her mind began to grow dizzy with the warm emotions he aroused in her. He was a skillful lover, she thought, while she could think. He was slow and gentle with her, returning again and again to her breasts, kissing and suckling them as a low moan escaped from Betsy's throat. He drew her closer, so she felt his hardness against her.

Betsy clasped her hands at the back of his neck, and deliberately willed herself not to think of anything but this man and the passion he was arousing in her. How muscular he was! Her fingers explored his back, and found the sensitive places along the spine. Vic shivered, bent over her, sliding his hands along her inner thighs, until she was trembling with excitement, then he drew her to him with an easy motion. It was an explosion of pleasure for them, unexpected and the more delightful for that. She half-sobbed in his arms, and his breathing was heavy as he finally drew off.

"I knew you would be sweet in your giving," he murmured in her ear, kissing the lobe. He settled back to sleep, keeping his steel-like arm about her.

Betsy knew by his breathing that he was asleep almost at once. She lay awake, blinking into the darkness, amazed at her own joy. It hadn't happened often like that, only with Lowell sometimes.

It was strange to sleep with a man beside her, but it felt good. To be with someone hard and strong, his even breathing close to her ear, his body relaxed and warm next to hers, giving her warmth. Even her slim feet were warm now; they were usually cold as ice, as she lay in bed alone.

Before drifting off to sleep, she had another thought, and it jolted her awake for a few minutes. Years ago, a more sophisticated actress in a play with her, in a burst of confidence, had told her, "I can tell what a man is really like when he makes love to me. He shows what he is inside. If he's a brute and a bully in lovemaking, you can bet your life he's really like that, no matter how he pretends and brings you presents. But a really sweet man is a gem. You don't often find them like that."

Vic had been very sweet to her, and gentle, even at the height of his passion. Was that Vic, the real man? Was his toughness assumed for the world to see, a protective veneer to keep himself alive? She would think about that some other time.

Betsy sighed, snuggled closer to her lover. She put her flaxen head on his dark shoulder, and let sleep and sweet dreams claim her.

11

Vic was gone when Betsy finally woke up the next morning. October sunlight streamed in through the windows. She peered over the edge of the bed—Bryn had disappeared also. It must be late.

She reached for the nightdress draped across the foot of the bed, put it on, slid out of bed, and her feet felt for the slippers. Just then Vic pushed open the door and walked in. He was wearing a sober dark-blue suit.

"Hi, honey, I was just going to wake you up." His gaze moved over her intimately, and she blushed and put her head down.

"Is it . . . late?"

"Past eight o'clock. We're going to the funeral at ten, you remember."

Memory flooded back. Uncle Hubert, the funeral, the murder. She shivered, stood up, pulled on her robe. He hesitated, standing at the door.

"Shall I fix you some breakfast?"

"I'll just have coffee when I come down." She frowned. "I didn't think what to wear, Vic. I don't have a black dress."

"You have a black scarf, wear that over your head. You'll be wearing a coat, anyway."

"Okay," she nodded. "Where's Bryn?"

"Eating in the kitchen. I took him out so he wouldn't wake you early. You slept hard last night."

She knew her face was red when he left. She went to the bathroom, found the water hot, took a bath. Last night—she wondered if he would take everything for granted now. Probably. He was that kind of man. What he wanted, he took. But he was generous also. She was thinking about him throughout her bath, how sweet he had been.

She dressed in her dark-blue dress, found her black scarf, and went downstairs. Vic had fixed breakfast, anyway, and it was ready for her when she came. She gave him a smile.

"You don't listen to me," she joked.

"Not when you need food, honey. More cream?"

She nodded, and enjoyed the luxury of fresh cream in her coffee. They ate in a leisurely way, talked more about redecorating the taproom. Then Betsy nodded toward Dora's room and asked, "Is she awake?"

"No. She won't wake up till noon. I think she read one of my books last night, said she had trouble sleeping."

Then it was finally time to go. They shut Bryn in the kitchen, though he whined and scratched at the back door.

"I hate leaving him," Betsy said as they got into the automobile.

"Dogs don't go to funerals," Vic said firmly.

She was glad he was with her. He was so strong and so sure. When they arrived at the church, they were both surprised to find a crowd outside, and more people inside.

"Must be the whole town here," Vic said. He put his hand in her arm, and must have felt the trembling of her body. "Take it easy, honey. I'm right here."

He *was* right there, and Betsy was passionately grateful for that. How would she have managed alone? She would have run away, scared to pieces. She took a deep breath, greeted some of the people. They were kind and nice about Uncle Hubert, saying good things about him, and how sorry they were.

One older man, a farmer by his clothing and reddish complexion, came up to them. "I'm Ned Palmer," he introduced himself. "Hubert was renting the tavern from me."

Betsy shook his hand, felt the calloused palm against her slim fingers. "It's good to meet you. Uncle Hubert—I think we should talk—"

"Mr. Halstatt here says you're thinking of carrying on

the Greystone restaurant," Palmer said, his keen dark eyes studying her. "You seem a mite frail for all that hard work."

"I'll be helping her," Vic said firmly. "As I told you. How about coming over this afternoon, and we'll discuss it?"

"I'll be mighty pleased to come this afternoon. I have to get back to the farm by tonight," he said, and they agreed on it. Betsy went on into the church, and an usher took her up the aisle to the front. She looked one last time on the face of her uncle, then the casket was closed by the man from the funeral parlor.

The preacher was a tall thin man, with a gentle face and a shock of white hair that stood straight up. He had dreamy eyes and a glow to his cheeks. She listened intently as he talked about death and resurrection. Vic's attention was wandering, he was looking at the altar curiously, with its simple wooden cross and the plain wood lectern. The windows behind the altar were of stained glass, flowing in the morning sunlight.

The preacher spoke then of the life of Hubert Olsen. Betsy wondered where he had found out so much. Maybe from Dr. Cameron, he had seemed to know Hubert. "A good man, a kind and simple man who lived only too short a time among us," said the preacher. He spoke only once, indirectly, of the manner of his death. "Taken so violently from us—" Betsy felt Vic stiffen to attention beside her. But the man went on to generalities, then recited a long prayer.

It was over. The people filed out. Betsy and Vic sat still, while the ushers took out the casket. Then they followed it to the back of the church, to the simple graveyard with the white tombstones. Some of the stones looked old, their inscriptions faded and blurred. They came to the raw open grave, and the men with shovels in rough blue workclothes stood back as the casket was set down.

There was another prayer, a long one. Then the casket was lowered into the earth. Betsy watched somberly as the first clods covered the casket, then Vic turned her gently away.

She rubbed her eyes with her fists. She would not

cry, it was not right. She was not weeping inside for Uncle Hubert so much as for herself. He was at peace after a long and rough life. She was still alive, in danger, scared. She wondered if that was the way it always was. The people who were left were the ones who wept. Dead ones were at peace and calm.

"You can cry later, honey," Vic said quietly, holding her arm closely to himself. She nodded, and wiped her eyes with her handkerchief.

Tall red-haired Dr. Cameron and his wife approached them. Betsy shook hands, tried to smile at them.

"We want to have you over for dinner sometime soon," Mrs. Cameron said. "We want to get acquainted." She looked curiously at Vic. "You'll be staying?"

"Yes, ma'am. She'll need help," Vic said firmly.

She must have wondered about their relationship, but she only said, "Then you must come also. Mr. Olsen was a fine man, and he spoke highly of Betsy."

"You're very—kind—" Betsy's voice broke. She felt weak and dizzy for a time, but Vic's hand steadied her as he walked her back to the automobile. He set her inside, and they started back for Greystone.

"That's over," Vic said. "Pretty church. Old one."

"Yes." She cleared her throat and tried again. "It was pretty. Old. Must have been there a long time. The town is old, too. Maybe a couple hundred years."

"Seems odd to think it was started so long ago. Dr. Cameron said Greystone Tavern was built about 1725, or 1730, near as they can figure. Did he tell you about the pirate?"

"Mrs. Cunkle did. Strange story. I wonder if it was true?"

"Oh, it could have happened," Vic said, and she realized he was making conversation to calm her. "Pirate ships could have come into the Sound. They don't draw very deep, and the Sound goes deep in places." He discoursed on early sailing vessels for quite ten minutes, until they drew up behind Greystone.

"She told me about a highwayman also, back in the

early 1800's. Seems someone hid him out here in the tavern, while everyone else was looking for him."

"Did they ever catch him?"

"I don't think so. The story goes that they believe he kept the money, and went west with a wagon train, started fresh."

"I think it's possible to start fresh," Vic said, his eyes dark and thoughtful. "Don't you?"

"I hope so," she said simply. "That is what I want to do. Put the past behind me, and start over in a different kind of life." He squeezed her hand hard, until it tingled.

Bryn whined and barked his delight and reproach when they came in. Vic took him outdoors and let him run around, for a treat. Dora was up, yawning and cross. "That dog, he did nothing but whine while you was gone," she complained. "I couldn't sleep a wink. Where was you?"

"At the funeral of Uncle Hubert," Betsy said simply, took off her coat, and went upstairs.

Dora stirred herself to set the table, much to Betsy's surprise.

"I wish Gino would come back and give me the money to go to Florida," the woman complained again. "Do you think he'll come soon?"

Betsy thought that what she wished was that Gino would never come back. But he would have to come and do something about Dora, and she hoped it would be soon. The woman grated on her nerves.

They ate luncheon, then Dora retreated to her bedroom with "Father Brown" Vic's short-mystery collection. Betsy decided to start sewing the draperies for the private dining room, pinned a hem into one of them, and carefully measured along the top for the pleats.

She sat down in the taproom while Vic measured the windows there, and began sewing. Vic climbed up on a small stepladder and muttered to himself, writing down numbers. When a stiff knock came on the front door he about fell over.

"I'll go," Betsy said, starting up, the fabric falling from her lap.

Vic gave her a scowl. "No, *I'll* go." His hand was at his pocket. He went to the front door and she heard the voices: the easy drawl of Vic, the quiet masculine voice of the farmer.

They returned. Ned Palmer smiled at Betsy. "Hate to disturb you today, ma'am. But I often don't get to town from one week to the next. My sons went West, you see, so I handle it all myself."

He was a man probably in his late sixties, she thought. He sat down, and the oil lamp struck gray from the fine hair and the alert black eyes that saw everything. He had a slow, practical way of speaking, as though he thought deeply before he spoke.

"Sons went West, you say?" said Vic, seating himself across the long table from Ned Palmer.

"That's right. I thought one of them would take over the tavern here, though *I* never cared to run it. Jonathan, my brother, did that—with his pretty wife Megan Marie. They had one boy, John, who's in insurance in Albany, New York, and two pretty daughters: Marie, who died when she was but three, and Louise, who married and moved to New Hampshire—Megan's there with her now, I judge. Has been since poor Jonathan died in the flu epidemic, winter of '18–'19. But, to get back to what I was sayin': my boys got itchy feet, like John, and both went to Wyoming, got a cattle ranch out there. They tell me to come out, but shucks, I've lived here all my life, and my people before me. Go back to before the Revolution, you know," he said with pride.

Betsy wanted to hear all about his family history, but Vic was impatient about more current matters. "I heard Hubert Olsen had a year's lease on Greystone," Vic said directly. "Does that go for his niece here?"

"We-ell, that's what I wanted to discuss with you." Palmer looked across at Betsy, who had picked up her sewing, and was putting small neat stitches into the hemming. "You're an actress, aren't you?"

"Not anymore," she said quietly. "I had pneumonia twice last winter, and I got pretty sick. The country air agrees with me. Uncle Hubert said I could stay, and I hear I've inherited all he had. I was his last relative. I didn't know he had made a will in my favor, I'm still not sure. We have to wait till the will is read."

"Oh, I think he did," Mr. Palmer said. "Said he had a nice niece in New York, all the kin he had in the world. Wanted to leave you something. He had a year's lease on the tavern, it was up in July, and we signed for another year. I've had a couple other offers, however."

Betsy stared at him, the sewing dropped to her lap. "You—have? To lease the Greystone?"

"That's right." He frowned at the table, his big tanned fingers moved unseeingly over the wood. "Don't rightly like to take them up, though," he said, after a pause. "If I thought you would keep the place open— keep it up and have a good place I wouldn't be ashamed to own—"

Vic jumped in with, "That's exactly what we have in mind." His jaw jutted out belligerently. "I've been a wanderer all my life, and I'm sick of it. I want to settle down. I know folks, I can cook, too. But Betsy here and Mrs. Cunkle will do the most of the cooking. I'm handy, and can fix the electric wiring. And I am going to get up on the roof and nail down the shingles. I've been looking around, seeing the places that need fixing." He paused for breath, his dark eyes anxious.

Palmer looked him over thoughtfully. "You plan to stay here?" he asked.

"That's right. Betsy needs help, and I aim to give it to her. With me, she can run the place fine."

"We-ell, wc can see, can't we? Why don't you go on as Hubert would have. I see you're fixing up the old private dining hall," he said to Betsy unexpectedly. "Got the dust out. Hubert didn't bother with it."

"Yes. Well, we thought we would make it into a nice salon for folks to wait while their meal was cooking, or if we have a lot of guests . . ." she said breathlessly. "We'll still take in folks overnight, you see, if they want. There's the first-floor bedroom, and three upstairs besides mine and Uncle Hubert's. I'm strong, when I'm not sick, really I am."

"I had an agreement with Hubert Olsen. He signed the lease on the understanding that he wouldn't turn it over to any stranger. That's the way I would agree with you. I'll let you keep the lease if you don't turn it over to anybody. I don't want strangers coming in on the strength of a lease. I'm proud of the place: it's been in my family for so long. You agree to that?"

Betsy looked at Vic, he stared straight back at her. She nodded, so did he. "Agreed," Betsy said, taking a deep breath. "We'll hold the place and run it—like Uncle Hubert would—or better if we can! And then you'll let us have the lease?"

"That's right. No need to go to a lawyer over it. Your word is good with me," Ned Palmer said contentedly. He rose to go. "We-ell, I'm glad to have this talk with you. Got things settled in my mind. I'll sleep well to-night. Any troubles, you let me know. I have a farm ten miles north of Saymore. Anyone can direct you. I'll be by in another month or so to see how you're making out."

Betsy shook his hand and thanked him for the chance. Vic saw him to the door, and when he came back, he was rubbing his hands, beaming. "Well, that's that, Betsy! We got us a place!"

"Oh—yes, isn't it great?"

She smiled up at him. Impulsively, Vic bent and kissed her cheek, then took her chin in his fingers and held her face uplifted while he kissed her mouth. His lips were warm and gentle against hers.

"It's going to be a great life, honey," he said. He went back to the stepladder, and pulled out the paper to write down more numbers. "I wonder who it was wanted the lease so bad? Mighty quick work, going to Ned Palmer so soon after Hubert died."

Vic's back was to Betsy. She set down the sewing again, felt her heart skipping a beat.

"Oh—I don't know," she said blankly. "It isn't as though we have a lot of customers. Who would want the business? We have to build it up first."

He turned around, gazed at her steadily. "Ever think it wasn't the business of food they wanted? It was the business—you know—" He yanked his thumb downward toward the cellar.

The rum. That horrible rum. And those cases of

Madeira and brandy. It made her ache just to think of the moonlighting someone wanted to continue.

She remembered that handsome Bradford Schuyler. He had wanted to take over from Uncle Hubert. And there was Alva. It would be convenient to Alva Stern to have the business, and all the profit, instead of just part of it.

"Any ideas?" Vic asked sharply, watching her face.

She looked up at him, troubled. He came down off the ladder, sat near her. "Go on, honey," he said in a soft dangerous voice. "You're thinking something."

"I was thinking—maybe Alva Stern," she whispered. "He could have all the money instead of part of it. He is a greedy sort of man. But he is a small man—could he have, you know, killed Uncle Hubert—for the lease?"

"Greed and fear can give a man great strength," Vic said grimly. "You think he could have done it? Damn it all, I'll have a talk with him—"

"Well, there's another man," she said hurriedly. She hated it when Vic's face took on that cold hard look, that deadly look.

"Who's that?"

"Bradford Schuyler. You know, you met him. Big red-headed man. Maybe close to forty. He was here a couple of times, he came to talk to Uncle Hubert."

"Did he know about the rum?"

She nodded. "Somehow he knew. He warned me against staying here, said it was dangerous. Then he and Uncle Hubert went to talk, and drank brandy together. He wanted the lease, I know that."

Vic was scowling. "I'll have to find out more about that character. Where is he from?"

"From Newport, Mrs. Cunkle says. He had a family there, a very important one in the old days. You know, in the nineties, when the rich social people came up this way, and built huge homes? His family lived in one. But he came over to Saymore to start a business."

"What business?"

"I don't think I know."

"Well, I'll find out. Anyone else?"

She thought, shook her head. He patted her hand,

said, "It's a clear day. I think I'll do some painting. The window sills on the outside need it. I bought some white paint." And he went out, whistling, his humor restored.

The day was peaceful. Betsy sat and sewed, and tried not to think about the funeral and all the people who had come. Could one of them have been Uncle Hubert's killer? It was horrible, to think someone in that crowd at the church might have been the murderer. Betsy fought away from that line of thinking and thought of Vic instead.

That night, he came to her again, and their loving was gentle and sweet. She rested in his arms afterwards, with a peaceful feeling. He was half asleep, and she ran her fingers slowly over his muscular shoulders. He was a hard man. What would happen to them?

Vic hadn't said a word about marriage. But she didn't know either if she wanted to jump into any marriage with him. She thought it best to wait, and find out if they were compatible, and if he would stay, or if the dullness and hard work would drive him to search once more for excitement. Maybe Gino would come beckoning, and Vic would go off with him in search of more money, the thrill of being chased by the Coast Guard, the bright lights of Miami and Havana, all the girls at his beck and call.

"You tease me like that, honey, I'll wake right up," Vic growled against her hair.

She laughed softly, and her fingers came to rest on his chest, and the mat of strawberry blond hair that curled down to below his stomach. His hand caressed her naked back, down to her hips, then rested there. His breathing slowed to sleep.

The next day was quiet until noon. Betsy was sewing on the draperies and Vic was painting outdoors, when Bryn began to bark.

Vic came racing in, his face shocked and pleased. "Customers, honey! Come to dinner! What have we got?"

She squeaked, dropped the curtains. "Customers! Oh, my goodness!" She picked up her stuff, cleared the table hurriedly, while Vic went to the front door.

She heard him apologizing easily for his paint-streaked clothes. "Didn't expect anybody today, but come right in, come right in! We're just getting the place fixed up."

"We wanted to see Greystone again," said a bright feminine voice. "They used to have the best home cooking! We came her years ago for my wedding breakfast."

A man growled something about not wanting to disturb them, but Vic reassured them, seated them in the taproom, and came back to Betsy.

"They'd like chicken or beef, whatever you can fix. What about it, Betsy?"

Her cheeks poppy-pink, her blue eyes shining, she was already taking fixings from the icebox. "Our first customers! Oh, Vic!" He hugged her from behind, gave her a little spank, and laughed.

"I'll get the table set. Think I should ask if they want drinks?"

"Oh, I don't know!"

"I'll see if they mention it," Vic decided. "We got some beer. Maybe that would do. I'll fix a plate of appetizers while you start the dinner."

They worked together like a team, smoothly, Betsy thought with delight. Vic put a nice lace tablecloth over the long pine table and set places efficiently. She gave him some pink glass candlesticks and red candles to create atmosphere. Two plates of appetizers were quickly prepared—pickled watermelon, candied kumquats, sweet pickles, corn relish, rye bread, and three kinds of cheese.

While the chicken was frying nicely in the skillet, Betsy put potatoes on to boil. She would cut them up with plenty of butter and salt and pepper. They had dried peas which she set on to steam. Then she cut fresh cucumbers in fancy patterns with the rind still on and added little cauliflower buds to the plate.

Vic served, an apron over his hastily changed shirt. She heard him kidding the couple good-naturedly. He knew his manners, and he knew people. She would have been shy, but he was easy as anything, yet respectful.

Two hours later, it was all over. Betsy collapsed onto

a kitchen chair as Vic carried in the last of the plates. "Oh, Vic," she said, wearily but happily.

"Tired, darling?" he said, worriedly, and leaned over to nuzzle at her neck. "They loved it. But I'll get Mrs. Cunkle to come in days after this."

"Oh, our first customers. Did they really like it?"

"They loved everything. They'll spread the word, they're from farms over west of Saymore," he said. He whistled happily as he set the plates to soak, and began washing up the glasses.

Betsy got up again and began preparing their own late luncheon. Dora had discretely hidden in her bedroom. She came out now, curious as a bird.

"You're really going to have a restaurant here?" she asked. "I didn't know you was serious!"

"Oh, yes, we are," said Vic over his shoulder. "We'll build it up in no time."

"Well, I must say you'll feed them well," Dora said graciously, sitting down in her place. "If this was Florida, I'd stay myself!"

It was her handsomest praise. Betsy felt so happy she could burst. They had done it, they had started anew!

12

Betsy had the satisfaction of hanging the drapes in the front parlor before she went to bed. It had been a great day.

Vic came in as she was sliding into bed. "I'll get Mrs. Cunkle to start coming on Monday," he said, scratching the back of his neck, then raising his arms in a great yawn. "Think I'll go see her tomorrow. You know, we ought to put in a telephone."

"A telephone? Really, do we need one?" Betsy asked, curling up under the sheets. It was strange to think that less than a month ago she had been alone and ill, in a one-room apartment in New York, not knowing what would happen to her.

"Sure, I bet the telephone company could set up a few poles and run a line across the bridge over here. I'll see about it," he said confidently, sliding into bed beside her. Jonathan Palmer never would have one, the groceryman told me in town, said his business was mostly Saymore and Torbury and Cornerbrook. And he or Megan were driving about all the time. Also, the two of them didn't like to be disturbed. Said a phone would ruin their little island existence, ringing at night. Tired, honey?"

"Um, pretty tired. How about you, you worked so hard today."

"Yep. But it is satisfying, you know. I can see the changes already. Tomorrow I'll paint the rest of the window frames—if the wind dies, I'll get up on the roof and nail down the shingles."

He gathered her into his arms and patted her head down onto his shoulder in a now-familiar gesture. It was a gathering-in, a comforting movement, as he settled

himself to sleep. It was as though they already belonged
to each other.

Vic went right off to sleep, but Betsy lay awake a
little longer, thinking how easily they had fallen into a
pattern. She could love Vic easily, she thought, he was
so good to her. If only she felt certain he had given up
his roving ways, she would let loose and love him. If
only— But he was a wanderer. How soon would he
grow tired of playing house with her?

She went to sleep on the thought, but wakened a couple of times in the night, and heard Bryn padding
around restlessly. "Go to sleep, boy," she whispered. He
came over, stuck his nose in her palm, then, satisfied,
went back to his place under the window.

Her home. It could be her home, with her man, her
dog, maybe her children later on. It was a big place,
one to raise children in, she thought, with growing hope.
If only Vic wanted to settle down also . . .

In the morning, Betsy found Vic had risen already
and taken Bryn out. She could hear Vic's raised voice
calling to Bryn. "Come back, you fool pup! You don't
go chasing birds!"

Bryn barked. Betsy grinned, and got up.

It was Friday. She wondered if any customers would
come today. Maybe over the weekend, they might.
They ought to get more food in. There was some in the
pantry, but they needed more meats and chicken. She
should count the canned goods down in the cellar. But
she hated to go down alone. Maybe Vic would go with
her, or even Dora.

She washed, dressed in her long blue dress, fixed her
hair in an upsweep with curls about her ears. It was
growing, she might let it get much longer if Vic liked it
that way.

How her thoughts revolved about Vic! Betsy paused
in brushing her hair, gazed into space; if he left her—
she would be desolate. She could never manage by herself.

Already she leaned on him. As long as he didn't get
tired of that. She went downstairs, her face sober, and
saw him as he came in from outside.

"Morning, honey."

He was grinning, looking so much happier than when she had first seen him. She smiled back at him shyly. "Good morning, Vic. I was wondering if we might have more customers this weekend."

"Might. I better see how much grub we have around."

"I thought I might count the jars in the pantry. I know we need more meat and milk and cheese and eggs."

While she started the ham, he filled the kettle for coffee, then sat down at the kitchen table with a pad and pencil. He began to make out a list.

They talked about food. She told him about the water supply from the well, and what Uncle Hubert said about getting fresh water when it went brackish. Of course, Vic had to go out, look down the well, and draw some water in a bucket, to see for himself. He came back inside, his cheeks ruddy from the cold.

"It's okay now. But I bet this winter when we have storms we'll have to depend on bottled water."

They ate, talking easily. They were sipping coffee, and adding paint supplies, soap, and various other items to the list when a knock came at the back door.

"I'll get it," Vic said, the suspicious look coming into his face. "I didn't hear a car, did you?"

She shook her head, gazing past him toward the door at the tall red-haired man who stood there. Bradford Schuyler. A little chill feathered down her spine.

Vic opened the door, said easily, "Come on in. Just in time for coffee."

Betsy saw a movement out of the corner of her eye, turned her head in time to see Dora Johnson peering from her bedroom door, staring at the man, then drawing back in alarm. She shut the door very quietly. Dora hadn't wanted to come out, she seemed startled. But she had been all dressed to come out of her refuge.

"Well, well, you seem cosy here," Schuyler said, his handsome face all smiles. Betsy got up to get another cup and saucer. He sat down easily at the end of the table, his sharp look taking in the dirty breakfast dishes, the pipe Vic had laid in the ashtray, the shopping list.

"Just settling in," Vic said, and sat down again. "Saw

you at the funeral, didn't get a chance to say hello. It was good of you to come."

Betsy echoed it, "Yes, it was good of you. You knew Uncle quite well, I think."

"Well enough. I liked and respected him. I had hoped to go into business with him, matter of fact," Schuyler said, easing back into the chair cautiously. He accepted the cup of coffee with a smile up at Betsy. The smile seemed meant to convey admiration, respect, consolation all at once. It was a masterpiece, that smile, Betsy thought, sharpened by her years on stage. She wondered if he had ever been an actor.

"Too bad," Vic was saying. "He's gone now. Betsy will inherit all he had."

"So I understand. Heard it over at the courthouse. I don't know that he had much, except for the lease of the place. Thought I might talk to you about that." He turned definitely to Betsy.

"Oh, what did you want to say?" Vic was glaring at Mr. Schuyler, so she gave him a light kick of her slipper under the table. His hand went automatically to his shin, and he turned to look at her. She frowned at him. "I—I wondered what you were planning with my uncle," she said to Mr. Schuyler with a sweet smile.

Vic was silent, sullenly pouring himself another cup of coffee, sipping it black. He picked up his pipe, deliberately dumped out the ashes, filled it again.

"Well, actually, Betsy—I may call you Betsy, may I not? Your uncle and I were on first-name terms. And please call me Brad." The charming smile again.

She did not call him anything. Vic was on the edge of explosive anger, and she wanted to hear what Bradford Schuyler had to say. She wondered if he had pressured Uncle Hubert about the rumrunning business, getting in on that, or the lease of the restaurant.

"How kind of you," she murmured. "What had you and Uncle planned?"

"Well, actually—" He leaned forward, his elbows on the table, his big, well-manicured fingers closed about the sturdy coffee mug. "He and I were going into business together. I don't know if you had heard about—the rumrunning." He lowered his voice to a murmur, glanced at Vic sharply.

"Rumrunning?" Betsy allowed her slim eyebrows to arch high as she looked at him with wide, innocent blue eyes. "On the Sound here?" She was willing to sound stupid if it would draw him out.

"That's right. Actually, your uncle earned all his money with rumrunning, I know it for a fact," he said, with growing confidence. "Now, I'm not against it, I'll have you know! Too fond of brandy and rum myself," and he gave a soft little satisfied laugh. "The law is foolish, they'll never enforce it. With all the miles of Sound to cover, and only a few stupid law officers to go blundering about—they can't possibly track it down. I mean to handle it all myself, with your permission. I'll let you have a generous commission for doing what your uncle did, turn a blind eye to the use of the cellar. I'll keep a watch—"

"Sounds like you're taking a lot for granted," Vic burst out, unable to contain his anger any longer. Betsy could have kicked him again—harder. She had just gotten the man to talk. "She's not having any part of that trading! It's a chancy thing, and you deal with tough guys who stop at nothing. You know her uncle was murdered?"

"Of course I know it!" Bradford Schuyler blazed. "It's all over Saymore. And you are willing to let her stay here and take her chances? I'm not! She needs protection, and I can give it to her. I'll keep her out of the business, just pay her for the use of the tavern."

"That's big of you—" Vic began bitingly.

Betsy reached out and put her hand on Vic's hard arm. She felt it tense with fury. "That's kind of you, Mr. Schuyler," she interrupted. "I'm sure you mean well. But we mean to run the Greystone as a restaurant. I'm not sure what Uncle was involved in, but whatever it was probably caused his death. We mean to run a dry place, serve meals, offer overnight lodgings, and that's all. The rumrunners won't be welcome, if indeed they do come here!"

Bradford Schuyler stared at her, his light-green eyes

flaring with fury. "A restaurant! You two, run a restaurant? That's a laugh! Nobody will come—not way out here—are you insane?"

"We had customers yesterday, our first ones. And they said they would come back, and spread word," Betsy said proudly, her flaxen head upraised, her pointed chin tilted. She felt Vic's arm stir under her hand, and she tightened her restraining grip on it. Schuyler stared at the slim long fingers on the dark cloth of Vic's sleeve.

"You two—going to run it? You two? Together?"

Betsy flushed at this insinuating tone and Vic stirred in his chair, as though he meant to jump up. "That's right," she said clearly.

"Well. Well." Schuyler took a deep breath, as though to calm himself. "Very commendable, I am sure. Well, my offer still holds. I'll back you in the restaurant, if that's what you want. I was a good friend of your uncle, and he spoke highly of you, Betsy."

"Back her in the restaurant!" Vic seemed to be biting the words like nails. "You've got a nerve! We're in this together, and we don't need your help, we don't want it—"

"Vic is helping me," Betsy said hurriedly. The two men were glaring at each other like strange dogs, she could fairly see the hackles rising on them. "We shall manage very well, thank you."

Schuyler turned fully to her, ignoring Vic though watching him sideways, like a sly animal. "The offer is for you, Betsy. I'll back you, you'll need money to fix up the place, get you started. I'll be your silent partner. You need protection, I can give it to you. I am respected hereabouts—"

"Betsy is not your concern!" Vic rose abruptly in spite of Betsy's attempt to hold him down. "You get out! We're going to manage this together, and I'll thank you not to poke in where you aren't wanted!"

Schuyler rose slowly, still speaking to Betsy. "I know his kind, Miss Olsen. He'll run out when he's bored enough. He won't stick, he's not the sticking kind. When he goes, you can come to me, and I'll look after you, I promise you that!" He was furious, the green eyes were blazing as he backed to the door, Vic menacingly after him.

Vic backed him out the door, and slammed it after him. Betsy watched the man coming around the building, past the windows, walking out toward the bridge. He must have parked his car across the bridge somewhere.

Vic turned on Betsy. "And what do you mean, encouraging him? You know I'm staying."

"Of course," she said, though she wasn't sure of it. "I wanted to get him to talk. Don't you see? I know Uncle turned him down, yet he was here bragging about how he and Uncle were going into business together. If you had just let him talk . . ."

Vic stared at her, his hands on his hips. Finally he said, "Women!" And stalked down the cellar stairs, where he banged around for a time.

Betsy sighed, shook her head, and began to clear away the breakfast plates. Dora Johnson came out timidly, her plump form quivering.

"Is—is that man gone?" she whispered.

Betsy stared at her curiously. "Yes, he went. Want some breakfast now?"

"Yes, yes, some coffee," Dora said. She sat down. "Do you . . . like that man?" she finally asked. "I heard him offering to back you."

"Vic's here, he's all I need," Betsy said flatly.

Dora scratched a match on the table and lit a cigarette. "I mean—do you trust that big fella?"

Betsy thought about it. "No, I don't think so. He lied to me, I do know that. No, I don't trust him particularly."

"Well . . ." Dora stopped, and began to drink coffee, her face rather pale and drawn. She was quiet that morning. She did wonder aloud when Gino would come and give her some money to take the train to Florida.

Gino came that night. Betsy had just gone to her bedroom to undress when she heard the sounds downstairs. Bryn got up at once from his rug, and began whining and barking uneasily.

Vic came to the open doorway of his room and listened. "Lord God Almighty," he said, and his dark eyes were furious. "If that goddamn Gino hasn't come again!"

"Maybe he just came to give Dora the money . . ."

Vic shot her a contemptuous look. "You kidding? Gino doesn't do any favors. He's unloading cases. I'm going down and stop that goddamn bastard. He can do his moonlighting elsewhere, damn him!"

Vic went down after sticking something dark into his pocket. Betsy, fear catching her throat, picked up her sweater and followed him. She was stuffing her arms into the sleeves as she followed him down the stairs. Bryn came after her, curiously, sniffing at her heels.

Vic ran down the stairs to the cellar. Candles were lit, stuck in the little metal holders on the pantry shelves. Gino in his shirtsleeves was lifting cases up into the cellar; Oscar, in a dark coat, was receiving them.

"Stop right there!" ordered Vic, holding the gun at them. Betsy, at the top of the stairs, held Bryn back from racing down. She was deathly afraid what would happen. The cold chill air from the open cellar slabs struck at her, swirling about her feet.

"Oh, come on, Vic, don't play games," Gino said, with a grin up at him from the motorboat. "There's good money in it, and I got the pay from the last time. Alva managed to pick up the load, and did he get a good price! Should set you up for a long time, you and that blondie of yours."

The gun did not waver. "Don't unload. Get those cases back in the boat, and get away," said Vic. "I meant what I said. You're unloading no more rum here. We're going to have a respectable place. Did you hear Jim Burton got shot?"

Oscar stiffened, set a case down carefully. Gino lost his smile. "Burton, the young officer? How did it happen?"

"I thought you could tell me," said Vic. "But not now. You can load up again, and then come pay Dora to get away. She wants to take the train to Florida."

"Damn Dora," said Gino. "You don't mean this, Vic. We didn't shoot nobody, honest. Stern didn't say a word about any shooting." He lifted another case easily, set it into the cellar.

"No more cases! Get them down into that boat! You want me to shoot?" Vic was shouting now, dark with rage.

"The shot will make quite a lot of noise," Gino said, good-temperedly. "Come on, Vic, we're friends. We can settle this peacefully. You want a bigger share of the money? Okay, I'll take it out of Stern's part. He's a greedy hog, anyway."

Dora came to the doorway. "Oh, Gino, you come for me! You're a good sort. Come on up and talk afterward. You want to meet me in Miami?"

Gino hesitated, looked from Dora to the gun in Vic's hand. "Talk him into putting up that pistol, that's a good girl," he said to Betsy. "We can't talk friendly-like with that gun around. It makes me nervous, and it makes Oscar downright angry."

Around the grin, there was menace.

"We can't leave the cases in the boat," Oscar said in his deadly monotone. His face was gray and weary in the candlelight. "Come on, Vic, put it up. If you missed, I'd get you anyway. You ain't that good a shot in this light."

Betsy put her hand to her throat.

Dora said, "You boys fighting? What about?" There was simple bewilderment in her voice. "Come on, Gino, finish up, and come up and talk. I got to have money to get to Florida."

"I'll come up when I get the boat unloaded. Come on, Vic, let us unload. I'm too damn tired to get them back on the cruiser tonight. Lord God, we miss you, boy! The motor went out on the way up here, and I thought we'd never get it fixed. Got a new boy, claims he knows motors, but he's a damn liar."

"He on the cruiser?" Vic asked cautiously.

"Right you are. Come on, let me unload, and we'll talk it over tonight. The waves are bad, and the cruiser is in a nice hidden spot. We can stay overnight and discuss it, how about it, Vic?"

The coaxing tone won. Vic looked keenly at Oscar, then nodded, and the gun disappeared into his pocket. He came on up the stairs. "Come on up when you're finished, we'll talk," he said harshly.

"Ain't you gonna help us, Vic?" Gino asked anxiously.

Vic sighed, gave Betsy a shove out of the doorway, his hard hands gentle on her shoulders. "You go up to bed, honey, I don't want you around them. Get Byrn to stay near you, shut your door. Dora, get some clothes on if you're gonna stay up. You looked downright indecent."

Dora gave him an outraged glare, then padded back to her bedroom to add to the flimsy pink nightdress.

Betsy whispered, "Vic, I'm afraid. You won't give in to them, will you? The officers will come around—"

"I know, honey, and I got to be firm, or they'll keep on coming. This has got to be the last load, and I'll tell them so in language they understand."

His mouth was a hard line; she tilted her head up to kiss it. His lips clung to hers, his eyes softened. "Take care, Vic, please," she whispered.

He gave her a quick hug, then turned her to the stairs. "I will, baby doll. Now you go to bed."

She retreated, snapped her fingers for Bryn, who was inclined to linger near Vic. The two went up to her bedroom, and she shut the door and went to bed, as he had told her.

Betsy could not sleep, no orders could get her to do that tonight. She lay tensely awake, hearing the rumble of voices, and Dora whining occasionally as she raised her voice. Only once in a while did she hear the hard, deadly, cold tone of Oscar Kawecki. Gino was doing most of the talking, persuasively. She heard the clink of glasses. They must be drinking and talking. Gino could be very beguiling with his Italian accent, his laughing eyes, his easy ways, his promises of more money. She could only hope Vic would not give in to him. It would be the beginning of the end for her. She could not last, she knew that. Hubert Olsen had died, so would Betsy, one way or another.

Finally she heard the voices cease. Vic came slowly upstairs, hesitated at her doorway, then went to his room. She lay tensely wakeful, shivering in the lonely bed, her feet cold, her hands cold. But he did not come. He was moving around for a time, then she heard his bed springs creak, and muttering to himself as he tossed and turned. Then finally it was quiet.

The tavern seemed full of white wraiths tonight, muttering, whispering, the old forms of those who had lived here, had come and gone. Every creak of the floorboards, every sigh of the wind against the panes of glass, the flapping of a loose shingle on the roof reminded her of those who had lived here, had loved and feared, and hoped and lost. Was she to be one of those who had lost?

Betsy sighed deeply in frustration. Vic might have given in to them. With enough wine and promises, he might have given in. Gino knew Vic's weakness—excitement. Gino might have persuaded him to come with them. Hope was dim, and flickered more weakly than a candleflame in her heart. Tears trickled down her cheeks, she closed her eyes tightly. It had been a nice dream while it lasted.

13

Betsy rose at dawn. She hadn't slept well, all night she kept on waking up and listening for sounds. All she heard was the soft sighing of the wind, the soughing of the waves under the tavern, the monotonous undercurrent of the sea.

She glanced toward Vic's door as she came out of her room. It was closed. Bryn sniffed at it, and she whispered to him and took him with her down the stairs to the kitchen. She opened the back door and let him out, then stood gazing at the outside through the window. It was dark today in the West, looked like it might brew up a storm. The wind whistled through the barren trees; it had blown off most of the red and yellow autumn leaves, and they lay piled on the ground.

Bryn gave a run through the pile of leaves under the oak tree, scattering them, giving a muffled bark as he encountered a startled squirrel. The squirrel flirted its fluffy gray tail, and ran back up the tree. Bryn stood back, gazed up in amazement, then tried a running jump to the tree the way the squirrel had. He failed, scrambled down again sheepishly. Betsy was laughing softly as she turned from the window.

She wondered what Vic had decided last night. She went over to the stove, lit it, filled the kettle with fresh water.

Dora's door opened and she came into the kitchen wearing a neat dark-blue dress, with a frill of white about her throat. Betsy stared at her in surprise. The woman had hardly been dressed properly in days!

Dora whispered, "I want to make sure Gino pays for me to go by train today, or takes me with him. He has got to take care of me!"

She looked tired, with dark, bruised-looking pouches under her eyes, as though she had not slept. She smelled of liquor. She must have stayed up drinking with them.

"You have another dress. . . . Did Gino—?"

"Yeah, he brought my suitcase from Florida. Damn him. Let him think he's done with me. He's mistaken! If he knew what I knew—" She broke off abruptly, turned to the stove. "Got any coffee yet? My tongue is dry as sand."

Betsy went on to fix the coffee, set the table. Dora sat down heavily, her face troubled. Her blond hair had been twisted into a bun at the back of her neck, only a few curls struggled free. She looked older than her early thirties, fleshy and plump and fearful. It must be awful to feel your looks going, Betsy thought, to be getting older and less attractive, and depending on a man who could not be trusted. Yet wasn't that what she herself was doing? The thought hurt.

When the coffee was finally ready, Betsy poured it out. She added cream and sugar to her own, Dora drank hers black.

"What did they finally decide last night?" Betsy asked. She tried to sound casual and idly curious.

Dora gave her a hard look. "Damned if I know. They was still talking when I went to bed. Vic was giving them a hard time. He has his nerve! He owes Gino plenty. Gino gave him a job, took care of him for a couple years."

"Maybe Vic wants to go straight," Betsy said, challenging those bleary green eyes. They flickered nervously, glanced away from her.

"Go straight? Vic? Don't make me laugh. He loves the money and the excitement as much as Gino," Dora said contemptuously. "And what's wrong with giving people the drink they want? The law is crazy anyhow. Maybe with the election next month, a Democrat'll win —they say John Davis, of West Virginia, is less of an old Puritan than Cal Coolidge!—and the laws'll change!"

Betsy fell silent. She was not going to argue the merits of Prohibition to this woman. They went on drinking the coffee. Dora was increasingly nervous.

"Damn that Gino. Didn't he get back yet?"

Betsy started. "Isn't he in bed?"

"In bed? Hell no, he and Oscar took the cases back out to the cruiser, at least that was what he said he was going to do."

"He did?" Betsy's heart gave a great thump. "You mean—Vic persuaded him—"

"Hell, I don't know! All I know is Gino said he was taking the cases. He said he'd come back for me. They want a safer dump, I think." Dora got up restlessly, stepped around clumsily in her heavy shoes. "You can't see the Sound from here, can you? I'll go see if the boat is coming back for me."

Dora went over to the bedroom, stared out the windows. She returned, shaking her blond head, her painted mouth hard and petulant. "Damn it, it's too dark. A storm is coming up. Damn that Gino, I told him to leave me the money for the train. I don't want to ride that damn boat again!"

Betsy clasped her hands together. If Gino was leaving with the cases, then Vic must have won the argument. Except—where was Vic? Would he go with them? Had he deserted her completely? Was she wrong in her conclusions? Were they going to find a safer place along the shore to dump the liquor?

Would Vic leave her?

Without a word?

She licked her lips. Dora was prowling the tavern hallway, up and back, up and back, then going to the windows again.

Betsy sighed, turned back to the stove. She needed eggs, she had better go down to the cellar pantry and get them.

"Listen, I think I heard a boat—" Dora was back in the kitchen, eagerly. "I'm going down—"

"I have to get some eggs, anyway," Betsy said quickly. She would be glad of company, she hated going down into the dark cellar alone. She lit a candle, picked up the metal stand. "Come on, we'll go down and see."

She started down the cellar stairs, her soft slippers making no sound as she descended. Dora thumped behind her.

"Damn it, I can't see. Hold the candle higher. I never

heard of a place not having electricity," Dora complained.

Betsy reached the bottom of the stairs, and turned to light the candles on the pantry shelves. She lit one, held it up for Dora to see her way.

"Any signs of Gino? Gino?" Dora called out. "Where do they bring the boats up?"

Betsy walked over toward the open slabs. Cold dark water was rushing below, and she saw a single rope hung over the side. Betsy leaned over to peer down. At the end of the rope a small rowboat was fastened.

"There's a rowboat here," she reported. Dora made a muffled sound. As Betsy turned, the candle went out, its stand knocked from her hand.

A shadowy form in the darkness was holding Dora, who was squirming, kicking, trying to protest. But the hands of the form were holding her throat silent.

It had happened so quickly that Betsy stood shaking with paralyzing fear. That form had flung the candle away. He must have crept up on them in the dark cellar, blown out the other candle, then grabbed Dora when she discovered his presence.

Betsy could not see beyond the struggling bodies swaying back and forth. As she backed up toward the pantry shelves, the shadows detached from each other. Then she heard the impact as Dora was flung to the floor with a sickening thud.

In the very dim light from the opened cellar floor, Betsy saw the creature bend down, pick up Dora's limp form, and incredulously—saw him fling the woman into the icy waters of the Sound! She heard the splash, saw briefly the mussed blond hair, the navy dress, the white frill at the throat—then the woman was gone in the swirling rush of the sea.

The attacker turned on her.

Betsy could back up no further. Warily, she circled away from the shelves. She stared wide-eyed at the figure, but could not make out his face; there was nothing to recognize in the darkness. Then he was coming toward her!

She circled slowly, backing further away. The waters of the Sound swirled before her as she paused. The man was coming around the opening, hands out before him—he was coming—he would kill her . . .

Her breath came in gasps. She felt shaky, unable to fight. She would faint, she felt her head swimming and her knees went limp. She could never fight him off. Dora had been killed by his hands, her neck wrung like a puppy's.

Betsy glanced quickly down at the swirling waters of the Sound. The rowboat? No, she could not aim for it. She would have to reach for the rope, steady it, climb down carefully . . .

Her attacker came around the open slabs—was close—reaching out—Betsy closed her eyes and desperately, with a fatalistic certainty she would die one way or another, dived down into the dark waters of the Sound.

The cold chilled her to the bone instantly. She went under, her thin dress clinging to the flesh, the waters sucking at her, pulling her down. She struck out desperately—her arms flailed the water ineffectually. Betsy had known she could not swim well—but she *had* to swim—she must—if only the water was not so cold. Helplessly, she gave herself up to the current.

It was lighter when her head came up this time. Her hair hung in limp strands over her eyes. She pushed them back with a wet hand. Betsy was coming out from under the foundations of Greystone. She glanced back fearfully over her shoulder. The rowboat bobbed below the cellar, empty.

Could he be in the water, following her?

With the strength that only despair and fear can bring, Betsy struck out. She must make it to land, it wasn't very far—just the length of the little island on which Greystone stood. But what if her attacker came after her by land?

She was growing numb with cold and fear. Her arms splashed feebly, but she was getting closer to shore. Betsy tried to swim with more strength, but only splashed herself. "Calm yourself, Betsy," she said to herself. "Keep on—keep on—Vic will come—he will hear you—Vic—oh, Vic—"

She held on to the thought of Vic. He must be somewhere close. He must be up—she should have waited for him to get up. Poor Dora, dead of her eagerness to escape . . .

Dead. She must not die. Life could be precious. She had wanted to die last winter, but some spark in herself had kept her fighting for life. She thought of the story of the two frogs in the butterchurn going to market. They had fallen in, and one gave up and sank to the bottom. The other kicked and fought, churned up a lump of butter in the process, sprang onto it, and jumped out, to life and freedom.

The funny things we think when we are dying, she thought. Last winter—ill—feverish—she had had such strange dreams.

Stroke, another stroke—she could do it . . .

Her feet bumped into land before she realized she had come to the bank. But it was so high. It was sheer here, she could not climb out. Her fingers grabbed for a hold, but there was only mud where the waters washed relentlessly against the land.

"Help!" she cried out feebly. Then more strongly, choking on some water she had swallowed: "H-help! Help! Oh, help me—!"

Then she heard a bark so close to her ears, it startled her. Betsy looked up at the bank. Bryn stood there, ears cocked forward, staring down at her in great surprise.

"Bryn—get help!" But he just stood there barking.

"Help!" she cried again. "Help, help, help!"

"Where are you? Betsy? Where are you?"

It was Vic!

She called more strongly, searching frantically with her hands to find something to cling to. There was nothing. Vic ran to the spot where Bryn was standing.

"Betsy—my God!"

"Get me out," she sobbed. "I'm so cold— I can't last—"

He leaned down, kneeling on the bank. She reached up her arms weakly, he grabbed her wrists, and hauled with brute strength. Betsy felt the agony through her body as the cold waters sucked at her one more time. Then she was free of the water, swinging free in the air, out—and up—and on to the bank.

She landed almost on Bryn. He came nosing at her curiously, licking her face. On his knees beside her, Vic demanded urgently, "My God, Betsy! What happened to you?"

She was shuddering in great convulsive shivers. Vic took off his jacket, wrapped it around her, picked her up and carried her toward the bridge. She glanced up at his learn dark face, saw him more hard and terrible than she had ever seen him.

But she was safe. Vic held her. She was safe.

With Bryn barking at his heels, Vic strode up into the small porch at the front of the tavern. He kicked open the front door and carried her inside. She could hear the drip, dripping of her sodden garments as he carried her back along the hallway, and up the stairs.

He carried her right to the bathroom, and set her down. Betsy was so limp, she sagged to the floor. Vic turned on the taps, began to strip off her dress. She let him, too weak to protest. He stripped her to her blue goose-pimply skin.

Then he dunked her into the hot tub. It was so warm it made her burn inside. He grabbed a washcloth, washed her face, her hair. Bryn came prancing back and forth, whining in a high-pitched yowl. Vic took a towel and began drying her hair, moving the towel over her head, her face, her shoulders in the most gentle, yet thorough fashion she could imagine.

Betsy was crying, tears streaming down her cheeks.

"There, there, honey, oh, darling. What in the name of hell—?"

She gulped, tried to tell him. "Dora—killed—"

"Try again, honey," he said patiently. "I can't understand you."

"Dora—someone in the cellar—attacked—killed her—threw her into the Sound—someone hiding down there— Oh, Vic—I jumped in—oh, Vic—"

She shivered in the warm tub. He was kneeling beside her, wiping her hair dry with gentle movements of his big hands. She gazed into his face, her blue eyes filled with tears.

His face had turned dark and taut, the cheekbones standing out. There were white lines beside his mouth.

"Someone in the cellar? Who?"

"I don't—know—we went down—candle out. Dora wanted to make sure—Gino not leaving—"

"I can't make sense of it, calm down, honey, calm down. We'll get you warm and dry, and then you'll tell me," he said, with forced calm.

He lifted her out of the tub, rubbed her dry with a big warm towel. He got her nightdress and robe, which warmed her some. Then he carried her back to her bedroom, and tucked her into bed. Bryn settled down on his carpet, satisfied they were all right.

"Okay, now, honey. Tell me," Vic said, with something hard and terrible in his tone. "The whole story."

14

Betsy clutched at Vic. The numbness and fear were beginning to merge. "Listen, Vic. Someone was in the cellar. Maybe he is still down there. He killed Dora, threw her in the Sound. Can you get the sheriff?"

He stared down at her. "I'll go myself," he said grimly. "You don't know who it was? You didn't see his face?"

She shook her head. "But don't go down—he will kill—oh, Vic, please, get the law—"

But he went to his bedroom, came out with a small black revolver in his big hands. He checked the load, then said sharply to the dog, "Bryn, stay there. Right there." He pointed to the entrance to her bedroom. "Listen, honey, you hear one single thing, you let out a big yell. I'll hear."

She nodded her wet blond head. "Okay, Vic. But be careful—oh, please—"

"Sure, honey." But it was mechanical, that comment. He went quietly down the stairs, she strained to hear the sounds. The cellar door opening, that was all. She could not hear more. Bryn, his ears cocked, listened also, his head to one side.

It seemed to take ages. She did not know how long it was, but huddled under the covers, she grew warmer in bed. She rubbed the towel absently over her hair, still listening. Then Vic finally came back, relaxed, the gun pushed back into his pocket, the handle sticking out.

"Nobody's down there, I looked all around. Okay, honey, you feeling warmer?"

Betsy nodded and sat up against the pillows. Vic took the towel, rubbed her head gently, caressed the soft flaxen hair. "It's getting dry. Feel like talking now?"

"Yes—I must tell you." She swallowed with difficulty. He put his hand to her cheek.

"I think you're in shock, baby doll. I'll go down again, and get you something hot to drink."

She didn't want him to leave her again. But he seemed to know best. He went out, presently returned carrying a tray with a teapot, cup, and bottle of brandy.

Vic poured out the hot tea, added a generous portion of brandy. "Drink that." He held it to her lips. It was so hot it about burned all the way down. She drank in little sips. Soon she felt better, as the brandy and hot tea settled in her stomach.

Betsy began to relax and felt the ache in her shoulders and back, where the tension had gripped her. She sank back into the pillows, sighed with relief.

"Can you talk now, Betsy?" he asked gently. He sat down beside her, took her in her arms, stroked her back soothingly.

She nodded, put her head down on his hard chest. She felt so safe with him, as though nobody could hurt her while he was near. She rubbed her cheek against his rough shirt. It felt deliciously sturdy.

Betsy began to tell him what had happened. "Dora came out of her room all dressed up. She was afraid that Gino would leave without her. She said Gino had taken the cases out to the cruiser, they were loading up. Were they going away, Vic?"

"Yep. I told them to find another drop," he said shortly. "We argued half the night, but he finally gave in. But I don't think he meant to come back for her."

"Ohhhh—" she whispered. "Poor Dora. She thought he would come back, or give her the money to take the train. But she was worried. She kept listening for the cruiser. But only the rowboat was down there!"

"What? Only the rowboat?" he interrogated her sharply. "No—wait—go on with the story."

"Well—she thought she heard a boat. We went down—I needed eggs anyway. I had lit a candle, I lit another one on the pantry shelf. We searched—I looked down—the cellar slabs were open—then—a man came—"

"When you looked down," he interrupted. "What did you see? A boat, two boats?"

"Just the rope, and the one rowboat."

"Okay, go on."

Betsy shivered, pressed closer to his comforting presence. His arms closed tighter about her, reassuringly.

"Dora—he grabbed Dora," she said in a muffled tone. "A big shadow—no, first he knocked the candle out of my hand, blew it out, then knocked it down on the cellar floor. Then he grabbed Dora. I could just make out a shadowy form as he held her neck. She was trying to scream, but she just made sounds. He choked her, flung her to the floor. I heard . . . the . . . thud—"

She was shivering again; he stroked over her back, drew the blankets up about her.

"Then he picked her up and just flung her into the water. In the dim light from the open slabs, I could just make out her face, all puffy, the dark dress, the white frill about her neck. She splashed when . . . she hit the water. Then he turned on me. I backed up—backed up—he followed—" Her voice climbed hysterically, broke.

"Easy, honey. So what did you do?" His voice was the calm of someone under incredible strain.

"I dived into the water. I thought I could swim if he didn't follow. I was afraid but kept swimming. The water was so cold—"

"He didn't follow you?"

"I don't think so. I got to the bank, Bryn barked at me, then you came."

"Thank God I heard Bryn barking, then I heard you screaming. My blood went cold," he said, holding her tightly against him.

He was quiet then, holding her. Thinking.

Then he said, "There was just one rowboat there? Not two?"

"Just one, Vic."

"That's the one we used—the one your uncle had. So he must have come some other way. Through the house probably. I didn't see any cars about. So he could have walked."

"You mean—the boat—wasn't his?"

"Nope. The boat is still down there, tied up. So when he left, he must have walked out, up through the house. Maybe while I was rescuing you— no, I would have seen him. Hmm. You were near the bridge. I would have seen you, Bryn would have barked at him. So he must have waited until we came into the tavern, and I took you upstairs. Then while you were in the tub, he left."

"Oh—Vic!" She shuddered. "Then, he was still in the cellar when we came in—oh, Vic—"

He gave her more of the tea and brandy to drink, then took a long swig of the brandy himself. "God," he muttered. "I wonder if it could have been Gino. He was mad at Dora for bothering him. And if he didn't find a place to dump the cases—he was pretty angry."

"It could have been," she said faintly. "But wouldn't he have come from the cruiser?"

"I don't know. Anyway, he would have had the motor launch." Vic was silent again, thinking.

Presently he went down and fixed breakfast, brought hers up to her, fed her tenderly, anxiously.

"And you just getting over pneumonia," he said, stroking back her feathery blond hair. "God, I could kill the guy, whoever it was. You're so fragile, it could have hurt you bad." He drew his fingers down over her cheek, gently. "And I meant to take such good care of you, nurse you back to health. Get some pink roses in your cheeks."

Impulsively, Betsy took his big hand, pressed it to her face, then rubbed her cheek against it. "Oh, Vic, you're good to me," she whispered. "If it wasn't for you, I would die, I think."

"Don't talk like that, you aren't going to die," he said gruffly. "The way I see it, you need me, and I need you."

Bryn barked sharply. With laughter in her tears, Betsy said, "And Bryn needs us both. Oh, Vic—"

Gino walked into the open door. Bryn barked again, straining and growling. "God, what are you two doing, cuddling in bed? Can't you get enough at night?" the man said sharply.

Betsy went stiff. Vic shot off the bed, his hand going to his pocket. Gino gestured.

"None of that."

Oscar Kawecki came in the door after him, a gray shadow sliding in, his slim gray hand holding a revolver on Betsy.

"What the hell are you doing here?" Vic asked sharply.

"Can't dump the stuff. Stern is scared as hell, says he's being watched. We got to leave the cases here till I can get them inland."

"No, you won't!" Vic said sharply, keeping one eye on Oscar Kawecki. "They're watching us here, also. You keep the damn stuff, dump in the Atlantic, if you want."

Gino scowled, his pleasant face marred with weariness and fury. "All the money I give you, and you're turning on me, Vic. All for little blondie here."

Betsy spoke up, her voice taut. "Dora is dead, Mr. Pescara."

He stared at her, blankly. "What?" His black eyes flickered, he seemed genuinely shocked. "What happened to her? Choke to death? She was drinking all night—"

"Someone killed her in the cellar," Vic said sharply. "You wouldn't know about that, eh?" His look went to Oscar Kawecki. The man stared back, expressionless as always.

Gino sagged against the wall, his hand went over his beard-stubbled face. "I can't believe it—what the hell was she doing in the cellar?"

Betsy told her story slowly, Gino watched her face sharply as though to tell whether she lied or not. Oscar lowered his revolver slowly then slid it into his pocket, but remained at the doorway.

"So—I jumped into the water, swam to land. Vic rescued me," she ended wearily. "I think Dora was—dead—before he threw her into the water."

"She'd have drowned, anyway, can't swim a stroke," said Gino. He was pallid under his reddish tan, lines marked his mouth. "God, what an end. Poor Dora. She hated the water."

"Good riddance, she was a pest," Oscar Kawecki said.

Gino turned on him. "Don't say that! Dora was a good woman, for all her ways. Known her for ten years. She was good to me."

"She would have sold her own mother for money," Oscar said. He stared right back at Gino unwaveringly.

Gino relaxed, shrugged. "That's beside the point. Poor old girl is dead. Do you suppose they'll find her body?"

"It might get washed up on the shore, might go right out to sea," said Vic. "I don't know about the Sound here. Some places it would come right up."

His head down, the black hair shining in the dim light from the windows, Gino meditated. It was a gray October day, the clouds were massing in the west. Maybe it would rain. Poor Dora, out there in the cold water, the water she hated so dreadfully. But she would not feel anything now, Betsy thought.

"Well—we got to decide about the cases," Gino said abruptly to Vic. "Come on, Vic, be sensible. Do you know anybody inland, anyone who would take the stuff up to Massachusetts? You ought to know the people by this time."

Betsy thought of Bradford Schuyler, but she kept her mouth shut. She didn't want to get involved, nor have Vic involved.

"That's your problem," Vic said. "You're not unloading here. I told you, we're going to run a clean restaurant."

"We'll talk about it," Gino said, giving a jerk of his head. "Come on, let the blondie rest. She's had a tough time of it. We'll talk downstairs. I'm starved, ain't you, Oscar?"

Oscar did not answer, merely slid out into the hallway, like a gray shadow disappearing. Vic hesitated, then nodded. "Okay, I'll come on down and we'll talk. I want Betsy to rest. Bryn, you stay and guard—guard, Bryn!"

Bryn whined, and settled down on the rug beside the bed. Gino went out. Vic said, quietly, "You rest, honey, get some sleep. Bryn will take care of you. He hears everything."

She wasn't so sure of that. Bryn could sleep like a worn-out child at times. He did seem alert now, but she felt safe only when Vic was near.

She clung to his hand, lifted her face. He kissed her lips tenderly. "You'll be careful?" she whispered. She wanted to beg him not to listen to Gino, not to give in. But Vic had to make up his own mind, take his own stand.

"Sure, baby doll. You be quiet and get some sleep. I'll come up later and see how you are."

He ruffled up her hair, smoothed it down again. Then he went out, shutting the door after him. Betsy settled down in the pillows, drew up the covers. For a time she could hear the muffled sound of voices, when Gino raised his voice, or Vic answered him back. Then the voices dimmed, and she slept.

It was evening before she wakened. Betsy blinked uncomprehendingly at the gray dusk outside, then began to remember. Bryn whined as soon as she sat up. Presently Vic came up, and peered in.

"You awake at last?" He came in, shut the door after him.

"Hi, yes, I'm awake. Are *they* still here?"

He nodded, frowned. "They'll stay the night. They're going over ideas for contacts. The cruiser is still out in the Sound. God, they take chances for money!"

She leaned back, intensely relieved. Vic had not given in. She managed to smile for him. He came over, sat down beside her, took her in his arms, kissed her cheek, nuzzled down to her shoulder.

"When I think—" he said in a muffled tone. "God, if anything happens to you . . ."

She caressed his thick curls in silence. She felt the same way about him. She needed him, she wanted him near her always. She had been so lost, she couldn't endure to be so lost again.

Vic pushed back the edge of her nightdress, pressed his lips to her slim shoulder. His warm generous mouth on her flesh made her feel hot inside, all warm and dizzy and happy. His hand moved over the nightdress, paused at her breast, his fingers moved gently over the rounded softness. Then he stopped.

"Not now," he said, with a sigh. "You're tired out. And I bet you could use some food."

Betsy was conscious of a keen disappointment, but she managed to smile. "I am hungry. Shall I get dressed?"

"No, stay up here in bed. I'll bring up a tray. Gino and Oscar can fix their own dinners. I left word for Mrs. Cunkle to wait to hear from us, now I wish I'd had her come and fix the meals. I won't have you waiting on them."

"It would be good practice for later, when we have our customers in the restaurant," she told him happily. "If we can handle Mr. Pescara and Mr. Kawecki, we can handle anyone!" She giggled.

Vic gave her a smile, his lean face looking younger for a moment. "Maybe you got something there, but for now, I can't wait till they get out of here."

She detained him with a hand on his sleeve. "Vic—do you think that Dora's death—it might have been—Gino?"

He did not deny it forcefully, as she had hoped. He scowled. "I was thinking about it. It could have been. He doesn't seem much upset about it. Oscar never gets upset about anything. He would kill as easy as a fellow would wring a kitten's neck. The sooner they leave, the better."

"I thought Gino was fond of Dora. But he treated her so casually—"

"He was tired of her," Vic said abruptly. "I don't think he cared what happened to her. He sure didn't mean to give her money for the trip to Florida. Well—that's past." He got up, stretched. "What do you want for dinner?"

"It doesn't matter . . ." Gino's words, that *he was tired of her*—that made her feel sad. Dora must have been attractive once, she had held Gino for years. But now he didn't care—what if Vic tired of Betsy one day? And how soon would that day come?

She brooded as she waited for Vic to return. She was up and down, happy and sad, hopeful and depressed. If she leaned hard on Vic, wanted him, loved him, would he desert her one day? Should she take a chance on it? He had never said he loved her, he only wanted her, and sexual attraction didn't last very long, not when it was unaccompanied by affection, respect, mutual interests.

Vic returned with a loaded tray, and set it down on the dressing table. "I'll eat up here with you, they make me tired," he said crossly, a scowl on his face.

Betsy guessed they had been pressuring him again. Silently she accepted the thick soup, and the roughly cut slice of brown bread and butter. It tasted good to her, she ate hungrily. Vic ate also, sitting on the side of the bed, feeding bits of meat to Bryn. He had brought up a plate of sliced roast beef, a dish of cauliflower and cucumber slices. When she finished the soup, she made a sandwich.

"Good, honey?" Vic asked, calm again.

She nodded. "Tastes good. I think I'll recover," she said cheerfully.

"You'd better, or I'll get mad." He touched her chin with the edge of his fist, gently. She gave him a smile.

He took the tray down, remained a while. She fell asleep again, and wakened only when he came up to bed. He slid in beside her, taking her into his arms.

She settled her head down on his hard chest. He patted her head in that soothing way she was beginning to expect.

"You tired?" Vic whispered.

"No, I slept all day."

"I want you, honey," he said simply. "You feel like it? Or would you rather not?"

"I want to," she murmured, and pressed closer to him. His mouth brushed her cheek, moved over it to her lips. The warm generous lips opened, Betsy opened her mouth, and their tongues touched, caressed. Oh, he could be sweet.

His hand slid over her body, pressing her breasts, then down to her waist, to her thigh. His big hands, so gentle and so knowing. His fingers moved over her flesh, he pushed up the nightdress, and caressed her rounded hip. Presently he leaned up, and helped her remove the nightdress completely, and took off his own pajamas.

She leaned over him briefly as he lay back, and her lips touched his rough cheek, his chin. "Oh, Vic—how can I thank you for saving me today?" she whispered.

He stiffened. "Is that what this is for?" he demanded, his pride wounded.

"No, silly, I want to," she said, understanding at once. "Can't you tell I want to?"

"Show me," he demanded. She laughed softly with pleasure as she realized what he wanted. Their bodies came together with ease and joy for them both, arms clinging, lips together, her soft slimness against his lean hard body, fire against timber, aflame with desire.

Again it was good for them both, and Betsy was sobbing with delight as she lay back on the pillows. He drew off, whispered, "It's good all the time with you, Betsy. Have you—I mean—often?"

She caressed his roughened cheek tenderly. "No, not much," she said quietly. "I did years ago, with—with my boyfriend. After that, it was all mechanical. Until you. I never felt this way with anyone but you."

His caresses rewarded her, his lips on her breasts, her body responding eagerly to his touch as they made love once again.

Betsy was settling down to sleep when Vic whispered urgently, "You know, Betsy, we never . . . I want to— I want to marry you. Make it permanent. Do you?"

She caught her breath, suddenly wide awake. "Marriage! You really want—" She was incredulous and happy as his arms closed about her.

"Yes, if you want. I love you, Betsy. I never felt this way about a woman before. I want to stay with you always, settle down, look after you, take care of you. I want—you to have—my children, Betsy. That's for life," he said seriously. "Do you want to?"

"Ohhh," she whispered against his neck. "That would make me the happiest woman in the world! Oh, Vic, I really do want to. If only—"

"If only what?"

"If only—we both love—and it lasts," she murmured. "I hope it will last—oh, Vic, I do want to—we have to think about it, maybe tomorrow we can talk again . . ."

She was conscious of his disappointment, she sensed it in his stillness as he held her. But he finally said, quietly, "Okay, honey, we'll talk tomorrow. Go to sleep now."

And presently he slept, his breathing regular, his arm about her waist, clipping her securely to him. But Betsy lay awake for a long time, listening to the cracks of the flooring, the creaking of the walls, the soft soughing of the Sound under the building, where Dora lay—dead.

So much had happened that day. She felt dazed by it all. She did not know what she truly felt. She must be quiet and rested before she could think clearly. Marriage was a long-term affair, was it what she really wanted? And what Vic wanted?

Vic, by his own admission, had always craved excitement, adventure, travel. He was a restless man. Would he be content to settle down and work hard, living in a small town off the Post Road? Content to talk to people who traveled, instead of traveling himself? Content to wait on travelers, on diners?

How long would this mood last? Could she trust him?

She lay awake a long time, but no solution came to her.

15

On Sunday morning, they got up early. Vic seemed restless, and Betsy had slept herself out the day before.

"I've been thinking . . ." Vic had dressed and returned to her bedroom, where she was brushing her hair and thinking how much longer it was getting.

"What, Vic?"

"I think I'd better go to the sheriff," he said very quietly, the blue-gray eyes grave.

She caught her breath. "Yes, yes, we have to—about Dora. But what will Gino think?"

"I'll have to take my chances." He paused, leaning against the door frame, watching her as she swirled the brush deftly and made little curls at each ear. "Lanahan seems like a smart fellow. Maybe he can figure out who did it. He should be informed, anyway. What if her body gets washed up on the shore? We'll be in bad then, for not reporting her disappearance."

"They know she was here."

"Right. Of course, we could say she left, but it means more lies. And we didn't do it. We better report it."

Betsy felt a surge of relief. Vic was doing the right thing. He thought things out. She could depend on him.

"Let me go with you," she urged in a low tone. "I—I don't want to stay here—in the tavern with Gino and that Mr. Kawecki—"

"Right you are," he said briskly. "I'll take you and Bryn with me. We'll go right after breakfast. It's Sunday, we'll have to go to his home, I expect."

She had put on her gray skirt and white blouse. She added a blue cardigan for warmth, and they went downstairs. Vic was casually dressed in his black slacks and a gray flannel shirt. How handsome he was, she thought. He glanced down at her as they descended the stairs. "What?" he asked.

"Oh—just thinking how good-looking you are," she whispered, with a blush.

He grinned down at her, and the tired lines around his mouth dissolved. "Oh, we're a handsome couple, we are," he murmured, squeezing her arm in his hand. His gaze drifted from her blond hair to her mouth, to her white blouse. She remembered the gentle feel of his fingers over her, and she tingled as though he touched her now.

Bryn had bounced down before them, exuberantly. Now he waited in the kitchen, expectantly. His black glossy coat shone in the sunlight from the kitchen windows, his wistful dark-brown eyes gazed hopefully. Betsy leaned to stroke the large floppy ears, and feel the silky texture of his head. He drew his head back so she would stroke his soft throat, and she scratched at it obediently. He whined with pleasure, as Betsy thought, We're a family.

Vic opened the back door. "Feels like spring, not winter coming," he said with a lift to his voice. "Sunny and warm. We better enjoy it before the snows come and the winds start howling again."

The cool air carried the fragrance of grass and late roses into the kitchen. If only they could relax and be happy here, she thought, as Vic filled the kettle and she got out the huge iron skillet. Over Greystone hung the threat of darkness and death. First her uncle, then Dora—and that attack on herself . . .

"Who would try to kill me?" she whispered to Vic.

He shook his head. "No more talking about it now," he murmured, jerking his head warningly toward Gino's bedroom door.

She nodded. He was right. She laid ham slices in the bubbling skillet, got out some eggs. Vic began to slice the loaf of whole wheat bread, took butter from the icebox. "Got to stock up today," he said aloud. "We're low on butter."

"I'll make up a list."

"It's Sunday, but we might find a store open somewhere," he went on casually, giving her a wink as she looked toward him.

Betsy lost the eager, hopeful feeling she had had with the spring-like morning, the sunshine. She nodded again, her mouth drooping a little at the corners.

They ate in silence. The ham was delicious, the eggs sunnyside up, as Vic liked them. The coffee was hot and fragrant. He spooned strawberry jam lavishly on his bread. "This is the life," he said finally.

She put her hand on his free hand for a moment. "I wish—I wish it would last . . ."

"It will, honey."

He sounded sure. She wished she could feel that way.

It was after nine before they got up from the table and stacked the dishes in the sink. They got their coats, and went out to the car. Bryn followed them eagerly, and darted into the back seat happily, curling up on the seat, then standing to stare out the windows with interest.

They bounced across the bridge; the wooden planks groaned under the weight of the little car. "Have to look at the bridge soon," Vic said absently. "Might need some mending. I'll get some planks and bigger nails in town."

"You'll have the place all shipshape soon," Betsy said, moving closer to him on the seat and putting her hand on his knee. "Do you think we'll have customers this winter?"

"We're bound to. Folks get tired of their own cooking. And there'll be travelers. We'll put up a sign in the railroad station, giving directions. Can you draw?"

"Yes. I was tops in my art class in high school—until I had to leave."

"I bet you were," he said warmly. "I can do mechanical drawing. We'll fix up a nice poster."

They rattled up the hill, then down again into the valley where Saymore lay. It shone in the sunlight, the red roofs and gray stone and white-painted wood; the white steeple of the church against the vivid blue sky looked like a painting. But the grass was drying, the trees had lost most of their leaves.

"Late October," he said.

She calculated. "It's the nineteenth. I think they get winter early here. The storms on the Sound can get bad."

"Think I'll work on the roof right quick, make sure the shingles are all nailed down. There's a patch near one of the chimneys needs fixing bad." Then he fell silent as they approached the sheriff's office. It was closed and locked. Vic went up to the door, studied the sign there, came back to the car.

"He lives over by the tobacco warehouse, behind the railroad," said Vic. "On the end of Maple Street. Do you know where Maple is?"

"Yes, I walked down Maple when I first came." Betsy pointed. "There's Lyme, where the church is. The main street is Southampton. And Maple is where Lyme and Southampton come together, there."

He nodded, started the car again, and they drove to Maple, turned onto the street, and proceeded slowly. "There's the railroad," he said. "Ah—and there is the warehouse. And that must be the sheriff's home."

He pulled up in front of the pleasant-looking dwelling. The front door was open to the October sunshine. The blinds were drawn up, the curtains open in the front window. Betsy and Vic got out, Bryn was told to stay put. They went up to the door, to find the sheriff coming along the hallway.

"Come in, Miss Olsen, Mr. Halstatt. Saw you coming," the sheriff drawled. "Parlor is right here. Something wrong?" The keen dark-brown eyes looked them over.

"You might say so," Vic said, his hand firmly on Betsy's arm. "We came to report a death."

"Ah—that right? Well, come on in, have a seat."

He showed them in with grave courtesy, seated Betsy in an old-fashioned rocker with a cushion seat covered in bright-red cotton. She clutched the arms as she sat down, looking to Vic.

Vic sat down in a straight ladder-backed chair. The sheriff sat down on the horsehair sofa, leaning forward to listen.

Vic started right in. "Early yesterday morning, Betsy went down to the cellar with Dora Johnson. Dora Johnson was staying in the tavern for a short time. She was waiting for a—a boat to leave—"

The sheriff listened gravely, his whole attention on Vic. "A cruiser was waiting to take her off? What kind of cruiser?"

"Thirty-foot," said Vic baldly. "Pleasure cruiser up from Miami."

"Ah," said the sheriff, without changing expression. Betsy knew, however, that he was thinking about rum-runners. How would Vic get around that?

Vic got around it by concentrating on the story. He told how Dora had been attacked, thrown into the Sound, how Betsy had had to flee the killer. Vic and Bryn had rescued her.

"And this was yesterday morning?" asked the sheriff. "Why did you wait to report it?"

"Because Betsy was in a bad state, I wasn't going to leave her," said Vic, his chin outthrust. "She had pneumonia twice last winter, and she was shocked, too. And I wouldn't leave her there."

"Who else is at the tavern?" asked the sheriff gently.

Vic hesitated then, looking at Betsy; she gazed back at him with wide blue eyes, willing him silently to keep on telling the truth.

"Two friends of mine, friends of Dora Johnson. They came to take her back to Miami," he said finally. "Name of Gino Pescara and Oscar Kawecki."

"Hum." The sheriff sat, his big capable hands between his knees. "And the body was thrown into the Sound? You didn't see it anywhere?"

"No, I looked about the Sound a little, but I was more concerned with looking after Betsy. Could the—body—be washed up soon?"

"Might be, might never be found," the sheriff said. "It could be washed out to the ocean. I think I'd better go back with you and question the others. They might have heard or seen something."

"They weren't there," Vic said abruptly. "They were off in the cruiser, returned later."

The sheriff eyed him carefully, then nodded. "But I'll have a talk with them anyway, since they knew the deceased."

Vic hesitated. "They don't know we came to town for you," he finally said bluntly. "They won't like it. They won't want to get involved."

"Nobody wants to get involved when there's a killing," the sheriff said blandly, and got up. He reached for his hat and coat on the peg in the corner of the parlor. "I'll follow you in my automobile," he said politely.

Vic's face was taut and hard. He nodded, went out with Betsy, and waited for the sheriff to come around the corner of the house with his large black sedan. "Wonder if Robert Ming is still around," he said, out of nowhere.

Betsy gave him a quick startled look. "Ming, the federal officer? Do you think he should—I mean, it's nothing to do with that, is it?"

"Might not be," he said. "I think they took Burton back to New York to the hospital. Maybe Ming didn't come back."

She twisted her slim hands in her lap. More worries. It was more and more complicated. All she knew was that Gino would be furious.

He was. He was raving mad, when Vic drove up with the sheriff coming right in after him. He had just gotten up and was shaving, with no shirt on and his pants hanging about him, suspender straps down to his hips.

As the sheriff walked into the room, he stared and whirled about, his hand going to the dresser drawer.

"Don't bother," Lanahan drawled easily. "This is just a little questioning I want."

"What the hell are you doing here?" Gino looked at Vic at once. Vic shrugged.

"Had to tell him about Dora Johnson," he said easily, leaning against the doorframe.

"We can wait until you have shaved and are dressed," the sheriff said politely. "Where is Mr. Kawecki?"

"Right here behind you," said Oscar's voice behind them on the stairs. He came on down, dressed in his usual gray slacks and gray shirt, looking at them without expression. "What's going on?"

"I came to question you about the death of one Dora

Johnson," Lanahan said at once. "Will you come into the taproom with me, Mr. Kawecki? Might as well begin with you." He took him along with him.

"Damn you, for an idiot and a bastard!" Gino snarled at Vic. "What the hell did you have to do that for? She might never have showed up."

"We're going to live here," said Vic. "We want things straight."

Vic closed the bedroom door after him. They could hear Gino muttering to himself. Once downstairs, Betsy sat down limply on a kitchen chair. Vic sat down beside her, and took her cold hand in his. "Take it easy, honey, it's all right. His bark is worse than his bite anyday."

Betsy wasn't so sure. They sat in silence until the sheriff came back, Oscar Kawecki trailing behind him.

"He doesn't know anything at all," said the sheriff without a smile, but with a gleam of humor in his dark eyes. "I'll try to get Mr. Pescara to tell me a little more. Is he dressed?"

Gino appeared as if on cue. "I'm ready," he said sullenly. He had dressed hastily in black slacks and black shirt, his hair shone wetly from brushing. He gave Vic a hard look before following the sheriff to the taproom. They soon returned.

"I'll file a report," Lanahan said smoothly. "If you think of anything else, please let me know. As things stand, I'll have to report her death as murder at the hands of someone unknown." He hesitated. Vic had stood up. "I appreciate your reporting this, though I could wish you had come to me yesterday, Mr. Halstatt. I'll be in touch."

He went out, and the others stood tensely in the kitchen as they heard the car starting up, moving away. Then Gino said, with quiet violence, "God damn you to hell, Vic, how could you do this to me?"

"He's a sucker for dames," Oscar Kawecki said softly, his hand at his hip easily. "Blondie here has him all in a dither."

"Keep her name out of this," Vic snarled. "I told the sheriff because I want it straight, get that? Someone had to tell about Dora, she couldn't just disappear."

"You couldn't wait till we left, could you? You had to mess us up in this? I could have sworn I could trust you, Vic," Gino sighed, his eyes bright with anger.

"Never trust him, I told you that," Oscar said.

"I've been thinking," Gino said. "Easiest thing in the world, get rid of a dame, then report it all innocently to the law. Vic, I'm surprised at you. Did you hate Dora that much?"

Vic started. "What the hell—"

"Sure he did it," said Oscar. "He kept telling us we had to get rid of her."

"I did not!" Vic blazed, his fists clenched. "I told you to take her with you, or give her money for a trip on the train! I never said get rid of her—"

"Sure you did, Vic, sure you did. You didn't want her around while you spooned with blondie here. You always did like to keep your affairs private and confidential," Gino sneered. "Well, listen to me. If I hadn't been tired of Dora, I wouldn't let you get away with this. But you are going to pay for this, you are, one way or another. You'll keep on taking care of the rum for us."

Betsy was standing rigidly, her hands clenched on the slat-back of the chair. She licked her lips. She could not speak, she was paralyzed with fright. They could not be accusing Vic of killing Dora: he would not, he could not!

Yet he had been the only man in the tavern that morning. His bedroom door had been shut, she had not seen him. She had thought he was sleeping late—but he had turned up soon after, to rescue her from the icy waters of the Sound. Could he have killed Dora—could he have turned on Betsy, thinking she had seen his face?

Vic was furiously angry, his face hard, the sunlight striking against the high cheekbones. His head was flung back. He kept his hands away from his pockets, though. Oscar Kawecki was holding the handle of his gun at the hip, not pulling it out, but keeping it ready.

"You're crazy," Vic said flatly. "I wouldn't kill Dora, I had no reason to. I just wanted you to take care of her—"

"But you took care of her instead," Gino accused, his black eyes flashing. "God damn you, Vic, you was my friend—I took you in, gave you a job—and this is the way you reward me."

Betsy could not help feeling he was over-dramatizing the situation. She relaxed a little from her fright, listened sharply to their words, the tones of their voices.

Vic turned right to Gino, ignoring Oscar. "Listen, Gino, I am grateful to you. You helped me when I was down, gave me a job. All right. I repaid you by working hard, and I was honest. I never cheated you. Right? But now I'm through with rumrunning, I got a chance for a really good job, handling this restaurant—"

"Restaurant," Gino scoffed. "You'll tie up with some other rummie and leave us out in the cold. You can't make a living here, not the kind of money you like to spend! Don't kid me, Vic, you think you're going to get a better deal with someone else—"

"You're wrong," he said clearly. "I am going to go clean! You're to stay away, and you can pass the word for other rummies to go elsewhere. I'm not doing any moonlighting for anyone! This place is going clean, and it's going to stay clean!"

"The hell it is," Gino growled. "Listen to me. I don't trust nobody to the limit. Hell, I trusted you, look where it got me! Dora dead, poor Dora . . . Well, that's water under the bridge—or under the tavern." He looked momentarily pleased at his own joke. Then he turned serious again. "You're going to string along with us, Vic—"

"No."

The two men stared at each other. "Then little blondie here will get it," Gino said in a soft deadly voice. "You want her to go the way of Dora? You string along with us, or she gets it. You're not going to go on betraying us, Vic. I don't take that kind of treatment—"

"You'll leave her alone! You won't touch her, or I'll kill you, Gino. That's my final word." His voice was hard as steel clanging.

Gino drew in his breath in a hiss. "You would kill me? Your friend?"

"She's my girl, she's under my protection. You won't touch her!"

"If you don't play along—"

Oscar's monotone interrupted with, "This is wasting time. That sheriff wasn't fooling. He'll go get the feds, and look over the cruiser."

Gino started, turned to him. "What?"

"I said—we got to get that cruiser away, unload the dump somewhere," Oscar said patiently, fingering the handle of his revolver with lean fingers. "We could take it inland ourselves. You know, find someone,"

Faced with another problem, Gino seemed to calm down. "Oh—yeah—we got to get moving. Come on, Vic, forget the angry words. You'll come with us, huh? Give you a fatter share than we gave Hubert—"

"No. You get out and stay out. Don't come back. And never dump stuff in the cellar again!"

"That's gratitude," muttered Gino. He shook his head, Oscar watching him coldly. The two men went into the hall, conferred together. Oscar went upstairs, they could hear him moving around.

Presently the two men returned, bundled up against the cold in coats and knitted caps. "We're going," said Gino. "But you will be sorry, Vic, if you don't cooperate." He gave Betsy a flick of a look. "She's fragile, isn't she?" he remarked casually, and went on down the stairs to the cellar, his boots clattering. Oscar followed him, with silent footsteps.

Vic closed the door after them, with a bang. They heard the motor cruiser starting up, the two men went off. Betsy collapsed into the hard chair, propped her chin on her fists.

"Vic, did they mean it?"

"Naw, Gino gets mad and says things he doesn't mean," Vic said. He went out with Bryn and she heard him banging savagely on the car's engine with some tools. He wasn't whistling.

She felt frightened and frigidly cold all over again. Vic was deeply worried, and that worried her. He would try to reassure her, but she knew as well as he did that Gino was capable of killing either or both of them. Gino was furious about Dora's death, about calling in the sheriff, about Vic's refusal to help in the rumrunning. They would have a lot of trouble setting up new connections they could trust. It wouldn't be a simple operation for them for a long time now. And they had had an easy time of it for more than a year with Uncle Hubert.

Vic was defying the whole murderous gang of rumrunners. The men stuck together. They wouldn't take betrayal by one of their own. Many who had tried to inform against rumrunners had disappeared, never to be seen again. She could disappear, into the Sound. So could Vic—into the waters or aboard the large cruiser. They could take him south, and dump him anywhere along the coast.

She pressed her cold hands against her face. Was that what had happened to Dora? Had she tried to force Gino to give her money, in return for not ratting on them? Why else had she been killed? Surely not just to rid Gino of an inconvenience he had wearied of.

Gino's pride had been touched deeply. His woman had been killed—though he might have killed her himself. His work had been endangered. Vic had reported to the sheriff. The feds had been coming around. Gino would feel he had to do something, either get Vic back on his side, or get rid of him.

And if several of them ganged up on Vic, how would he keep himself alive, how could he protect himself? With despair Betsy saw her new life ending as quickly as it had begun.

16

It was quiet in Greystone. Betsy thought, pensively, how nice it could be there, if only she were not worried silly about the murders, and whether or not Gino would return.

The big building was comfortable, they had plenty of food and water. Vic began to whistle at his work. In the afternoon, he went up on the roof and tacked down some shingles. She could hear the rat-tat-tat of his hammer, his whistling, from the open door of the kitchen.

For a time he was whistling his own variations of "Oh, Johnny," and "Little Sir Echo" and "There'll Be Some Changes Made." Then he got more sentimental with "Look for the Silver Lining," and "Three O'Clock in the Morning," and "Wonderful One," and "Ah, Sweet Mystery of Life!"

She hummed along with him softly, though he could not hear her. She sang when she knew the words. She thought of the old days, tramping the streets of Broadway, asking for parts, worrying about where next month's rent would come from, if she had enough to buy a decent lunch. She shook her head in remembrance.

"No more of that for me, Bryn," she confided, and the cocker perked up his ears with interest. "I've had that, all the way. It's safety and security for me, I don't care about hard work, I just want us safe here, and Vic looking after us."

Bryn barked once, as though he agreed. Presently Vic came in, hungry, sniffing with appreciation at the frying chicken. She set the table quickly, and had the vegetables on, mixed corn and limas, and a salad of cold red and green beans.

"I guess we'll have a lot of beans this winter, Vic," she said cheerfully. "The pantry is full of them."

"I like them, the way you fix them." He held her chair for her, and sat down opposite her. She spooned up the vegetables and salad, he put a big piece of chicken on her plate. "Hot rolls! Honey, you spoil me."

"And there's honey for them." She offered the jar. "Will you have some honey, honey?"

They both laughed because they were happy and hungry and together. His face seemed more relaxed and pleasant, he had lost that cold hard look she hated. He talked about the repairs he would make, which would come first. "The place has been neglected. I better get after that bridge soon, or it'll give under the automobiles. And that pile of wood that was the stables and the casino-room addition before it became the private dining room and they tore the extension down. I'll stack them up and we'll burn it this winter. Save buying fuel. I wonder who owns the trees across the bridge? A couple are dead. I could cut them up for firewood."

He pulled out a pad, reached for a pencil, and began listing the repairs, putting checkmarks next to the most urgent ones.

"And we'll make a poster for the railroad station," Betsy reminded him.

"Right. And I'll ask the man in the hardware store if he'll put one in his window for a time. He's right on the main street. Wonder if they have a village paper? We could put in an ad if we don't get much business."

After dinner, Vic went out and Betsy saw him looking over the bridge, critically, climbing down under and looking up at the planks. Bryn had bounded out after him, and was scuffling through the leaves. The sun shone down through the bare branches of the trees, making lacy patterns on the grass, and the sky was vivid blue, with only a few fleecy drifts of windblown clouds.

After doing the dishes, Betsy went out to examine the flower beds. She weeded out one bed, cut back the rosebush a little, examined some other bushes. "I think we have forsythia and lilacs," she told Vic when he came back. "But I don't know what's in here."

"We'll see in the spring, when it comes up," he predicted cheerfully. He looked down at the flower beds, smiled a little. "Seems funny to think we'll be here in the spring, doesn't it? I haven't stayed in one spot for more than a week or two—since I was a kid."

She slipped her chilled fingers into his big warm hand. "I like the idea, don't you?" she whispered. He gazed down into her questioning blue eyes, leaned over, and kissed the tip of her small nose.

"I like it very much, sweetheart. We'll make a go of it, you'll see."

She walked around the tavern with him, hand in hand, Bryn bounding ahead of them, then hanging back to investigate an interesting odor at the base of a bush. As they stopped to look out over the Sound, and beyond toward the Atlantic Ocean, where cruisers laden with rum sailed, Betsy's hand tightened on Vic's, as though she would hold him back from his former trade.

Feeling the pressure of her hand, and seeming to know her intent, Vic turned to gaze at the dilapidated yet somehow permanent-looking greystone building on which their hopes were pinned.

"Greystone Tavern," he said. " 'Tavern.' Does that mean restaurant, or should we change the name?"

Betsy hesitated, studied the sign her uncle had put up. "Oh, it's been Greystone Tavern for almost all its life, Vic," she said impulsively. "It'll *mean* restaurant; that's what *we'll* mean for it. But let's leave the lettering the same."

"Okay, sweetheart. Think I'll get some black paint and go over the letters, and shine up the ironwork around the top. Look how the roses have grown over it. I'll have to cut them back just a bit so you can read it."

"It's a lovely place. I wish Uncle Hubert could have—"

"I know. He deserved some peace and quiet. If only he hadn't gotten involved . . ."

But regret was futile. They had to look forward, not back. Both had things in their past they wanted to forget. Today was shining clean, tomorrow was theirs to make beautiful.

They went to bed early, sleeping peacefully after their work outdoors. They got up early, eager to begin again, and over breakfast talked over the chores. Betsy wanted to put up some more vegetables against the winter, tomatoes, peas, and corn. "We'll get pretty tired of beans otherwise."

"I could start a vegetable patch next spring," he mused. "That would save money, and we could serve fresh vegetables from our own garden."

"Maybe where the stables were, when the wood is cleaned out," Betsy suggested. "The soil looks rich, and it hasn't been used. We could have fresh lettuce and cucumbers."

And so they planned and hoped.

They were about ready to sit down to luncheon when they had visitors. Vic sighted them from the roof, where he was repairing the brickwork in the chimney. He came down fast.

In the kitchen, he went to the sink, said grimly, "Two cars coming, honey. Looks like the sheriff is coming back."

"Oh—I wonder if—if she—" She could not say the words, thinking of Dora's body being washed up on some sandy beach.

"We'll soon see. Let me handle it, though."

She nodded. The two cars drove across the bridge, and pulled up near Uncle Hubert's car parked near the back door. Three men got out. Betsy frowned as she recognized the tall red-haired man, Bradford Schuyler. The others were the sheriff and Robert Ming.

They went around to the front door and knocked. "Going formal," Vic said in his slow drawl, and went to the door. Betsy heard him say, "Good morning, gentlemen. Come right in. Why don't you step into the taproom? We're still fixing up the front parlor."

"Where's Miss Olsen?" Bradford Schuyler asked sharply. Betsy stiffened, held onto a kitchen chair. Bryn was growling uneasily.

"In the kitchen, fixing lunch. Is this a formal call?" Vic asked.

"You might say so," the sheriff answered. "Would you please ask her to step in?"

"Sure." Vic came back. His jaw was set and hard, his

dark eyes gleamed. "You still let me do the talking, all you can, honey. Something funny is going on."

She nodded, motioned to Bryn to stay where he was. He settled down near the warm stove, whining a little.

Betsy wiped her hands, took off her apron, and followed Vic to the taproom. Robert Ming nodded courteously, the sheriff gave her a grave greeting.

Bradford Schuyler, his bright green eyes flashing, burst out, "Well, I'm glad to see you are still alive!"

She gave him a cool look. "Thank you, I'm sure. You are still alive also, Mr. Schuyler?"

The sheriff passed his hand over his mouth, coughed a little. "Um—may we sit down for a short spell, Miss Olsen? Mr. Schuyler has something to say."

"No need to be so formal and polite," Schuyler said angrily. "I told you what I wanted. I want you to arrest this man for the murder of Hubert Olsen and Dora Johnson! There is plenty of evidence to show he is guilty."

Betsy gasped and sat down limply in a chair, holding to the arms of it. Vic showed little emotion, his hands casually at his sides. The tall federal officer seated himself slowly near Betsy, listening, as though he had little to do with this. Betsy wondered why he had come. Murder was not in his line, was it? Just rumrunning.

Schuyler turned on Sheriff Lanahan. "Well, Sheriff, are you going to arrest him?"

"I thought we came to talk it over," Rob Lanahan said mildly. He sat down also. Finally Vic sat down next to Betsy, leaving only Bradford Schuyler standing, shifting uneasily from one foot to the other. "Mr. Halstatt, where were you when Mr. Olsen was—ah—murdered?"

"We went over all that," said Vic tightly. "I'll repeat my story in court, under oath, if you like. But not to please *him*." He nodded his curly head at Schuyler. "I didn't kill Olsen, I liked him. And Dora Johnson—well, I was sorry for her. I didn't kill her, didn't want to. Why should I?"

"To get this place free and clear," said Bradford Schuyler before the sheriff could speak. "You wanted to take over the tavern and its profitable business! You wanted Miss Olsen in your power—"

"Why should he want the tavern?" Mr. Ming asked in his cool distinct voice. His dark head turned in mild inquiry to Mr. Schuyler. "I understood the tavern was not doing much business. Hardly any travelers stop here, and the restaurant business was poor. Why should he want it?"

"For rumrunning," Schuyler said wildly. "We all know it was used as a dump for rum."

"Do we?" Ming asked. "What proof do you have?"

"My God, Hubert treated me to the best rum whenever I came! He handled it openly! Everyone knew—"

"So you received some of the smuggled rum," Sheriff Lanahan said briskly.

Schuyler gave him a furious glare. "Don't be an idiot," he said in a grating voice. "Everyone drinks around here. It's a stupid law, against drinking. But everyone does it. Hubert Olsen had rum from Jamaica, brandy from Spain—I saw the bottles and cases myself. He had a thriving business. I've seen him pull out a roll of bills that would choke a horse."

"Ned Palmer informed me that you were one of those who wanted to lease Greystone," Sheriff Lanahan asserted in his easy drawl. "Why did *you* want it, Mr. Schuyler?"

The man's jaw dropped. "Why—why? But—but that's not the object of our trip here! I want you to arrest this man! He is guilty of murder!"

"What evidence do you have?" asked Sheriff Lanahan.

"Evidence! He was the only man here strong enough to commit the murders! He was right on the spot! He has the motives to do them!"

Vic was sitting there quietly, letting them argue it out. Betsy clutched his hand, holding on to him for dear life. Ming looked thoughtfully at their clasped hands, the small slim white one and the large tanned one, with the fingers entwined.

"Why did you ask for the lease of Greystone?" Ming asked, abruptly entering the conversation. "Did you plan to do some rumrunning?"

Schuyler gulped and turned red. "Why—of course not! I meant to run a respectable restaurant! Why, this place could be a goldmine. It ran well in the old days, folks tell me. It's right beside the Post Road, and if it is well handled it could mean a mint."

Vic's hard fingers squeezed Betsy's quickly. "Thanks a lot, that's exactly what we thought," he said pleasantly, with a note of steel under his tone. "That's what we aim to do, to build up the business. I'm fixing the roof, the bridge comes next. By the way, boys, drive easy over the bridge, will you? The supports near the mainland are a bit shaky."

The three men stared at him silently. Vic stared right back.

Schuyler looked away first. "I demand that you arrest this man," he said grandly. "The evidence shows he is the only man who could have committed both murders. And he had the motives—"

Sheriff Lanahan stirred, fingered his chin. "Don't see that we have the evidence," he murmured. "Nope, don't see it."

"What are you going to do—wait until he murders Miss Olsen?" asked Schuyler furiously. "She'll be dead next! And you'll have only yourselves to blame for not protecting her!"

"I'm protecting her," Vic said coldly. "She's going to be well looked after—by me."

"And you're going to run a restaurant," Ming said. "Without rum or brandy or wine?"

"That's right. Just Mrs. Cunkle's cooking, and sometimes Betsy's. I figure that will draw them all right. I'm going to manage it, and fix up this place right. You're all welcome to come and try a meal—say, next week sometime. Our pleasure."

"I hardly ever turn down a free meal," Ming said and rose to his considerable height. "Well, I best be getting back to the office, I'm expecting a message. Coming, Lanahan?"

"Right you are," said the sheriff, rising. "We'll go back to my office, Mr. Schuyler. Pleasure to talk to you folks, we'll be coming back."

Vic escorted them to the door. Betsy could hear

Schuyler beginning to rage at the other two men for not arresting Vic. She stood there, her finger on her lip, thinking.

Why, she had not believed him one bit! She hadn't believed his charges against Vic at all! Neither had the other two men, and they surely knew their business! They had just let him rave on, and punctured his ballon of vicious lies as easily as anything.

Vic returned, looking tired and grim. She gave him a big smile, and said, "Oh, Vic, wasn't he silly?"

"Silly? What do you mean?"

"Oh, such stupid accusations. He has no evidence at all, and they knew it. You know, they accused him more than they did you! Oh, Vic, I didn't believe one word of his. You could not have murdered them, and I knew it."

He gazed down at her, into the wide blue eyes, at the smile. Slowly he put his arms about her, and drew her tight. He put his cheek down on her soft flaxen hair, and rubbed against it.

"You believed me?" he whispered.

"Of course, silly. I know you you're good and kind and strong—"

"Oh, darling." He drew back, gazed down at her again. "You know, I loved you the minute I saw you? I came up into the kitchen, took one look at you, and fell plunk in love? Oh, honey, I can't believe my luck. Maybe one day you'll love me, too."

Betsy caressed his cheek tenderly. "I love you already, Vic," she said simply. "I would trust you to the end of the world and back."

His face grew radiant. He pulled her closer, so that her slim body felt the warmth of his lean strength. "Tell me again," he demanded softly, his lips close to hers.

"I love you, Vic, I love you."

His mouth pressed down on hers, so gently, so sweetly, that she melted right against him. He molded her body to his, his arms close and tight and warm about her, so that she arched into him. He nuzzled against her cheek, then returned to her lips, and she responded more wildly to the pressure.

One hand went to her soft fluffy hair, and the lean

fingers caressed the back of her neck, up into her hair. "Listen, Betsy, I want us to get married. Will you, Betsy?" he urged seriously. A flush stained his high cheekbones, his pale eyes shone. "Will you marry me? I never wanted anything so much in my life. I want you to belong to me, and give me the right to take care of you forever."

"Forever. Oh, Vic, that's the sweetest word in the world." Tears choked her throat, she rubbed her cheek against his rough shirt. "Oh, Vic, yes, yes, yes—if you really mean—"

"No ifs, honey. I mean it. We could get married soon. Better, anyway, for your reputation. Since we're often here alone. I've been thinking . . ."

When he had proposed before, in bed, she hadn't believed he meant it. But this was in the sunlight, in the clear light of day, and he was talking seriously.

"If you'll marry me, we can settle down, raise our family here. You like children, don't you? I'll look after you, I swear I will—God, I've wanted a home for the longest time."

"So have I, Vic." Her doubts had disappeared finally, like dew when the sun rises. She stroked his hard arm. "I love you, Vic. I know that now. I do want us to marry. Forever and ever."

He kissed her, his lips clinging to hers. "God, you are the sweetest woman in the world. I never thought I'd meet anybody like you, didn't know they made women like you anymore. The others are so tough and hard— so cold right through—they give you a chill like ice. But you—warm and sweet right to the bone, so loving and giving—oh, honey, I'll make you happy!"

"I want to make you happy, Vic," she whispered. "Make up for the years of drifting and feeling alone—I know how that is. I hate feeling alone, it's so horrible. We'll be together, and never lonely again—"

"Yes, yes, yes," he said. "Let's get married soon. Listen, I bet we could have a marriage in that pretty church. The Camerons would fix it up with the preacher. Would you like that, a church wedding? I bet you'd be the prettiest bride in the world."

She laughed, shakily, rather incredulously. Her a

bride, in a church, going down an aisle while the organ played? It could not be—but Vic wanted it that way.

That afternoon, they planned—working spasmodically on the repairs outside, talking, sitting over coffee in the kitchen, dreamily, hands clinging. Ideas for fixing up the tavern. Plans for the wedding. Plans for a family. Ideas for the future.

They went to bed early. They were weary from working outdoors, but not really sleepy. Vic's kisses that day had been more and more ardent, he couldn't seem to keep his hands from her. She felt the same way, warm and passionate and wanting.

She was in bed when he came into the dimness of her room. He slid into bed with her, and she turned at once into his arms.

He patted her head down onto his shoulder, and gathered her into his arms. She felt like she was coming home after a long absence. This would be their home, Greystone Tavern, their work, their life, and that of their children.

He was so sweet and ardent that night that she felt as though her very bones melted with love of him. His touch was gentle, yet urgent. He stroked his hands over her naked body, until the flesh tingled and her fingers clutched more tightly on his shoulders. When they came together, it was a meeting of heart and body and soul, each wanting the other to be happy, each finding joy. Vic skillfully made their loving last a long time, and she whispered her delight to him.

"I love you—Vic—you're so good to me—oh, oh, I love that—oh, Vic—I love you—"

"How did I get so lucky, to find you?" he murmured against her shoulder. And she felt the same way.

17

Betsy wakened early the next morning with her cheek on Vic's bare shoulder. She felt warm and safe, but something had roused her.

She lifted her head, listened intently. Bryn got up, walked to the door, whined uneasily.

Vic wakened completely, all at once, the way he always did. "What is it?"

"Noise. I think—oh, Vic—I think it's a boat. The motor cruiser."

He listened, then got out of bed. He went to his room, got into his clothes rapidly, reappeared with his face taut and hard. Betsy scrambled up. She washed quickly. She could hear voices in the cellar already.

Bryn barked once. She hushed him. She got out her dark-blue dress with the long sleeves, the morning felt cold. Was it going to start all over again? Why had Gino returned?

She heard the footsteps as they came up into the tavern. "You best stay up here, honey," Vic said. He was putting a revolver in his pocket.

Before she could answer, Gino called upstairs. "You up, Vic, come on down! We could use some food and coffee."

He sounded natural, his jovial self. Vic hesitated, his mouth grim, his eyebrows drawn together in one ominous line.

"Okay, Gino, be right down," he finally called back.

Betsy went with him, and Bryn scampered ahead of them down the stairs, his paws clumping on the wooden planks. They went into the kitchen. Bryn sniffed at Gino, barked briefly at Oscar Kawecki. They were sitting at the kitchen table.

Gino got up slowly, nodded to them. Oscar stayed where he was, his face gray with fatigue, his eyes blinking.

"Well, we dumped the stuff," said Gino, with a grin. He had dark bruised-looking bags under his eyes, as though he had not slept much lately. "Alva gave us a lead, bless his hide. Proved out."

"That's good, that's good," said Vic, with evident relief. "Why did you stop off?"

Gino shrugged. "Can't we see an old pal without you asking questions?" he said with a laugh. Vic looked at him keenly, his dark gaze going over the man.

"I'll start breakfast. How do ham and eggs, hot biscuits and honey sound to you?" Betsy asked quickly, in an attempt to be friendly to the two scoundrels.

"Sounds great, doll," Gino said with joviality that somehow rang false. Betsy thought that Vic seemed suspicious, too. She noticed he was careful not to turn his back to the men.

"You sit down with them, Vic, and have a good talk. I'll fix the breakfast," she said easily. That way he would never have his back to them. She filled the kettle. Vic sat down with his back to the stove, between the two men who sat at either end of the long table.

The men talked, idly. The weather had been good. The dump had been arranged "up the coast a ways," Gino said casually. "We'll be able to do it again. Not so convenient as here, but okay, okay."

Vic changed the subject. He told them about repairing the roof, getting wood for the bridge, deliberately emphasizing the work he was doing on the tavern. They listened, drank coffee as soon as it was ready. Betsy kept a nervous eye on Oscar Kawecki. He did little talking, just listened with one hand under the table. If he pulled a gun, she thought she would dump the whole pot of coffee on his head.

The ham sizzled in the skillet, the scrambled eggs were fluffy and light. She warmed plates on the stove, then turned the food onto them, and set them carefully before Gino, then Oscar, wary of standing between them and Vic. She opened the oven door to see the biscuits turning golden brown. She closed it again, wiped her hands on her apron.

"Great cook. No wonder you want to stay, Vic," Gino said, his mouth full. He waved his fork at Betsy genially. He was just too nice, Betsy couldn't believe in it.

Oscar stuffed his food down methodically, as though stoking a furnace, because it was necessary, not because he enjoyed it. She wondered if he enjoyed anything in his life. Maybe killing. She got the feeling that Oscar Kawecki would enjoy killing. She wondered how many men—and women—he had killed. The feeling she got when he was near was similar to the way she felt near snakes.

She did not eat, content to feed the men and stay out of their way. She put the biscuits on the table and the men opened them, spread them with butter and honey, popped them whole into their mouths. She noticed that Vic ate slowly, looking from one man to the other, using his left hand only. The right hand sat easily on the table, the wrist resting near his plate.

Gino mentioned Havana. "It'll be great down there, while the weather up here is turning nasty. Listen, Vic, why don't you close up here, and come on down? Think of Havana, hot in the sunshine, cool in the moonlight. And that babe you had down there. She'll be hot for you, Vic." He punched Vic in the ribs, chuckled.

"Which one?" asked Oscar, in his gray monotone. "They was all hot for him. Regular Valentino. Call him Rudolph. Regular sheik." His gray eyes met Betsy's.

There was a red flush high on Vic's cheekbones, a dangerous glint in his eyes.

"I bet he was," Betsy said in a false friendly tone, bright and sweet. "He's as handsome as Valentino. But he's tired of all that, wants to settle down." She turned back to the stove, took out another pan of biscuits.

Gino gave a guffaw. "You think so? Wait another month or so, honey."

Vic said, in a tight controlled voice, "Betsy is right. I plan to settle down, have a home and family. Nothing like children. Always wanted several. What about you, Gino? You used to talk about having a family. Thought all Italians wanted a big family. If you don't start soon, you won't make it."

Deflated, Gino scowled at Vic's statements. He shifted uneasily, reached automatically for the plate of hot biscuits. "Aw, plenty of time. I want to make my fortune first. Plenty of time. I got my eye on an Italian girl in Havana, she's only seventeen, her father half-promised her to me."

"You should get married," said Vic easily. "You got plenty stashed away, don't kid me. You'd as soon get tight with feds around as spend that stack. Marry the girl, and raise a family. Turn respectable. You could send for your mother from Italy."

Gino turned gloomy. Oscar was frowning slightly, watching him sharply with those expressionless gray eyes of his. Gino leaned his elbows on the table, spread honey on another biscuit, popped it into his mouth.

"Mama. God, I ain't seen her in ten years. I always meant to send for her. When she writes, she talks about the bank I work in. I told her I work in a bank. If she came to Havana or Miami, and found out—God, she would be sick! My older brother, he works in a bank, she thinks he's the berries. And my sister's husband, that's my older sister Giovanna—"

"Going to talk about your family all day?" inquired Oscar. "Thought we come here to talk to Vic."

Gino frowned. "Don't interrupt me. I got things to think about. You know, that little girl, her name is Maria, and she's dark and sweet as a grape. I saw her last time I was down, she's getting prettier all the time. If I don't speak for her, her damn father will marry her off to somebody else."

"Better get it all settled soon," Vic said calmly. "Girls like that, they mature fast, especially Italian girls, you always said that. She'll want her own husband, and babies. Probably have pretty children. Remember Donna, who you didn't marry? Got two of her own, pretty as pictures, boys both of them. Saw her a year ago. The boys could go straight into the movies."

"I know, I know. God, Donna was sweet for me. But her papa— God, he wouldn't have nothing to do with a rummie."

"He's talking at you on purpose," Oscar said. "Getting you all soft. Got to watch Vic, you know."

"Vic's a clever bastard," Gino said, with no animosity. "Sure, I know what's going on. But he's right. You wouldn't know anything about it, Oscar, but Vic's right. Damn right. Man ain't nothing without a family. Got to have sons and daughters, children to live after him, or he's nothing. You die today, you're nothing, you're a piece of dust. But with children, you're immortal. Know that?"

"Damn," Oscar said.

"Don't damn me!" Gino said seriously. "It's true. Man lives on in his children. Reason Vic wants to marry blondie, here. She'll have pretty children." His gaze went up and down her slim form critically. "Once she has more fat on her, she'll be a damn nice woman."

"Keep your looks away from my woman," Vic said quietly, but with that hard ring of steel in his tone. "She's a good girl, we're going to get married."

There was a little electric silence in the kitchen. Betsy went around the table, pouring more coffee in their mugs, careful not to come between them and Vic.

"Married?" Gino said. "You going to marry this bum, honey?"

Betsy said, "Vic and I decided to get married. We love each other, we're good for each other. We're going to run the restaurant, and raise a family. Here, in Greystone." She set the pot down on the stove with a ringing sound.

"I told you," Oscar said in his tired voice. "Get a woman mixed up in it, and it goes all to hell."

"Married," Gino said, leaning on his elbows, staring down at the red checked tablecloth, moving a fork slowly. "Married. You getting married, Vic. Never thought you'd leave me and get married. Thought we'd make our fortunes, and then retire, be best men at each other's weddings. Remember, we talked about that?"

There was a sound like a sob in his throat. Vic moved slightly. Oscar was watching Vic's right wrist, idly.

"*You* should find a girl and marry her. Marry that Maria. Go ahead, you won't be sorry. You got enough to buy a house and settle down. I can see you, Gino, with a fat bambino on your knee. A kid with black curly hair and black eyes, just like you." Vic's voice was warm and encouraging, but somehow ironic as well.

Betsy thought with admiration how clever Vic was. They had been all set to ruin him with her, by talking about his many women. She knew he must have had women before her, he was so skilled at lovemaking. But she wouldn't think of that, only of the present and the future. He would be faithful to her and work for her and the children.

Vic had cleverly turned the conversation, now he had Gino all sentimental and thinking about a family of his own. He knew Gino, and what appealed to him. Talking about his mother, his wife and children to be.

"Yeah, yeah," Gino said absently. He shoved back his chair, smiled at Betsy. "Damn fine meal, honey. Damn fine. I can see why Vic wants to stick by you. Listen, honey, why don't you come with us to Havana, or Miami? You can set up housekeeping down there. You'd love it, all warm and pretty. Nice beach. Fine for lovemaking, nights, in the sand, huh, Vic? Remember the nights on the beach in Havana? That pretty redhead you had? God, she was a hot number. Betsy here would like it down there too. All the dames like Havana."

"We like it here," Vic said, moving back slightly from the table, wiping his fingers carefully on his napkin. "We have it all set up. Have the lease for the tavern. Have the word of the owner to let us run it. Got a fine cook to work for us. Betsy won't have to work so hard. We're going to advertise for business, soon have the place humming fine. Only food and soft drinks, though—no rum," he ended, deliberately.

"No rum, huh? Can't supply you?" Gino asked jovially, a grin on his face.

"No, we promised the fed, you know, Robert Ming. He was over yesterday, nosing around. They have their eyes on the place. No, no more of that for us. We'll have a clean place."

"What was Ming doing over here?" Gino asked sharply. The smile had disappeared.

"Like I said, nosing around. Talking. The sheriff with

him. Nope, the business here is dead. They know this spot. Not safe to dump anything here anymore," Vic said cheerfully. His right wrist lay carefully on the table before him, his left hand was on his hip.

"That was your fault," snarled Gino. "If you hadn't called in the law, we'd still be sitting pretty. This was a good dump. Safe, easy from the sea. We could pull up in the night, nobody around, get the stuff unloaded and be off, with nobody the wiser. You killed that, wise guy."

"Not me," Vic said. "The guy who killed Hubert Olsen killed the whole thing dead."

There was another of those ominous little silences. "Well, I didn't," Gino said flatly. "And Oscar didn't. That leaves you, Vic. You killed him for your own purposes. Going to take up where he left off." He looked at Betsy deliberately.

"Doesn't make sense," said Vic calmly. "Nope, I didn't. I liked him. And I meant to make up to his niece, knew it the first time I saw her. We're going to be married, like I said. If Hubert had lived, he'd be giving her away—to me."

Gino was rocking back and forth, teetering dangerously on the legs of the kitchen chair. But Vic didn't seem to see him, he was gazing down at his plate, seeming to think deeply. Gino watched him, Oscar watched them both. Betsy backed away a little toward the sink, out of range. She could feel the tension, the explosive quality of the air between them.

"You betrayed us," Gino said finally. "We don't like that, you know. Someone works with us, they got to treat us straight. You know the boss, he knows you. You know the dumps, you know the places in Havana and Miami, and along the keys. The boss doesn't like it, that you plan to stay up here. And he didn't like it—not a bit—when we told him you called in the feds."

"Had to," said Vic. "A fed was shot, and bleeding to death."

"You should have left him in the water!"

"A human being, even a fed," said Vic. "He deserved better than that. He's in the hospital, coming along fine," he offered casually.

"You called in the feds, you helped a fed. The boss doesn't like it at all."

"Tell him he can shove it up—"

"Now, Vic, don't be foolish! The boss liked you. He said nobody could touch an engine like you. He trusted you, *I* trusted you," Gino said plaintively. "Come along now, don't throw it all away like this."

"I'm going straight. I'm getting married."

"You're coming back to Havana with us. Boss wants to see you in Cuba," Gino said.

Betsy cringed in terror against the sink.

In the space of an eyeblink, Vic had flicked his left hand, and a revolver was pointed right at Oscar Kawecki. Oscar was caught, his hand halfway to his right breast. The men stared at each other. Gino sat with his hands flat on the red-checked tablecloth.

"I'm going nowhere," Vic said in his cold deadly tone. "Get that—*nowhere*. The boss doesn't call me back to Cuba. Remember, I can shoot good with either hand. Forgot that, didn't you? Doesn't pay to forget— not anything. I told you, I'd let you alone if you let me alone. Tell the boss I'm not telling on him, but he's got to let me alone, or the feds will hear the whole long story, the song with all the lyrics. Tell the boss that, with my love."

"He won't like that, Vic," Gino said sorrowfully. "I tried my best to make you see reason."

"Tell the boss—kiss him for me. I won't be seeing him again. It's over, the cover here is blown to hell. He can look somewhere else for his trouble, because I'll be waiting—and ready."

Oscar hadn't moved a muscle, his hand still stuck in the air somewhere near his chest. Vic hadn't taken his eyes from him.

"We-ell," sighed Gino. "Look, Vic, I'm getting up slow. Okay? Just slow and easy. We got to be on our way. But we'll be back, kid. The boss wants us to come back and collect for him. See? I have to do it that way."

"You git, and don't come back. Tell the boss it's impossible. The job is too rough, you'd get all torn up. Tell him for me." Vic rose slowly, the gun still on Oscar Kawecki. It moved slightly, the deadly black barrel gestured. "Go on downstairs, get on your little motorboat, and go away. And don't come back."

"We used to be pals," Gino said sadly, starting for the steps.

"Used to be. I wouldn't want to kill you, Gino. You were good to me." There was a faint tone of regret. "But don't count on anything. This is the way I'm going to live, you can just get used to it."

"Boss will send somebody if we don't bring you back."

"I'll be waiting."

Gino hurried down the stairs, Oscar followed him. Vic waited, revolver in hand while they descended. He listened. They were both muttering. Then they heard the motor starting. Betsy, without being told, went to the front bedroom and looked out the window. In a minute, she saw the boat coming out from under Greystone Tavern, heading away, out to the open sea.

"They're both in the boat, Vic," she called back over her shoulder.

"Okay. Listen, I'm going outdoors, going to work on the roof. I can watch the Sound from there."

She returned. For a minute, she nested her head against his chest. "I was so scared, Vic," she whispered.

"I'll take care of you," he said, but his tone was still hard and cool, ringing like steel.

She stood up straight, and nodded. "I know. I'll— feed Bryn."

He went to get his thick sweater from the peg in the hallway. He came back, his face taut with strain. He had slipped the revolver back in his left pocket. Another bulge filled his right pocket. He patted her shoulder absently.

"You get some breakfast, honey. Cool it. We'll be fine. We'll watch today—"

"I'll help," she said quickly.

"Sure you will, baby doll. We're in this together. They can only come two ways, over the bridge, or from the water. And Gino and Oscar aren't good swimmers, they hate cold water." He did not smile, just lifted his hand, and went out the back door.

She fed Bryn, then heated some water for a poached

egg. She couldn't face a heavy meal. Her stomach was all churned up and her nerves ragged. The men could come back any time, silently, stealthily. Was there some way to lock up the cellar? Couldn't they close up the stone slabs?

She ate the egg and a piece of toast, slowly, and drank coffee till her hands stopped shaking and she felt warmer. When Vic returned for more nails, she said, "Can't we close up the stone slabs downstairs, can't we lock them up?"

He shook his head. "I looked them over. They can be opened from inside or outside, that's the way they're built. No way to lock them up unless you seal them with cement and close them entirely. But I can lock the hall door to the cellar stairs. I'll put a lock and key on it. That way nobody can come up from the cellar without making noise."

She watched in silence as he set on a lock and tried it. He must have bought locks in Saymore, she thought, in the hardware store. He must have thought of this. His face was half turned from her, she studied the hard, lean planes of his cheek.

Betsy felt tense all day. Vic watched from the roof as he worked up there. When he turned to the bridge, and began measuring for fresh wood for planks, she watched the Sound from the bedroom windows, sitting there in a comfortable rocker, sewing, with Bryn beside her. Her eyes felt weary from the strain, her shoulders hurt from the tension. But nobody came.

Toward dusk, Vic came in. "I saw a car come up and park near the Post Road awhile ago. Wonder if the fed came back?"

"Wouldn't he come in?" Betsy asked apprehensively. She would feel safer if Robert Ming were there!

"Not if he's waiting for the motorboat to come. Wonder if the cruiser is still out there? Maybe the fed saw it."

He went to look out the bedroom window, then returned. "Can't see far, the mist is closing in."

He went back to watch while she fixed supper. They ate, automatically. Vic would get up at times, and go out to look. He went out the front door, returned. "Can't see the car from here, just from the roof," he said. "It's hidden in the bushes, behind some trees. Can't tell the make."

She sighed. The tension was getting to her. How could they sleep under these conditions? How long could they wait? Days and weeks, and months? Years? Would the big boss in Cuba order Vic to be killed? She had heard of things like that. She rubbed her arms. Maybe they should leave Greystone, run away and hide, change their names. She looked at Vic, decided to say nothing—not yet.

They ate, cleaned up. Vic kept going to the windows and looked out, first from the taproom, then from the kitchen. He got out both pistols, cleaned them on the kitchen table, then reloaded.

"You know how to shoot?" he asked Betsy.

"Not—not much," she said. "I don't—"

She shut up. He gave her an understanding look. "Sit down, honey. I'll show you. Just the works of it. Take it in your hand, I unloaded it."

The revolver was heavy in her small hand. She tried sighting it, pointing at the stove, then a plate. Then he showed her how to load the pistol. "Just point about the middle of a man, and pull the trigger, you'll stop him cold. Don't worry about aiming for his heart, or anything."

She didn't say she could not kill a man. Who knew what she could do, if driven?

They sat at the kitchen table. Vic had stuffed the revolver in one pocket, the other lay at his hand. She sewed on a curtain tie, watched his face occasionally as he worked at a list of supplies he wanted from town.

She was just beginning to relax as it turned dark. Then all at once, they heard a sound.

Vic lifted his head alertly, like an animal in the jungle. His eyes narrowed, he listened. The sound came closer. A motor cruiser. He was on his feet.

He opened cellar door, listened. Someone was coming up into the cellar. But there were no voices. They were stealthy and quiet.

Vic held the revolver ready. Betsy was back near the

stove, holding her breath, keeping Bryn stock-still and quiet.

Then into the hard silence—the sound of shots.

One—two—three cracks blasted the silence.

Betsy let out her breath in a long sigh. She could not believe it. Shots. Down there.

Why? Why?

Vic was leaning over the edge of stairway door, searching the darkness of the cellar, tense, alert, the revolver in his hand. It was silent now, after the echo of gunfire died away.

18

All was silent in the cellar. Betsy held her breath, listening. Vic's face was expressionless.

No sound, nothing.

"I'll have to go down," Vic finally said, in a low tone.

Betsy swallowed. She took Bryn and shut him in the first-floor bedroom. Then as Vic started down the stairs slowly, his revolver ready, she followed him.

She wondered if she should take a candle. But there was a light down there, a flickering, wavering light. She went down, one foot after the other, slowly—wondering if she was mad. She should be running screaming out the front door to Saymore.

But she had to stay with Vic. She had to.

She followed him down the stairs. Then in the light of the single candle flickering on the pantry shelf, she saw the incredible sight.

Bradford Schuyler was bending over a limp form on the floor. Bradford Schuyler, his red head shining in the weak light. Looking up swiftly, his revolver in his hand, pointing at Betsy.

"Drop it," he snarled at Vic. "Or I'll kill the girl."

All cold purpose. No charm, no suavity.

Vic dropped the revolver on the steps. Schuyler came forward slowly, his revolver still pointed straight at Betsy, halfway up the stairs. "Come down," he said to them both.

Vic walked down slowly, his hands half up to his ears. Betsy thought of that second revolver. Vic reached Schuyler who had come forward toward him. Schuyler patted his hips, found the second revolver, and tossed it away toward the water. It fell in with a slight splash.

The red-haired man patted him all over, competently.

His face was a hard mask of determination. There was blood on his left hand. He found a knife, tossed that into the water also.

Then he motioned them on down. Betsy said quickly, "I'm not carrying a gun or anything."

Schuyler motioned her forward, reached out, ran his hand down over her body. She flinched. Vic's face was a mask of hate. He and the intruder stared at each other.

A voice—Gino's—moaned. "He's not dead," Vic said and started toward him. Schuyler let Vic go to bend over Gino, touch him. Gino moaned again.

Beyond him was the body of Oscar Kawecki. Vic went over to him, bent down. Touched his head, his throat. "Dead," he said. He straightened. "You did this?"

Schuyler ignored him. He kicked Gino roughly. "Wake up, you're not that hurt."

Betsy made a sound. She put her hand to her throat.

Gino groaned, spoke faintly. "God, help me. I'm bleeding like a pig."

"You'll bleed to death if you don't answer me," said Schuyler. "You're going to work with me, aren't you? You're turning over the business to me, and I get double what that damn stupid Stern got."

Betsy pressed harder on her throat, her blue eyes wide. Vic stood still as a statue.

"I can't decide now, while I'm feeling so awful," whined Gino, stirring on the cold cement floor. "God, have a heart, man. Get me bound up, I'm bleeding, I can feel it—"

"You'll feel another bullet if you don't answer me," said Schuyler callously. "Come on, agree. We'll go upstairs and make out our agreement."

Gino's dark eyes flickered toward Vic. "What about him?"

Schuyler hesitated. "Never mind, he's out of it. He doesn't want to be a rummie, do you, Halstatt?" His tone had a sneer in it.

"That's right, I'm through with the business," Vic said calmly. His hands were held out away from his body, not exactly up. His body seemed poised on the balls of his feet.

"Don't do it," warned Schuyler. "I can kill the girl faster than you can move toward me."

The revolver was still trained carelessly on Betsy. She stood quite still, arms down at her sides, watching. It was unreal. It was terribly cold down there, she felt as though she were chilled to the bone.

"We can talk," said Gino weakly. "But I got to get fixed up first. God, the boss ain't going to like this. You killed Oscar. Oscar was his close friend, you know. The boss isn't going to like this at all, I'll have to explain fast."

"You'll explain fast, over that radio you have out there in the cruiser, on our way down to Miami. I want to meet the boss," Schuyler said. "We can make a deal. I'm a sharp man, and he'll be glad to get me."

"The boss generally picks them himself," Gino said, almost apologetically.

"He'll pick me. I'm on the spot, and I know the angles."

"But you killed Oscar. He won't like that. He liked Oscar."

The man's cold patience seemed to break a little. "God damn you, you listening to me? I'm going to be the contact here. You're going to recommend me to the boss, or you'll bleed to death! Which?"

"I can't think down here, I'm so damn cold," Gino said, and closed his eyes.

Schuyler swore, a string of words that Betsy would never have dreamed he would know. He still looked the dandy, in a dark suit with a wide tie flowing down his white shirtfront. But his left hand was bloody, probably from checking to make sure Oscar was dead. And his right hand held the big revolver as though it were accustomed to it.

Vic was quiet and still. Betsy tried to control her shaking.

"Why don't we go upstairs and talk it over?" Gino asked, in a plaintive tone. "God, I'm freezing to death down here."

Schuyler hesitated, then nodded. "All right. Betsy,

come here." He grabbed her before she could shrink back, and stuck the cold rim of the revolver on her quivering neck. "All right. Halstatt, you get him upstairs."

Vic glared at him. Betsy was trembling. She could smell the big man behind her, a smell like that of a devil, strong and terrible. She thought then that she had smelled it before. The night her uncle had died. And the morning when Dora had struggled with a man, and lost, and Betsy had felt him coming after her.

He must have been the man who had hidden in the cellar, had attacked Dora, and killed her, and thrown her body into the Sound. Betsy remembered that hard strange smell, the smell like that of the devil, pungent and dreadful. The smell of the man who had stalked her in the darkness, and almost got her.

How often had he hidden down here? Waiting, listening, waiting . . .

"Go on," Schuyler said to Betsy, and pushed her to the stairs. He stood beside the stairs, with his bloody left hand clamped on Betsy's shoulder, and the cold rim of the revolver digging into her slim throat. "Pick him up, Halstatt. You can do it."

Vic nodded, bent down, and lifted Gino to his feet. The man cursed weakly, then bent over Vic's shoulder. The younger man staggered a little, then hefted him in a fireman's lift, and started for the stairs.

"No tricks, now," Schuyler said. "Take him to the front parlor and lay him down. I'm coming up with the girl right after you. One funny move, and she's dead. Nobody can hear shots from down here. It's too far away."

His voice was calm and conversational. Betsy wondered wildly what he would do with them both after he got them upstairs.

He needed Gino.

He did not need Vic or Betsy. In fact, they would be in his way. They had seen too much. They knew he had killed Oscar Kawecki. Betsy guessed he had killed her uncle and Dora. Schuyler could not afford to keep them alive.

She moved numbly when he pushed her to the stairs.

Vic had reached the top, carrying Gino, who grunted and groaned as though he were the one making the effort. Vic carried him into the kitchen, then paused while Schuyler came up the stairs pushing Betsy before him.

"Into the front parlor," Schuyler said. Now he reminded Betsy of Oscar Kawecki. She could not feel sorry that Oscar was dead, he was a cruel cold man. But he had met someone as tough and coldhearted as he was.

How many had Schuyler killed?

Betsy remembered the young federal agent, shot and left to die in the water, whom Vic had carried back to the tavern. Had Schuyler shot him also?

Vic carried Gino into the front parlor, struggling with him along the hallway past the large chests, the wooden pegs with their coats and sweaters hanging there. Betsy could hear Bryn whining anxiously in the closed bedroom.

Gino was laid carefully down on the parlor sofa. Vic bent over him, straightened his legs and arms, and then prepared to open his coat and shirt.

"Leave him be," Schuyler said brusquely.

"Just going to tie up the wound a bit," Vic said quietly.

"Let him bleed. He'll listen to me faster. Tie him up, though." He looked about. He motioned with his left hand to the neat curtain ties that Betsy had been sewing. "Take some of those. Tie his legs together."

Vic's mouth was hard and grim. He took the curtain ties and bound Gino's legs together.

"Now his hands together, at the wrists." Schuyler watched carefully as Vic worked. "Tighter, God damn you." The tone was all the more menacing for being without expression.

Betsy's breath was coming hard. Would he kill them now? He didn't need them any longer. Vic must have been thinking the same thing. He was tense when he was finished tying up Gino.

"Now, you two—" Schuyler seemed to be thinking, looking at Gino, I'll put you where you won't be any trouble to me. Gino and I have some talking to do."

"We have some talking to do also," Vic said casually.

"I'd like to know why you did all this. You must have killed Hubert Olsen. And maybe Dora Johnson—"

"Shut up," Schuyler snarled without a trace of his former finesse. His looks were an odd contrast to the bloody hands, the revolver, the wild expression in his light-green eyes.

"And there was the young fed officer, Jim Burton. You must have done that—and now Oscar Kawecki, and shooting Gino. Why—why did you do all that? Why do you want the rum business so badly?"

Vic's even tone was belied by the dark dangerous glisten of his eyes.

"For money, of course. I've got so many damn debts, and people hounding me—God damn you, shut up. I can't think—"

Vic took a slow step toward him. The revolver jammed into Betsy's neck forcefully, and Vic stopped.

"No, you don't. You go first, to that back room, the bedroom. Go ahead!" Schuyler's tone was wilder, his nerve was breaking a little.

He turned Betsy around to follow Vic, out into the hallway, then back to the bedroom. He opened the door. Bryn jumped up and down, licking his hand. Vic pushed him back sternly. "Go back, Bryn. Sit down!"

Schuyler shoved Betsy inside so forcefully that she stumbled against Vic.

"Go on in. I'm going to talk reason to Gino. You be quiet. You can't get out, don't make a fuss. We'll come to a deal together, you'll see." He attempted a smile, it was a ghastly grimace. "You be nice now, huh? I'll talk to you later."

He slammed the door, locked it from the outside, took the key out, and they heard his feet thumping along the hallway.

Betsy collapsed against Vic. He took her in his arms, and held her close, her head against his shoulder. "There, there, honey, we're still alive."

"Oh—Vic—"

"Take it easy."

"He must have killed . . . Uncle . . . and Dora—"

"I know. It's clear now. He must have come by car, left the car across the bridge—he always walked in, remember? And the doors were unlocked in the daytime. He could come in whenever he pleased." Vic's tone was hard, but his hands were gentle, soothing her, patting her head and back.

"It's—horrible. Coming to talk to Uncle, pretending to be his friend. Uncle had refused to let him join in the rum business, I know he tried to make Uncle join in a partnership with him. He wanted the money so badly— that he killed—poor Uncle—oh, poor Uncle—"

"He must have hidden in the cellar often. Could come in when he pleased, leave when he was sure we were upstairs. Snuck around the tavern, over the bridge, and away to his car. Must have been his car I saw to-day," Vic said thoughtfully. "I hoped it was the feds."

"Couldn't it be Mr. Ming? Do you think he's around?" Betsy lifted her head with hope.

"I don't think so, honey. If he had heard all those shots, as he would have from the car, he would have come in by this time. No, it must have been Schuyler's car. He must have seen the big cruiser out in the Sound, and come to wait for Gino and Oscar."

"Waiting in the cellar," she shivered convulsively. "The way he waited for Uncle—and Dora Johnson. But why would he kill Dora? She was harmless."

"Maybe she was, maybe she wasn't. If she saw him at some point—remember she found your uncle? I wonder if she saw Schuyler that time. Or saw him leave. She was bold as brass. She might have blackmailed him— well, it's a thought," he said, as Betsy gave him an incredulous look.

"She wouldn't have! It would be too dangerous. He must have killed her because she saw him in the cellar with me—"

"With you?"

"I mean, when I went down with her. Oh, I'm all mixed up," and she put her head down wearily on his shoulder.

They could hear a low rumble of voices from the front parlor.

"I'd give a lot to hear what they say," Vic said presently, moving restlessly from her. He prowled around the room, opened the drawers softly.

"What are you looking for?"

"Something to dig with. If I could remove some of the bricks, in the alcove where the bathroom is, I bet I could hear. I had a couple of bricks out one day, and I could hear you and Dora talking in the front parlor." He grinned cunningly.

"Oh, what did we say?"

"Never mind now. Look in the drawers, quietly now."

He was pulling out all the drawers, opening the doors of the wardrobe, peering everywhere. Finally he shook his head. "No luck. Nothing here but combs and brushes and a mirror. How about you?"

"Nothing but a couple candles and a few matches."

She wasn't thinking about burrowing instruments. She was thinking that when Schuyler had the information and the reluctant promise wrung from Gino, he would come back for them. And he would probably decide to get rid of them. Shoot them, dump them in the cold waters of the Sound.

He had done it before, he would do it again. Kill with a bullet, and let the Sound do the rest. Dora's body had never been found. All he had to do was make sure they were dead.

When Schuyler returned to the bedroom, he would kill them. She looked at Vic. Their life together had seemed to hold so much promise of happiness. Now it would be gone.

"What is it, honey?" he asked gently, finally looking up from his search.

"I think—I think he'll come back—and kill us," she quavered. Bryn whined at her voice, and came up to lick her hand in sympathy.

Vic came over also, and took her in his arms. "I think he'll give it a try, honey. But we're not dead yet. I'm going to listen in on that talk. You okay?" He gave her a kiss on her forehead, and a gentle little shake.

She nodded, fingered the teardrops off her eyelashes. He kissed the tip of her nose, then turned from her. He took a mirror he had found in the dresser drawer, wrapped it in a towel. He tapped it against the mantel, then gave it a hard crack. She watched, wide-eyed. He

opened the towel, showed the mirror in several frag-
ments.

"What did you do that for? It's seven years' bad
luck!" she gasped.

He grinned, a wide white slash across his dark face.
"I make my own luck, baby doll. This is going to scrape
away some of the cement between the bricks. You listen
for Schuyler coming. I'm going to work on the bricks."

She watched him silently as he shoved aside the thin
curtains that separated the bedroom from the little alcove where the tub and washstand stood. Then she sat
down in a straight chair near the door. Bryn put his
head in her lap. She fondled his floppy silky ears. Her
fingers were cold as ice.

What could they do? What could Vic do that would
keep that horrible monster from killing them? Schuyler
had killed before, he knew they realized that. He would
not leave them alive.

19

Vic took a couple more towels from the rack. His face was intent, keen, the way it was when he was figuring out how to repair the roof or the bridge. Betsy listened, could hear nothing from the alcove. Curiosity drew her to the entrance of the alcove.

Vic grinned at her. His eyes blazed bright with excitement. He mouthed slowly, "I . . . can . . . hear . . . them."

He pointed at the wall behind the toilet. Above the wall he was scraping away patiently at the mortar which bound the large old bricks. Through the wall she could hear the vague murmur of voices. Vic put his ear to the wall, and despite his closeness, couldn't distinguish any words. He shook his head, and began work again.

Carefully, he scraped away at the mortar, pried away one brick. He laid it carefully in the tub, then scraped around another one. The bricks must be loose, she thought. They came away from the wall rather easily. She stood and watched.

Vic kept listening, then resumed working. He lifted out another brick.

Betsy and Bryn watched him in fascination. There seemed no end to the things that Vic could do, thought the girl. He loosened two more bricks, drew them out slowly, laid them in the tub. He leaned to listen, then motioned to Betsy to come forward. She managed to climb around the tub, and sat on the end of it, her ear to the wall.

As she listened, her eyes widened in shock. Gino was talking quite clearly in the next room.

". . . did to Dora, can't forget that, you know," he

said, in his plaintive voice. "You killed her for nothing."

Betsy looked up at Vic. He nodded sharply, indicated she listen closely. He listened too, but continued loosening more bricks.

Bradford Schuyler's voice came through a little more muffled, he must have his back to their wall, thought Betsy. By listening intently she could make out what he said.

"Had to kill Hubert," he was saying. "That damn ass, he wouldn't let me get in on the business. Then he let his niece come and stay. I knew that would queer things. I tried to make up to her, but she wasn't the friendly type."

"She really went for Vic in a big way."

"Stupid dame," Schuyler snarled. There was a moment of silence. Vic squeezed Betsy's shoulder.

She nodded, pressed her hand to his, then leaned closer to listen.

"You bad in debt?" Gino inquired with sympathy. Betsy could just imagine his cunning face, all interest, his dark eyes melting with interest. The old fox.

"Bad enough," grunted Schuyler. "My folks turned me out finally. Damn them all. I came over to Saymore to make a new start. Everything I touched went rotten."

"Too bad. A guy gets bad breaks sometimes."

Vic growled something about bad breaks. Betsy squeezed his hand to quiet him. She knew how he felt about a man making his own luck, taking the bad with the good, and working it out.

"I sure as hell did. Then I got wind that Hubert Olsen had the dump for the rum. Alva Stern wouldn't let me cut in, the nosy old bastard. Laughed at me. I thought I could get him, sicked the feds on him. But they never caught him. Them and their big feet! They never caught him in the act. I started watching for myself. I'd park across the road, and wait in the bushes. Saw you come night after night, got you timed."

"You don't say, that was real smart," said Gino.

"Really, it was. Only I didn't really want the feds around," Schuyler said earnestly. "You see, I wanted the business. Make good money. I knew Olsen was making plenty. He had wads in his pockets."

"It is—real good money," Gino agreed cheerfully. "You'd be able to clear up your debts and have a good time. I'll put in a good word with the boss—"

"I want more than a good word," Schuyler said sharply. "I want your promise to give the business to me alone. I want it all. I can make good contacts north of here. I have a fine car, I can drive it up myself. Save you a lot of trouble. No need to get everybody involved in this."

"Say, you're a greedy cuss—"

There was the sharp sound of a blow. Betsy winced for Gino.

"Hey, don't do that—I just meant to be kidding—"

"Don't make cracks. I want what's mine. I worked for this, got rid of Hubert for you, and that stupid Dora Johnson. She tried to blackmail me, the fool."

Betsy stiffened, Vic pressed his hand harder on her shoulder.

"How did you do that? What did she do?"

"Saw me down with Hubert, I came up first, thought he was dead. Poking and prying—she saw me another time, told me to give her five hundred dollars, or she'd tell you all about it the next time you came. She saw me come up from the cellar. Saw him come up all bloody. Put on a good act, screaming and all. And she wanted to be paid for it. I paid her, all right, caught her down there and squeezed the life out of her squawking throat."

Their voices lowered. Vic went impatiently to work loosening more bricks.

Gino said, "About Betsy Olsen, she's not so bad. I think if Vic sees it our way, she'll go along."

"She knows too much," Schuyler said briefly.

"You don't trust her?"

"I never trust a dame. This is between men—" The voices lowered again. So he had tried to kill her in the cellar, thought Betsy, a cold chill shivering down her back. And soon he would come to the bedroom and kill both her and Vic. And Bryn, poor little Bryn, who was so cute and friendly, and had never harmed anybody.

If they disappeared, people would think they had gotten tired of trying to run Greystone as a restaurant. They had given up and gone back to the bright lights of the city, folks would say. They might not even conduct much of a search for them. And who would find them deep in the waters of Long Island Sound?

"But how much do the feds know?" Gino was asking.

"Oh, that damn Ming—he and the sheriff went to old Ned Palmer, asked him who wanted the lease on Greystone. And that Palmer told him Stern did, and me. God, I'll have to fix that character."

Kill *Ned Palmer?* Betsy shook her head and looked up at Vic. She mouthed the words, "He—is—insane!" Vic nodded soberly.

He pried out another brick, then another. Betsy thought Vic would take the whole wall down.

"What about it, Gino? Come on." Schuyler was getting impatient. "I can't wait all day. Do I have your promise? I'll get you to a doctor I know. He'll keep his mouth shut. Then we can go to the cruiser, and I'll go with you to the boss. We can get it all set up. Next trip you'll find me in residence here and all ready to work."

"We might have to get another dump, with the feds knowing about this one."

"So we'll settle on a place around the beach," Schuyler said. "I can watch for your signal and come and pick up the stuff. Come on, what do you say?"

"I got to think about it—"

Schuyler struck him, they heard the crack.

"Come on now, don't do that," Gino drawled. "I don't like that. Take it easy. We got business to discuss."

Vic pried another brick from its place, then frowned. He reached in carefully with his fingers, poked about. Slowly, he drew out a strange brown object, about the size of a lady's purse. It was a leather bag, all crumbling and dusty with age.

Betsy's eyes widened, she was close to exclaiming, but Vic gave her a sharp warning look. She held out her hands at his gesture, and he put the worn bag in her fingers. Through rents in the leather, she caught the glint of something gold within.

She unfastened it carefully, and Vic helped. He poked at the shining gold coins inside, shook his head in amazement.

"Who?" she whispered, indicating the hiding place.

"Maybe that highwayman they told us about, years ago. Some said he left gold here at Greystone, but they never found it." He lifted a coin curiously. "The date is on it," he whispered. "We can look at it later."

Later. If they lived.

The coins fell over in her hand. Vic's fingers darted to a dark object among the coins. His face glowed with amazement as he delicately lifted it out.

A knife, a small sharp knife, with the blade scarcely rusted at all. "God," he whispered, "a knife."

They had practically forgotten about the two in the next room. Sharply raised voices recalled them as Vic held the knife, and then strapped it against his pants leg.

Betsy leaned to listen. ". . . do about them two?" asked Gino. "Vic is my pal, you know."

"He isn't my pal. He turned you down, didn't he?"

"I can talk him into coming to Havana or Miami with me. Just give me the chance to talk to him. He's okay, my buddy. We've been through a lot together."

"I don't trust him."

"I do," Gino said easily. "Just let me talk to him."

"He would want a cut of the business. No, nobody but us two, Gino. You can hire who you want, but I'm taking all the money for this end of the deal."

"I got to think it over. The boss really does the deciding, Schuyler, you got to see that."

Crack! Schuyler had struck him again. Betsy flinched in sympathy. Gino sounded tired but patient.

"Oh, come on, Schuyler. This doesn't get us noplace. Untie me, and let's talk like partners."

"Are we partners? You going to work it out with me? I got to have money!" The man's tone was more and more hysterical. "Come on, I don't have all day!"

"Untie me, and we'll talk."

"We'll talk this way. What else is there to say? You going to take me in, or do I finish you off, too?"

"That would queer you with the boss," Gino said calmly. "He likes me a lot. You won't get nowhere like that. Okay, say I took you in, you'd want up to twenty-five percent?"

"Twenty-five, hell! I want fifty percent."

There was a short silence. "Did you get that fed, young Burton?" Gino asked finally. "Listen, if he saw you, it's no dice. He's alive—"

"Yeah, thanks to Halstatt! If he had left him alone, he would have died in the water, and no one know the difference—"

"Did Burton see you?"

"Hell, no, nobody ever sees me," bragged Schuyler.

"You talked like you killed before," Gino said casually. "Okay, okay, don't hit me again! I get the point, you don't like to brag about it, huh? Tell you what, we'll go out to the cruiser, and put in a call to the boss, ask him what to do. How will that be?"

"Now you're talking. I'll take care of those others, and we'll go out."

Gino did not reply. Betsy went stiff. Vic took the knife firmly in his hand, helped her over the tub and out. "We'll get ready for him. Courage, honey. I want you behind the dresser. When he comes in, duck."

Her lips were dry. Vic went over to stand flattened against the door, his back to the wall, in the shadows, the knife ready in his right hand. Betsy caught Bryn, shoved him into the alcove, and crouched down behind the dresser.

Vic glanced at her once, a flash of his dark eyes, to make sure she was all right. Then his attention went completely to the door.

In one hand, she still clutched the worn leather bag and the gold coins. And through her mind seemed to pass her whole life history.

The early years, the heartbreaking years of being alone. Her fiancé, his death. Then coming in complete desolation to Greystone, seeking sanctuary. Finding Hubert—and danger and death.

And Vic. Vic had come, and she had come alive

again, warm and wanting and eager for the future. Yes, she wanted to live, and love, and make a home for Vic and the children that would come to bless them.

Oh, was it in her hand, only to fall through her fingers like grains of sand? Was she unlucky that way, that nothing would ever go right? Had she found Vic only to lose him and her own life?

She closed her hands over the bag, squeezing the leather unconsciously tight, her fingers hurting on the gold coins. She had only wanted to find a place to stay, she would have worked hard for Uncle Hubert, she was willing to work and scrub and cook and sew—work all her life—only—only if she might live . . .

If she might live, and Vic would live . . .

Then she heard footsteps in the hallway. Schuyler was making no attempt to hide his coming.

"Hey, Vic Halstatt! I got a deal to make with you!" called Bradford Schuyler. Betsy stared at Vic wide-eyed. Was it true? Was he going to talk to them, suggest something?

Vic evidently didn't believe it. He was crouched against the wall, his arm lifted, ready—ready, with the knife shining in his hand, on his face the deadly cold look she hated.

Ready to kill.

She swallowed, and clutched at the leather bag as though it might be a talisman. Maybe it was. Maybe the highwayman who had hidden it there years ago hoped that someone who needed the gold and the knife might one day find it. Whatever had happened to him, that long-ago highwayman? Had he gone away, finding peace and a good useful life for himself, that he had never returned for the gold?

It must have slipped down behind the bricks. There were cavities behind the bricks, they needed chinking again. Betsy closed her eyes briefly, and then all thoughts but one were clear.

She wanted Vic to live, and she wanted to live with him.

"Oh, God, if it could only be—let us live!" she prayed fervently.

"Halstatt, you hear me?" Schuyler called from outside the door. "I'm coming in to talk to you. Don't act foolish now. I'm coming in!"

The door key clicked in the lock.

Vic was waiting, his knife hand upraised.

The door was flung open unexpectedly wide. Schuyler was turning on Vic, the revolver ready. He had guessed, guessed that Vic would be there. He would kill him!

Betsy, clutching the leather bag, stood up in the dimness.

"Mr. Schuyler! Look what we found! Gold!" she cried in a shrill voice.

In the dusk of the room, Schuyler was caught off guard for one precious moment. He turned toward her, swiftly turned back. The revolver fired, into the air. Vic had him clutched to him, the knife stabbed into the throat, once, twice, and stuck.

Schuyler groaned, gagged, the gun went off again in his hand, the bullet spatting into the wall. Vic held him, the knife in the man's throat, his face . . . Betsy closed her eyes.

Schuyler went limp. Betsy opened her eyes as she heard his body hit the floor. Vic crouched over him, his hand on the knife. Slowly he pulled it out. Blood flowed out in great red spurts. Bryn whined uneasily, crouching back beside Betsy.

Vic stood up. "He's dead," he said. "Come on, Betsy. We're getting out of here."

She stumbled across the room to him. His hands were covered with blood. She stepped around Schuyler carefully, her gaze fearful on the still form. He seemed to kick out.

"He's—he's still alive—Vic—" she gasped.

"No. Just death throes," Vic said. "Come on."

She followed him to the kitchen. He turned on the tap, washed his hands with cold water, then hot and soap.

Gino called plaintively from the front parlor, "Hey, Schuyler, what's going on? What's happening? Come on, man, untie me!" His voice was fearful.

Vic did not answer him. "Get your coat and sweater,

Betsy," he said. "Grab my coat, too. We're going for the sheriff."

She breathed again. Her chest hurt from holding her breath, from the fear that had clutched her. She slipped into her sweater, then her coat, grabbed Vic's coat from the wooden peg, and returned to the kitchen.

"Schuyler? Vic? Who's there? What happened?"

Vic opened the back door, motioned her out. Bryn scampered out before them, down the steps, paused to wait for them. Vic put his hand under Betsy's elbow, steered her toward the automobile. His hand was steady as a rock. And he had just killed a man.

To save them both, she reminded herself, feeling rather hysterical. Vic was a hard man, but he was not a killer. He had killed to save their lives.

They drove toward the bridge. In the distance, two cars were coming down the Post Road, sweeping in toward the bridge. If he did not swerve they would crash.

Betsy started to clutch at Vic's arm. She clasped her hands instead. "Who is that?" she asked sharply. "Did Schuyler have friends?"

Vic drew the car to a stop. He had to. The two automobiles had swung forward right in his path, blocking him. He stopped the Ford and waited. Robert Ming got out of one car, a revolver in his hand. Rob Lanahan got out of the other car with another revolver. They came forward, one on each side.

"All right—out—and hands up," snapped Robert Ming, glaring at them both.

20

Vic called to them, "Okay, we're getting out. We were coming for the sheriff."

"Come out easy and slow," Lanahan said curtly, his revolver trained on Betsy.

"Don't shoot, we'll tell you the whole story," Vic called, his tone hard.

"Come on out," repeated Lanahan.

Vic got out first, his hands going in the air. Ming came up to him, slapped his pockets, reached in his breast pocket. "Okay, no gun or knife. Come on out, Miss Olsen."

Betsy's knees felt as though they would not support her. She half fell out of the small automobile. Bryn followed her, whining, jumping around her. When Lanahan came up, gun in hand, Bryn snarled at him, growling deep in his small throat.

"It's all right, quiet, Bryn, quiet," Betsy said faintly. She put her hand to her throat. "It's all—right—"

"What were those shots?" snapped Ming, looking toward the tavern. "What's going on in there?"

"It was Schuyler, Bradford Schuyler," Vic said in an almost casual voice. "He was waiting for Oscar Kawecki and Gino Pescara when they came into the cellar. He killed Kawecki, shot Gino."

"Where's Schuyler?" asked Lanahan, peering uneasily beyond Betsy as though expecting the man to come out.

"I killed him with a knife," Vic said simply. "He tried to shoot me. I got him first."

The two men stared at him for a full minute without speaking.

"Come on," said Ming, with a sort of groan. "I got to see all this. How many bodies are in that tavern?"

"Three—two dead and one alive," Vic answered quietly, "You want to hear the story or not?"

A cold west wind bit into them as full darkness descended. Betsy was shivering from cold and excitement and relief.

"Let's go inside," Ming said. "Go on, lead the way, Halstatt." His gun was still on them. Vic didn't like it, Betsy could tell by the stiff way he walked. Oh, Vic, don't turn on them, she prayed. They are the law, please, take it easy. Shyly she slipped her hand under his arm as he came to her, and felt the tension in him. He patted her hand, and gave her a grin. She felt him relax a little.

"We'll be okay now, Vic," she whispered.

"Sure, baby doll," he said quietly. They went into the building through the front door. Bryn pranced before them, and led the way into the parlor, to sniff curiously at the bound form of Gino on the sofa.

The parlor was dark but for the light of the single candle Schuyler had lit. Ming found the oil lamp near it, lifted the glass shade, lit it, shook out the match. He carried the lamp over to survey Gino Pescara, who was staring up at him.

Blood covered Gino's shirt. His arms and legs were tied with once-pretty curtain ties. Ming shook his head at him.

"Feds," Gino gasped. "My God." That was the extent of his reaction, for he fell back and closed his eyes immediately after speaking the three words.

Lanahan took it all in, then went back to the bedroom. It was then that Betsy remembered the worn leather bag filled with gold coins. Where had she left it? She had dropped it on the kitchen table, she remembered. She looked at Vic. He was gazing down at her.

She mouthed the word. "Gold?"

"Safe," he murmured. He must have put it somewhere. She gave a little sigh of relief. If they got out of all this, she wanted them to have the gold. It would help them, for the future they now had a better chance of achieving!

"We'll need some hot water," Ming said, bending down over Gino. He ripped open the jacket and shirt, examined the wound. "Bullet wound. Who shot you?"

"Schuyler," Gino said, opening his eyes again. "Damn bastard. He killed my buddy, Oscar."

"In the cellar? Waiting for you?" Ming asked casually, prodding the wound.

Gino wrenched away. "Ouch—go easy, damn you! In the cellar, yeah." He seemed to gather himself together. "I—uh—we were coming back from an outing—fishing trip."

Gino winced. "Ouch—go easy, damn you! In the wound. "Hold that light closer, Miss Olsen, if you will."

She picked up the lamp, held it close so he could see.

"Looks bad. Bullet has smashed against the bone. Needs an operation."

Gino moaned.

Lanahan returned. "Schuyler is dead, all right. Knife wounds, in his throat. Who did it?"

"Vic did," Gino said quickly. "The man was after his girl, little blondie here."

Betsy made a sound. Vic said, gently, "Look, Gino, we're not covering up for you. The feds know you were rumrunning. Schuyler wanted a big piece of the business. We heard him tell Gino here that he killed Betsy's uncle for it. Dora Johnson saw him come up from the cellar that time. She tried to blackmail him—five hundred dollars for not telling Gino about it. So he killed her, tried to kill Betsy."

"God, the stories you make up, boy," said Gino loudly, turning uncomfortably as Ming cut him loose from the curtain ties. "It wasn't like that at all, mister. We don't know who killed all them—me and Schuyler were just having a quiet talk—"

"Before or after he shot you?" asked Ming. Lanahan stood with his hands on his hips, listening. The revolver was back in its holster, Betsy was relieved to see.

"Should I heat some water?" she asked timidly. The men seemed to pay no attention. She left the room and went back to the kitchen. A quick look around showed her the leather bag had disappeared. Only a little dust lay on the kitchen table. She brushed it off quickly, and dumped it into the trash bin. Then she filled the kettle with water, and set it on the stove. She put more wood on the fire, and drew the first deep breath she had enjoyed for more than an hour.

Her ribs hurt from the tension. She rubbed her side wearily. Bryn had come out after her, nosing the cupboard. She patted him, got out his bowl and some food. He ate contentedly, drinking noisily from his water dish, all very normal.

Lanahan came out for a pan of hot water and some cloths. She handed him torn-up sheet material and some salve.

"He will have to go to the hospital, won't he?" she asked timidly.

"Reckon so. The bullet will have to come out. After that, prison," he said, with a slight smile at her. "You've had quite a time of it, haven't you?"

She nodded. "I thought he would kill us. Mr. Schuyler, I mean. He was going to, and dump us in the Sound. Because we knew too much. I think—I think he had gone crazy. Killing all those people."

"How did you hear him?" Lanahan asked casually.

"Through the bedroom wall. Vic took out some bricks. He thought he could hear, and we did."

"I'd like to see it, if you don't mind."

Betsy wiped her hands on her apron, and led him to the bedroom. She shivered, and looked away, walking carefully past the big, limp body of Bradford Schuyler. There was so much blood on him and on the floor. She showed Lanahan the bathroom alove, the bricks Vic had dug out.

"How did he get them out?"

"He broke a mirror, and used the pieces."

"Not the knife?" asked Lanahan.

"No—no, he needed something sharper, I think," said Betsy, staring intently at the wall, keeping her gaze from the sheriff. She wanted desperately to keep the secret of the little leather bag and the gold coins and the knife. The gold was the start they needed, she wanted to hang on to that. "He broke a mirror, and took the biggest piece to dig with."

Lanahan seemed satisfied for the moment, and they

walked back to the kitchen. She poured out some hot water into a round pan, and carried the strips of sheet back to the front parlor. Gino was squirming, his face red.

"No, no, it wasn't like that! Don't listen to Vic Halstatt. We ain't rumrunning, just coming up for some fishing. We used to come up and fish with Hubert Olsen—"

Betsy realized with a sinking feeling that Gino was lying to save his hide. He wouldn't back up Vic's story and hers.

And the law officers, she could not tell by their impassive expressions if they believed Gino or Vic. Gino settled it by fainting, and they decided to take him to the hospital.

Vic went along, as did the bodies of Oscar Kawecki and Bradford Schuyler. To her relief, Vic was back by midnight, just as she was about to give up and lock up Greystone for the night.

He walked in, and gave her a big hug. His face was tired, but more calm and serene. "I'll have to go back tomorrow, honey, but I think they believe me now. They sent the Coast Guard out, and picked up the cruiser. The fellow Gino left there had gotten into some of the best Jamaica rum that Gino keeps for himself, and they latched onto two cases of the stuff. So they have the evidence they want."

He was too tired to eat. She fixed him some coffee, and he drank that, and strode around Greystone finally locking up the place. Then they went up to bed.

Vic was up early the next morning. He had rolled and tossed in the night, waking her. But she did not complain, even to herself. They were safe and alive. Vic had saved them. When she shut her eyes she could see his hard intent face as he lunged to kill Bradford Schuyler. But that had to be, she told herself.

The sheriff and Robert Ming returned that day, and they went over and over the story. Betsy told them what she knew, Vic went patiently over his story. And finally the lawmen were satisfied. They brought out a lawyer, and took down statements, and went away with them.

Gino had reluctantly given evidence when he realized he could not get away with lies. He was in the hospital, under guard until he could be removed to prison. The large cruiser and the small motor cruiser were registered in his name. And the drunken aide on board the larger craft had talked freely.

When they were finally alone, Betsy asked, "Vic, what happened to the bag of gold coins?"

"I would never tell. Only let me empty the trash bin today, honey. You might throw away something important."

Her hand flew to her mouth. "Oh, Vic, and I almost dumped it awhile ago!"

He laughed. "I was watching you, honey. That's why I asked for more coffee." He got up lazily, and went to the trash bin, full of coffee grounds, some bloody cloths from Gino's wound, old newspapers, a couple of cans. He dug around, then drew out a newspaper wrapped around the leather bag. Carefully he opened it, and set it on the table, slit down the sides, and scooped up a fortune in gold coins in his hand.

Betsy picked one up, examined the date. "My goodness," she breathed. "It says 1802. And it's a British gold coin! Look, isn't that the sign of Great Britain?"

He examined them critically. "They're all about the same date, brought from England. I bet they are worth more than the face value. Probably a coin dealer would give me plenty. I know a fellow in Havana—"

He caught the expression on her face.

"Oh, honey, don't worry! I'm not going back down there. There are contacts I can trust—"

"I wish we could keep them," she said wistfully. "But we need things for the restaurant, for us."

"Right you are. But we could keep one." He indicated the one in her slim fingers. "Keep that one, Betsy. For luck."

"I thought you didn't believe in luck!" she told him spiritedly, closing her fingers about the coin.

"Well, I think you make your own luck. But it doesn't hurt to have Providence on your side, and a quick right fist," Vic grinned easily. "Say, I know what we'll get with the money."

"New draperies for the 'taproom'?" she suggested eagerly.

"Sure, honey. But also something else, something important. A pretty wedding dress for a honey I know."

"Oh, really, Vic?" A blush spread over her cheeks at his look. "Oh, really?"

"Really." His big fingers closed over hers, and the gold coin. "I want to make sure of you soon. Right? We can speak to the preacher, and to Dr. Cameron and his wife. I bet they would come to our wedding."

The gold coins were sent through some of Vic's contacts to Havana and to Miami, where they brought more money than either of them had ever dreamed of possessing. And they had gone down to New York to see about some of Uncle Hubert's other affairs. They were stunned to find he had set back some of his runrumming income in a savings account. Vic insisted on taking it all out, and bringing it back up to the savings bank in Saymore. "We're citizens now, honey. We're going to support the town, and let it support us." Their new wealth paid for some sprucing up of the tavern and a wedding dress for Betsy.

The dress was of white crêpe softly draped over the shoulders, with sleeves like white wings. Over it was embroidered blue butterflies, small ones on the waist, and larger ones over the full skirts. It came to the tips of her white silk shoes. With it was a veil of white Brussels lace they had found in another shop. And on the veil were woven small butterflies and vines and flowers, frail and exquisite.

Mrs. Cameron said she was the prettiest bride she had ever helped dress. All Saymore turned out for the wedding, in the white church with the wooden steeple. That November day was bright and golden and blue, just like the bride, said Vic, as he touched the veil drawn back from the blond hair.

Dr. Cameron gave away the bride and Rob Lanahan came to the wedding. Jim Burton, somewhat recovered, attended the wedding on crutches, and gave a toast to the bride and to Vic. He was almost embarrassingly grateful to Vic for saving his life. The whole town was talking about the surprise, that Mr. Bradford Schuyler, of the grand Schuyler family, had turned out to be a killer.

There were many wedding presents laid out in the old private dining room of Greystone. Ned Palmer gave them a new sofa and chairs, since they were going to keep up his property. They were of blue plush on rosewood, and the prettiest Betsy could have chosen. The Camerons gave them a silver coffee service. Others gave linen, sheets and tablecloths and pillowcases.

Vic hid the card from one gift; Betsy saw it later. The gift was an ornate silver tray with a huge old-fashioned epergne to hold flowers and candles. Vic showed her the card. "In gratitude, to an old pal from his boss."

Her blue eyes opened wide, in shock. "From the boss?" she whispered.

"Yeah," said Vic. "It seems he was grateful that I avenged Oscar's death. He looked at it that way. I got word he isn't going to do anything against me, so long as I don't give him away. And I won't. I want to forget the whole thing."

Betsy held his wrist in cold fingers. "He—really won't? You can trust him?"

"I'll trust him—and keep alert," Vic said grimly. "That's the way of it, honey. Don't look so scared." And he kissed her.

Mrs. Cunkle had prepared the reception. They had coffee and tea and cold raspberry punch, cookies and cakes. Vic shook his head a little, amused. "No rum for me?" he murmured to Betsy.

She could not laugh. She wanted to forget everything about rumrunning.

After the excitement was over, they settled down in Greystone. The word of the restaurant and its good food spread. They often had overnight guests on the weekends. And many a party was held at Greystone, celebrations of birthdays, weddings, school reunions. And there were meetings monthly or weekly of the Lions Club, and the Rotary, and the Sunshine Ladies' Club, and the sewing circle, the musicians' club.

It became the thing to do, to come to Greystone for an extra-special meal, a celebration. The mellow stone walls echoed the sounds of laughter and singing and joviality.

And at night, Betsy slept better and better, when she finally got over listening for the sounds of a boat slipping stealthily into the waters below the cellar.

When she did lie awake, it was to feel the solid hardness of Vic's arm about her, to move her head more comfortably on his shoulder, and count her blessings thankfully. They were alive, happy, with a prosperous business. And presently she had more to be glad about, as she discovered she was to have a baby.

When Vic learned about it, he was amusingly shattered. He could not believe it at first, then he became anxious about Betsy and wanted her to sit with her feet propped up. She was not to lift anything, not even a tea kettle. She finally cajoled him out of it, and, eyes radiant, began to prepare for the baby's coming.

Whenever she walked to Saymore, or drove there with Vic, she thought of that first sad day when she had come, that October day when the world seemed ended for her. She had come to Saymore as a last resort. She would beg a job at Greystone, hope to make a living, just exist.

Instead, she had found a new life, hope, and a deep and abiding love for a man who was dearer to her every day. She had found a man to love, who loved and needed her. And together they began to forget the past and its grief and loneliness.

Today was theirs, and a radiant future was within their grasp.

IT'S THE PEOPLE WHO CHANGE...THE TIME THAT PASSES...BUT THE TAVERN STAYS THE SAME